I0781314

The Treasure of Loon Lake

THE SHORES OF LOON LAKE

RACHELLE PAIGE CAMPBELL

THE GHOST OF LOON LAKE

Copyright © 2025 by Rachelle Campbell Dio

All rights reserved. No part of this book may be used or reproduced in any manner whatsoever without written permission from the publisher or author except in the case of brief quotations embodied in critical articles and reviews.

This is a work of fiction. Names, characters, places and incidents either are the product of the author's imagination or are used fictitiously and any resemblance to actual persons, living or dead, business establishments, events or locales is entirely coincidental.

ISBN: 978-1-963705-09-6

Published in the United States of America by Harbor Lane Books, LLC.

www.harborlanebooks.com

Molly Maguire hated online quizzes. Pick a five-course meal to learn your ideal vacation. Choose an outfit and find out your princess type. The answers were as mind-numbing as the questions.

And what did any of the hypothetical scenarios prove? She liked steak, so she was destined to spend her next holiday in the woods? She hadn't taken a vacation since childhood. On the off chance she received a cash windfall, she was more likely to stay in the city than leave.

She preferred pants to skirts, so she was a swashbuckling princess pirate? With her predisposition for motion sickness, she wasn't likely to hop onboard a ship and set sail. The results were meaningless.

She didn't need a quiz to tell her what she couldn't live without. She had irrefutable proof of what she would grab in case of a fire. A phone, a blazer, a laptop, a camera, and an oversized tote purse. Because the terror of escaping flames in the early morning hours was her reality. And with no time to think, she'd grabbed what she couldn't live without, including the once-prized camera she hadn't touched in well over a decade.

What did any of it signify other than, at thirty-five, she had lost most of her worldly possessions and wasn't sure what she'd replace or how? The tragedy erased every illusion of comfort she'd created and forced her to live truthfully. On paper, she had less than nothing, thanks to her student loans. Reality finally matched.

Sitting behind her desk in the high-rise office building in the Chicago Loop, she tugged the blazer over her pajamas, glad she'd left the garment draped over her chair last night. A whiff of smoke tickled her nose. She frowned and pressed the phone tighter to her ear.

Her life's goals had been modest, scaled back after a series of creative failures discouraged her from pursuing her passion. Support herself and maybe—one day—own a home. Have a family. Those were far-off dreams in the wake of her morning.

She had grabbed the purse she used every day. It was big enough for her laptop and camera, and she kept her keys and wallet inside. The black bag hung on a hook near what had been her front door. On the rush out of the apartment building, she hadn't spared a thought for her splurge purchase, the designer bag still in its box on the top shelf in her closet. The old cliché—use it or lose it —wasn't so far off the mark.

She propped her elbow on the desk, resting her head against her hand as hold music droned. After the unwelcome morning wake up, she had headed to the office. She had nowhere else to go. While she might have idly pondered how she'd respond in a worst-case scenario, she'd found herself shockingly unprepared for the reality.

Her only family, her mom, lived a six-hour car ride away. Without a vehicle, Molly couldn't spontaneously drive there. Besides, Mom was off on a once-in-a-lifetime vacation around the world. She shouldn't have to deal with an interruption because her adult daughter's life crumbled under the weight of the real world.

Molly modified her goals to one immediate need. Call her insurance company so she could recover something. In the interim, she'd have to check into a hotel, floating by on her credit cards. Fear kept her from checking her bank account balance. Cash hadn't magically doubled overnight.

Calling her insurance company about her renter's policy violated her boss's rule of no personal business on company time. If she used her cell, she might be able to get away with it. But she didn't have a charger and wouldn't waste the battery if she didn't need to. Maybe she'd get an exception for extraordinary circumstances. Or she could finish the call before her boss showed up. She needed one moment of good luck. With her home gone, how much worse could her day get?

A knock shook the propped-open door, rattling the wall stopper.

She jerked, dropping the phone to the desk, and widened her gaze.

"Sorry, I didn't mean to startle you."

A kind-looking, older man in a gray suit filled the doorway. With thinning silver hair, he entered the room belly first. If Santa was real, he'd just strode into her office. Was he here to tell her if she'd been naughty or nice? She didn't need more judgment. Not today.

She cleared her throat and pushed back her chair, clutching her blazer closed as she stood. "My apologies, I'm sure. Do we have a meeting?" She waved her hand to the seat in front of her desk.

The man pulled out the chair and sat. "Well, not exactly, though I have been eager to make your acquaintance, Ms. Maguire." The chair groaned. "You must forgive my impertinence."

If she started a tally of everything that had gone off course so far, she'd be in the thousands. Whatever he wanted would only promise more distraction and trouble on an already full day. She nibbled her bottom lip and sat.

On the wall above the door, the clock flashed seven forty. Molly had twenty minutes tops before her boss strolled past the door. With her discerning eye, she'd spot the pajamas at a glance. Molly needed to steal herself and keep calm. Her boss hated emotions almost as much as unwanted surprises.

The stranger would draw attention. In her role, she sat behind a desk most of the day, entering clerical data for a plastics manufacturing company. The job was repetitive and mindless. It was the latest in a long line of data entry jobs she'd taken since college. Her ability to sit down and get work done kept her employed but never advanced. Not that she particularly had ambitions to climb the ladder in the world of plastics or any other corporation. She did her job and got a paycheck that kept her going. It wasn't the worst profession. But she didn't have visitors.

She had to get this man out of her office. "Oh? I'm sorry, you seem to have the advantage over me, Mr.?"

"Baird. Leonard Baird, attorney at law."

Her stomach dropped. Lawyer? Was she being sued? How much could go wrong? Why was trouble hounding her like she wore a jinxed talisman?

She looked around anxiously, and her gaze dropped to the bag that held her camera as a long-ago memory resurfaced. During her study abroad program in London, she had stopped in a restaurant for an early dinner in the busy theater district. Like so many other nights, the rain propelled her to seek shelter, and she wasn't alone. The restaurant was packed with tourists and theater ticket holders taking up every inch. She squeezed through the crowd to grab the last table, a tiny bistro-sized setup for two crammed against the front window and a wall.

As she set her bag onto the free chair and tugged it next to her, clammy, wrinkled hands covered hers. Molly lifted her gaze off the bag holding her prized possession, her camera, to meet the tanned visage of a frowning, dark-eyed, silver-haired woman speaking in another language and shooting daggers with her eyes. A server called her a gypsy and pulled her away from Molly. And nothing happened despite the chill she'd felt down to her bones.

Was this morning's events undeniable evidence of a long-awaited gypsy curse? "How may I help you?" She managed to keep her voice even.

"I've been searching for you, Ms. Maguire, to settle

an estate. In fact, I have to conclude the business within the next seven days, or the property defaults to the city."

She shook her head. "Excuse me? Property? Estate?"

"Yes, I fear I have rather unfortunate news to share. Your great-aunt has passed."

She scrunched her nose. She didn't have family besides her mom. "I think you must be mistaken."

"Oh, indeed, I am not. Finding you was a lucky break. On a whim, I submitted a sample of DNA, God rest sweet Lily's soul, to an ancestry tracing company via their mail-order kit. And boom, we got a hit. You, through your father's family."

Was he joking? Or—worse—did he represent a criminal? The ambush was the very worst-case scenario she'd warned Mom about.

Molly had been against the idea of sending off a spit sample. Mom had insisted. As she aged, she worried about what illnesses Molly might be susceptible to, thanks to her genetics. Dad's accidental early death provided more questions than answers.

Humoring her, Molly sent in the vial after Christmas and hadn't spared a thought in the months since. And now she had proof. Extending herself in any way only opened her to more complications on a day she really needed none. Would she be liable for estate taxes? Was this great-aunt in debt? "Oh, you'll forgive me. I don't know that I'm prepared to assume any sort of property at the moment. Let Chicago take the property."

"No, ma'am. The city in question is a little town on the shores of Lake Superior. Loon Lake, Wisconsin. Have you ever visited the North Woods?"

She frowned and shook her head.

"Well, you are in for a treat. The people are friendly. The air is fresh. And your property is quite a sight."

Not my property. Not my problem. "Forgive me," she managed through gritted teeth. "Not to be rude, sir. But you're catching me on a rough day. My apartment building just burned down. I have only the clothes on my back. I have a lot to figure out. I can't take on another responsibility." Why was she oversharing with this insistent, inscrutable stranger? Because he was a cross between Matlock and the jolly old elf himself?

She never believed in Santa as a kid. She definitely wouldn't imagine for a second that this man had weighed her behavior of the past year and determined she was nice enough for her heart's desire—her own home.

And if he really was a small-town litigator, she'd better have her wits about her. Any slip in demeanor or language at a vulnerable moment could haunt her later. She knew that from all her years watching true crime documentaries. Whomever he was, he needed to leave. She'd had her share of drama for the day. She stood.

"I am sorry to hear that." He pressed his hand to his heart. "But you're in good health?"

Under his careful scrutiny, she faltered. She was a light sleeper and had awoken before the alarm. If she'd slept even another second, she'd have been trapped. Physically, she was okay with limited smoke exposure, but she was shaken by the experience.

She shrugged and sank back into her chair. He wasn't easily deterred. She was too tired for a fight. She'd give him time to finish his prepared remarks about her mystery inheritance. Then he'd leave. "I'm fine."

"All we have is our health. You'll forgive me for the sentiment, but perhaps this is the answer. You need a place to stay, and you own a building only a few hours away. Why not take a vacation? Come north. Sign the papers and accept the keys. You'd be doing me a huge favor."

Take a vacation? She nearly snorted. She didn't have cash on hand to fund a spur-of-the-moment trip. If she really did own property, she could visit for a few days to escape from her nine-to-five grind. With limited paid time off, however, she hated to waste a day.

Or she could sell the property and travel where she wanted. *Or, more likely, pay off my debts.* Frugal to her core, she always chose the practical option. "I can't just leave without notice. I really don't want to take on something without reading all the fine print."

"I understand, and I appreciate that. As a man of the legal profession, reading every detail is of the utmost importance to me." He rubbed his hand along his jaw. "You must do great work here if you are so needed you can't even take a few days to yourself after enduring a tragedy."

She stiffened.

"Or perhaps you just have a great passion for the job. Like I do." He nodded and smiled.

She rested her arms on her desk, gripping both elbows. The stranger's words—probably meant for polite and meaningless conversation—cut her to the core. No, her work wasn't her passion. Nor was what she did in pursuit of the greater good. But her bills were paid every month, and in the years since graduation, she had never asked for more. Gambling wasn't about gaining; it only resulted in losing. She didn't bet on anything, including herself. "I'm not the person you're searching for."

"Oh, you are, my dear. Without a doubt. And I should know. I left no stone unturned or body buried, as the case may be, to find you." With one hand, he crossed himself. "Exhuming Lily was the only option available after she'd been interred so quickly. I owed it to her to see this through. When she first laid out her estate years ago, she relayed the family legend. Without a Maguire in residence, the town will decline. *A Maguire in possession is prosperity for all.*"

A legend? Sure, she believed in a curse, but to add to her superstitions taxed her mental capacity to the max at a delicate moment. Perhaps she'd been born under a dark cloud. Maybe she'd start throwing salt over her shoulder as a precautionary measure. "I'm sorry, Mr. Baird. I really can't take on any more complications at present."

"I understand. I can help you if you'll let me." He slid his hand into his suit jacket and pulled out a card, extending it to her. "You've had a tough morning and need time with your thoughts. I'll see myself out. But if you do change your mind, please make your way north to Loon Lake, Wisconsin. One of the finest towns you'll ever see. If you can get up there by Sunday night, I'll hand you the keys and will have truly seen Lily's last will and testament fully executed and done." He stood and pushed back his chair.

Rising with surprising agility, he crossed to the door

and glanced back. With a wink and a nod, he left. After several minutes, Molly heard the front door of the office open and shut. She exhaled a slow sigh and stared at the card on her desk. He'd given her a deadline less than a week away. She hated the imaginary ticking now ringing in her ears.

A place to stay was tempting. Nothing ever happened without some sort of catch. Even the jolly old elf expected payment in the form of good behavior. Besides, Mr. Baird wasn't Santa, dropping off a present and fulfilling a wish. He'd have a demand.

Beep, beep, beep, beep.

She frowned and stared at her lap. She hadn't hung up the phone and now only heard a busy signal. Shaking her head, she pressed the receiver and dialed again. She was put on hold with an estimated wait time of forty minutes. She snorted. She'd been on hold for over an hour already. This Monday really lived up to the hype. Powering on her computer, she searched for Loon Lake on the internet.

Images of a quaint town, shops on a boardwalk, and a beautiful white Victorian resort flashed on her screen. She scrolled through the gallery of search results. Mr. Baird had good reason for the pride in his voice. The town looked picture-perfect.

She amended her search, adding autumn and clicking for updated results. With each new photograph, she felt a peculiar piercing in her heart. Her palms tingled. Her fingers flexed with muscle memory from her long-ago photography days. Then she searched again for spring, followed by summer and winter.

Did the green hills shine in the summer during a rainstorm? Was the sky truly so impossibly blue in frigid January? How could the trees glow so vibrantly orange, yellow, and red in the fall? The photos must be doctored. No place was so beautiful and pristine in the modern era.

For a little while, she lost track of herself, her predicament, and her location. With each updated search, she dove deeper into the dark waters of the lake. The act was almost meditation.

"Molly. What are you doing? What are you wearing?"

Her boss, Stacey's crisp, clear voice carried through the open doorway.

Molly dropped the phone, the receiver clattering on the desk as new-age music droned. Heat crept up her cheeks. Molly met the arched-brow stare of her boss.

A petite woman only a few years older, her boss operated in clear black-and-white terms. And she stared pointedly at the phone.

Molly hung up the call and pulled her hands off her keyboard and into her lap. "Oh, hi, so, not-so-funny story, my apartment building is gone."

"So you're just going to work in your pajamas and make your office your new studio apartment? You can't conduct personal business here. You know that."

"I understand." Molly tucked a strand of hair behind her ear, fingers brushing her burning cheeks. "It's just a one-time thing, and I thought—"

"No, we have very clear standards. I can't believe you're violating the rules. After so many years here." Stacey pinched the bridge of her nose. "I've given warnings. I simply... I was informed of this lapse and can't ignore it." She shook her head and frowned. "Don't make this difficult. You're out. Please pack your things and go."

Where? Shutting her gaping mouth, Molly nodded and dropped her gaze. She stared at her keyboard until her boss's steps echoed down the hall.

Packing her office into a banker's box was easy. Only a few personal items decorated the bland, beige space and fit into the cardboard box with room to spare. Where could she go? According to the itinerary, her mom was currently cruising through Central America. Molly had no other family. She had no close friends who would let her sleep on a sofa.

She never had much faith in destiny. Until right now when fate slapped her in the face.

She was heading north.

* * *

Grant Reem never wasted a day. His carpe-diem attitude wasn't because he scheduled every second of each hour. Despite reading books on time management and taking courses on optimization, he'd never applied the techniques he'd learned. His strict adherence to not planning was the key to his success in living and working to his fullest potential.

He had made some mistakes along the way and had his fair share of regrets. If he ever had the chance to right the past wrongs, he'd gladly accept the opportunity with a grateful heart. But he didn't focus on the past.

Once he'd proven himself an undisputed winner,

checking every box on society's vision of success, he'd found the top of the corporate ladder a lonely place. He climbed down. And now, he could embrace no demands on his time and truly be on his own. A life of contentment and peace, his future and time controlled by his own two hands. He didn't want more.

Scanning the display rack, he grabbed a bottle of sunscreen and a blanket emblazoned with the Chequamegon Bay Yacht Club logo. August on Lake Superior required both. Storms moved swiftly, promising fluctuating sunshine and temperatures almost on the hour. Summer slipped past. Autumn clamored for attention.

He'd stopped at the store several times since taking ownership of his new business and returning to the region for the first time in years. He'd grown so used to the convenience of stopping at a corner store whenever he had a need and forgot how different life was in the idyllic setting of the North Woods. Writing a list and planning ahead would save him from another visit and more exposure to the side-eyed gazes of the employees he'd gotten to know by name.

But he wasn't a checklist kind of guy. Neither was he used to having limited options or everyone so painfully aware of his actions. Taking over a bankrupt tour boat company in a tiny offshoot lake from Lake Superior, however, he'd had to adjust to both. Scrutiny was his constant companion in the sparsely populated region.

He'd come to nearby Loon Lake to build something for the rest of his life. A small enterprise he could manage by himself. A quiet life without any unnecessary attention or trials in the court of public opinion on a national stage. He could handle a few curious locals.

He approached the counter and set the goodies next to the cash register.

"Can I help you find something in particular?" Jayden asked.

The pimpled teen was young, pale, and gawky. He reminded Grant of himself at fifteen. In those days, his mom couldn't keep enough food in the house to satisfy him. She had forced him out of his bedroom and into the sunshine. She had complained video games and hours on the computer would get him nowhere.

He named the house he bought her *nowhere* so she'd be correct. She'd laughed and hugged him hard.

"I'm good, Jayden. I can always stop by again if I need something else."

The teen nodded and rang up the purchases.

Grant pulled his wallet from his back pocket. Dealing with physical currency was just another adjustment to his new life. With the money magnetically clipped to his phone, he pulled out his cell, too.

The screen flashed with a familiar number. He hit ignore call. Answering and explaining himself again would only bring him down on a sunny day. He pulled out a fifty-dollar bill, waited for the change, and deposited a tip in the jar on the counter. Slipping the phone and cash into his pocket, he grabbed the purchases and exited via the side door.

Drawing in a deep breath, he filled his lungs with clean, pine-scented air. His boat shoes slapped against each wooden plank. He loved the greatest lake of them all and the towns along its shores. Everything was brighter and crisper. From smells to sights to sounds, the southern shore of Lake Superior was unmatched.

In his pocket, the phone vibrated.

Nothing could ruin his day. Not even an unwanted voicemail. He blamed himself for the persistent phone calls. He should have formulated a better, more satisfying, and final response to the inquiries from the CEO of the conglomerate that bought his company a year ago. The leadership team remained unconvinced that he was enjoying a break from his workaholic ways at forty. Early retirement didn't always last.

The company hadn't known about the four years of what ended up being six years in undergrad. He was quite happy to take his life one day at a time. He hadn't gotten his act together until absolutely necessary, aka when his parents threatened to stop paying his tuition. He had changed for a woman, too, but it was too little too late to impress her.

Once he had started his business, he hadn't stopped. Never taking time off as he built a company from nothing to a multi-figure valuation. He could understand why other executives would think he was itching for a return. Perhaps he could have been convinced if he'd been asked earlier. He had spent much of the past year at his ailing grandpa's bedside. After his passing, Grant might have been tempted to return to work. Unfortunately for the corporation, an entirely new venture captured his attention, and Grant was not interested in returning to the West Coast.

"Mr. Reem? She's ready."

Grant raised one hand to shield his gaze against the bright glare off the lake. He spotted Jayden's older brother, Liam, at the pump on the fuel dock. Grant cupped his mouth. "Thanks." Jogging along the wooden walkway, he strode down the pier and hopped aboard the Tommy Buoy.

He had enough boating knowledge for casual pursuit. His thirty-five-foot yacht was pushing his capabilities to the limits. He liked the solitude of not employing a crew on his own vessel. After years of being responsible for others' livelihoods, he welcomed the peace. If he ran aground, he only impacted himself.

Soon enough, he'd have to hire a full staff to run his tour boat business properly. Tickets, merchandise, guides, and a website demanded as much attention as driving the actual boats. Before long, he'd be the boss again. He could do the role with aplomb. But he had no illusions. With a decade running a company, he was all too aware of the stresses of the job and savored his solitary start for as long as he could. He climbed aboard and hopped into the cockpit.

Liam untied the lines.

With a wave, Grant navigated away from the dock and into the open water. He passed the tree-lined southern shore of Lake Superior and motored in silence. The yacht club wasn't convenient for him to fill up his tank, but it was his current best option. His new business had had the ability to fuel its vessels. But, like many things he'd discovered in his money-pit purchase, it wasn't operating at its fullest potential and hadn't been certified and inspected for years.

Until he fixed the pump at his own dock, an absolute must to run tours efficiently, he enjoyed his scenic trips around the lake every week. He steered into the channel. Directly across lay the historic sawmill marking the start of Loon Lake. The vinyl-siding-clad structure rose like a modern-day colossus from its own dock, jutting into the icy water. The historic wheel was barely visible.

Scanning the opposite side of the lake's mouth, he frowned at the log cabin, wracking his brain to remember what it was. "Historical society and museum," he announced, snapping his fingers. As if on cue, Elise McKenna, the buttoned-up, stoic curator and one-woman town tourism board, rounded the building and spotted him. He waved.

She stiffened and—after a pause—tilted her head.

Her tight greeting made him chuckle. He was officially a part of the community now. He'd launched his website hours earlier, boasting of unrivaled tours at some future date to be determined. The statement was a verifiable fact as he had purchased the only licensed business operating on the water. He needed to get his bearings before the tourists realized he was still learning the area.

He headed to his newly acquired boathouse, raising the exterior rolling door remotely and steering inside to dock for the night. With a few more hours of daylight, he could find peace. As soon as he laid his head on his pillow, he knew he'd be plagued again by all the old haunts and taunts. The missed call from his former assistant stirred up his anxiety.

With his company sold and the pressure of the corporate world behind him, he vowed a new start with a break-even business, showing tourists the lakeshore he'd grown up loving. He found purpose in helping others, often in surprising ways. A quiet life spent giving back was all he could dream of for his next act. But he worried that he had let down his former staff despite their assurances they understood. He needed a better work life balance than he found in Silicon Valley. At the first chance, he'd jumped out of the rat race and straight into a lake.

He steered into the slip and lift, docking the boat and using technology to secure his position. For the time being, he'd only invested in what he could control himself. His lawyers and financial planners toiled behind the scenes, sorting through the mess of his newest venture and determining how to scale and grow. He believed in tackling problems step by step, and he'd start his tours one boat at a time.

"Need any help?" A deep voice called over the mechanical whirring of the lift.

"I'm good," Grant shouted. With the boat in position, he cut the engine and leaned back in his captain's chair to study the visitor on the dock.

In the dim, overhead fluorescent lights, Christopher Lewis still found a way to shine. He was a commanding presence. As the proprietor of the biggest business on Loon Lake, a historic inn Grant had enjoyed vacationing at every summer as a child, Christopher was involved in everyone's professional affairs. In addition to the inn, he oversaw the boardwalk as landlord of all the shops hugging the lakeshore. The community relied on tourism and each other in a symbiotic relationship heightened by the summertime season.

Grant respected that and was also grateful for the other man's wife, Ashley Hale-Lewis. He suspected that Christopher's visits would be even more frequent if not for the lady's influence in giving Grant a bit of space as he began to sort through his purchase and triage the business.

"I saw the website is up and running. Looks great. Cheers to progress." Christopher pumped a fist in the air.

Grant chuckled despite himself. Christopher was the closest thing Grant had to a close friend in town. He could handle a little meddling for the chance at human interaction. "I'm getting there. I promised I'd be fully operational by next spring, and I meant it." He scrubbed his hands over his face. "The financials were a mess. The debts have been cleared. I'm trying to determine what can be salvaged and what must be scrapped. At this point, it's such a disaster that I'd be tempted to throw out everything and start over. But I don't know how I'd get a construction crew started in time with your project."

"It's a chicken-and-egg scenario." Christopher nodded. "I wouldn't mind if we could bring in more construction companies and give people more job opportunities. It's hard to lure anyone here without a steady paycheck. After the lighthouse is built at the inn and this property is sorted, what next?"

Grant pocketed his keys and tapped the garage door button to lower the water gateway.

The mechanical clinking echoed off every surface

inside the boathouse. The loud cacophony gave him a chance to regroup and get onto the dock. His instinct to rush in and save the day with his finances had often proved counterproductive. He believed in giving a hand up whenever he could. But as a benefactor, he'd been burned several times.

"Do you think the town could support continued growth and development?" Grant asked as the room quieted. "Can the infrastructure be stretched for more residents? I'm asking for myself, too. Thanks for letting me stay past my welcome at the inn. It's nice to have a break from the boat and a shower I can stand fully upright in. I've had no luck finding a place to live."

Christopher waved off the comment. "It's a small price to pay to have this business in capable hands. The inn relies on the tour boats and vice versa. As for the second thing, I would hate for the lake to be overdeveloped, but I fear it's only a matter of time. Lily Maguire's heir might develop the building." He shuddered. "Can you imagine how overrun the town would be if it's turned into a high-rise?"

"Do you mean like apartments?" Grant couldn't picture it. "Are you sure?"

"I don't know. Just thinking about something Ashley mentioned a while back. But now I can't stop worrying about it. Hopefully, the search for the mystery successor will be a dud, and Elise will secure the land for the historical society."

"Any construction on the shore would change the lake forever. Especially in such a prime location."

"And I'd have to admit my wife was right." Christopher shuddered. "She warned me about the possibilities once the last Loon Lake Maguire passed."

Grant rolled his eyes at Christopher's dramatics. Ashley was often correct with her snap judgments and quick assessments. "Nothing she hasn't heard before. I wouldn't worry. I'm sure Elise won't let anyone change the lakeshore without a fight. She'll have to stare at the monstrosity from the museum across the water."

"And she's determined to claim the building for the town." Christopher stroked his chin.

Elise picked up the micromanagement where Christopher slacked. Between the pair, nothing happened in Loon Lake without a lot of civic oversight. Elise had threatened Grant with litigation almost as soon as he had assumed control of his rundown tour boat business and lakefront property. She'd tossed around words like historical landmark and cultural significance.

At first, he'd thought she was joking. The boathouse and dock better resembled a trash heap than an important institution. Once he had understood her seriousness, however, he'd changed course. He'd rather have friends than enemies, especially as a newcomer to the tight-knit community.

"If you need anything, you'll reach out?" Christopher asked.

"You'll be my first stop. You've done too much already."

"I need you to be successful. We all do." With a wave, Christopher strolled away, his footsteps echoing on the wooden dock throughout the boathouse.

Grant appreciated the weight of the words. In a

major demonstration of trust and respect, he'd been brought into the inner circle of business owners. The significance wasn't lost on him. The start of the summer had sparked major upheaval that led to his purchase. He still wasn't privy to all the details, so he minded his every step. He'd do his best for the community. He was ready to belong somewhere. What better place than a lakeside town?

Chapter Two

Molly approached the empty host stand at the brewery and grill. The sweet smell of spilled beer perfumed the air, and she breathed deep, inhaling the aroma like she strode through a rose garden. She'd never been so happy to see a bar in her life. She dropped her chin to her chest and rolled her neck.

To top off yesterday's string of bad luck, she discovered the few hours' drive Mr. Baird mentioned was actually eight from Chicago. She hated driving under the best of circumstances. Her current predicament was far from ideal. She rented a car and drove north, stopping at the outlets to buy a week's wardrobe and spending the night at a cheap hotel. This morning, she awoke and determined a plan. She called Mr. Baird and continued to her destination, parking at a red brick structure past the town's welcome sign.

She stood at the host stand, rocking front to back

and stretching her sore muscles and stiff back, grateful she didn't have hours more to spend behind the wheel.

"Table for one?" A young woman holding a menu in her arms asked.

Molly smoothed her ponytail. "I'm meeting someone. Mr. Baird?"

"The lawyer?" The woman cocked her head to the side and narrowed her gaze. "Are you from around here?"

Molly shook her head. "No. I had family here. My aunt owned the sawmill?" She could have kicked herself; phrasing her statement as a question was silly.

The woman recoiled slightly, leaning back as her nostrils flared. "Oh. Right. Welcome to Loon Lake. Mr. Baird isn't here yet. I'll get you a table and bring him over as soon as he arrives."

"Thank you." Molly fought the urge to sniff herself. Had she forgotten deodorant this morning in her hazy, pre-caffeine rush to get back on the road? Did she smell bad enough for the woman's unwelcoming behavior?

The hostess spun on her heel and strode through an open doorway.

Molly followed, scanning her surroundings. The historic brick building, a nineteenth-century neoclassical, was lovingly preserved. Inside the main dining room, a large open area boasted high ceilings and exposed beams. Overhead, a gallery of tables hugged the perimeter.

The hostess pointed to a table in the center of the room, keeping her distance from Molly and darting her eyes to the side.

Molly nibbled the inside of her cheek. She didn't want to be on display. While she had changed out of the smoke-scented pajamas into a sundress, she still felt conspicuous. Especially in a small town. Everyone knew everyone here, right? Wasn't that the deal? No newcomer went unnoticed. A table in the center of the room, fully visible, was too much. Her request might be registered as her being difficult. She'd take the judgment to get out of the way. "Can I sit in a booth?"

"Of course." The hostess strode to a vacant booth lining the wall.

Molly slid over the bench seat. After a day of driving, her body ached from another cramped position. But she didn't like the other option. "Thank you. This is nice."

"Your server will be over shortly." The hostess set the menu on the table and beat a hasty retreat.

"Thank you." Molly repeated, raising the menu as a shield. What had Molly done wrong? Had she been too presumptuous when she introduced herself as having family despite never even knowing her late aunt existed until Mr. Baird contacted her? Should she have made a better attempt at small talk?

Or, perhaps, exhaustion played tricks on her mind. Perception was easily swayed and not always a fair assessment of a situation. The hostess was working and didn't have idle time. Molly dropped her gaze to the text, the letters swirling before her. She rubbed her eyes, narrowed her gaze, and tried again. In her purse, her phone buzzed.

Abandoning the menu, she pulled out her phone, eager for any good news. She'd received an automatic reply to an email she'd sent asking about her insurance claims. She read the note and spotted the phrase *following interviews with authorities.* Authorities? Like the police? Or the fire department?

She'd had no formal meeting with either. Was she reckless in skipping town before she'd been formally questioned? She had left a message with her insurance company and filled out an online form. She had called building management, too. The landlord couldn't offer assistance finding housing. She hadn't expected any, but she had wanted to touch base.

No one told her she had to stay. Had her abrupt departure looked suspicious? With any luck, not that she had much these days, her explanations would be sufficient for any law enforcement agency.

The first meeting with the lawyer had stoked her dormant curiosity about her dad's family. He'd passed before her tenth birthday. She'd never known any of his distant relatives. A quick internet search pulled up a few mentions of Maguire Lumber, a sawmill begun in the late nineteenth century. Was her dad's family rich? She'd never imagined her last name posted anywhere, let alone displayed forever on a building in a show of strength and honor.

She wasn't sure what to think about being part of a legacy. Did the town hate her sight unseen? Or adore her because of the legend? Both options made her uncomfortable.

"PEANUT?"

Warmth spread through her as her stomach fluttered. She dried her trembling, clammy hands on her napkin and pressed her lips together to refresh her lipstick.

Shoot. She forgot her lipstick. Nerves and excitement tangled together.

No one had called her Peanut in fifteen years. The nickname was the invention of her slacker college boyfriend. The one she knew she shouldn't get involved with. The guy who entered his fifth year of study during her first. She gripped the smooth vinyl seat, securing herself to the present while her mind time traveled.

Handsome and charming, Grant Reem had lived life by an easy-going, the-universe-provides ethos that intoxicated and confused her. For two years, she succumbed to her desires and followed him in a dizzy haze of love and companionship.

He was a lot of fun. Until she realized she couldn't do the no-plan thing indefinitely. Her life needed structure and discipline, the two things standing in direct opposition to Grant's carpe-diem lifestyle. After her sophomore year, she stopped answering his calls and didn't see him again. Their breakup had been a fizzle and not an explosion.

Heavy footsteps approached.

"Peanut?" A deep voice asked.

She shut her eyes. Was she really about to see the only guy she'd ever loved now that she'd hit rock bottom? The breakup was mutual. He hadn't tried to change her mind. She hadn't thought she'd ever see him again. Couldn't the universe have warned her? Couldn't she have had a premonition? She would have preferred warning and time to put on a little makeup and something cuter than the off-the-rack, loose t-shirt dress.

"It is you. My goodness, Peanut. How have you been?"

She turned her face towards the voice and opened her eyes. She stared into familiar brown eyes, a startling warm and welcoming color. Her blood thrummed, and her skin tingled. She'd never get used to the rush of heat brought on by his attention. "Hi, Grant." She slipped her phone into her purse.

With one smile, she time traveled back to college. The first time she had tripped over the cute guy sitting on the floor in the stacks of the university library, she had stammered an apology and barely glanced at him. The second time, a few days later, she had huffed a slightly annoyed excuse. After the third encounter, when she tumbled over him and scrapped her tights-clad knees, however, she'd been ready to tell him off. But he had helped her to her feet, apologized, admitted the ruse to see her again and asked her on a date. He'd been unexpected at the best of times, lightening her serious moods with his light-hearted ways. And unreliable at the worst moments.

He slid onto the bench seat opposite. "I can't believe it's you. How are you?"

She studied him. With a full beard, worn clothes, and hair in need of a trim, he looked like he'd fallen on hard times. *Had he?* She hadn't kept up with him. She believed in a clean break, deleting his number and blocking him on social media. Over time, she had forgotten him. A chance meeting had seemed far-fetched only a few months ago. After the past few tumultuous days, however, nothing seemed impossible any longer.

She scanned him from head to toe again, and her stomach sank.

His rough appearance and undoubtedly difficult situation put hers into perspective. She'd lost her home and her job. But—thanks to the universe—she had an unlikely backup plan. She'd be okay. He wouldn't. "I'm fine. Do you live here?"

"Sort of. I'm docked past the inn." He scrubbed his hands over his beard and through his hair. A few streaks of silver were threaded into his mahogany locks near his temples.

His words hit her brain. "Dock?" she asked.

Did he mean he hadn't put down roots, or was he speaking more literally? *Like living on a boat?* She didn't like the picture. In college, he'd shared the back half of a neglected house with four other guys. Chores were no one's forte. To be in even tighter quarters must be unbearable.

"Yep. I'm living on my boat. Sort of. I have a long-term stay at the inn, too. Sometimes it's nice to not feel so cramped when I shower." He chuckled, resting his forearms on the table and leaning closer.

She grabbed a napkin, unrolling the utensils before smoothing the fabric over her lap. She was glad for the excuse to turn away from his harsh reality. She wasn't alone in her tough times. But he wasn't defined by his. He could always look on the bright side. She needed some of that right now in the face of a terrible, life-changing week. *Things could always get worse.*

"I'm starting a tour business," he said.

"Hmm." She smiled. At one time, she'd tried to get him to think about goals and write a plan. The best way to achieve something was to put it on paper and start breaking down actionable steps. Not that she'd gotten far on her path to success. Her current situation was a setback. She'd get ahead and make the most of the surprise opportunity before her.

"Are you still taking pictures?"

She sucked in a breath, her nostrils flaring. He didn't waste time with pleasantries. He couldn't have known the truth about her either, having private social media accounts that languished with old updates. She forced her body to loosen and shook her head. "Not for a long time."

"Are you visiting? I can't believe I ran into you. If you ever want to take a tour of Loon Lake or Lake Superior." He leaned forward and reached into his back pocket. He slid a folded-up sticky note across the table. "I don't have cards yet. But that's my cell number. Give me a call."

She pursed her lips. Same old Grant. Running a business on a wing and a prayer? She might not be living the life she'd dreamed about, but at least she had herself somewhat together.

"Ms. Maguire? I'm delighted you're here." A deep voice boomed. "My apologies for the delay in meeting you."

She turned and met the gaze of Mr. Baird, approaching through the restaurant. He announced his arrival to the entire dining room. Heat crept up her cheeks. She didn't want any of her business being made public in present company. "Thanks, Grant. Good to see you."

Grant slid out of the booth.

Mr. Baird nodded to him and took the vacated spot.

"Guess I'll see you around." With a wave, Grant walked away.

She slowly exhaled the sigh building in her chest. She reached for the phone number and slid it into her purse. She wasn't going to call him. Dating him the first time had nearly derailed her plans. He had a natural optimism that warmed her like the sun. Most days, she felt like a walking rain cloud. With her life falling apart, she couldn't be tempted to let go of everything and fall into his no-plans attitude. After all, his motto hadn't seemed to get him very far. They both ended up at zero, although he might have beaten her there in their race to the bottom.

"My dear, I was thrilled to get your phone call," Mr. Baird said. "After our meeting, you'll forgive my surprise. I didn't imagine you'd follow me here." He chuckled.

She shifted on the cushioned seat. His easy laughter grated. She fought off a shudder. "I didn't—"

"Semantics, my dear." He interlaced his hands on the table. "I'm thrilled you're here. Local legends are quite a tradition in Loon Lake. It's for all our sakes that you're here."

The server approached with two glasses of water. "Are you ready to order?"

Molly's stomach growled. She covered it with both hands. "I still need a few minutes."

"Patrick, do you know who this is?" Mr. Baird asked the server.

The server squinted and shook his head, frowning.

"This here is the last living member of the Maguire dynasty. I found her. She's come to save us." Mr. Baird rested both hands on his belly and leaned back.

"Oh, really?" Patrick tilted his head and studied her.

Under the close examination, Molly squirmed. Her cheeks burned, and her stomach roared again. "I'm just here... I... Umm..."

"I'll give you a few more minutes." Patrick turned and strode away.

She didn't like the incredulous stare or sudden departure. Mr. Baird arrived at her office yesterday acting like he'd come to save her. Now she was supposed to be the town's savior? Heat crept up her skin. Was Patrick spreading news of her arrival? Or gossip?

"Patrick is a good kid. Most folks are around here," Mr. Baird said. "We've had a bit of a tough year. Rebuilding and all that. You are a bright light, my dear."

She followed Patrick's progress across the dining room, pushing through a swinging door. After a few seconds, the door opened the opposite way, and three heads poked out, staring at her. She dropped her gaze to the table. The unblinking focus unnerved her. What wasn't Mr. Baird telling her? Many towns operated in a constant state of flux as jobs left or arrived and economies shifted. The significance of his delivery hinted at something more.

"Here are your keys, my dear," he said.

She lifted her gaze.

Mr. Baird dangled a keychain.

She wasn't sure what to make of the gleam in his eyes. "I came to assess the property and determine if I want to accept it," she said slowly. "You told me I had until Sunday to claim it. I need a few days to make up my mind."

"I understand."

She held out her hand.

He dropped the keys into her palm. "I can't wait to see what you do with the place. It's quite a prime piece of real estate. Lily mentioned renovating the building and subdividing it into multiple housing units. You could do that, too, if you're interested."

"Oh?" Molly's voice rose along with her hopes. Acting as a landlord wasn't something she'd ever had in mind but she eagerly welcomed a new revenue stream. Perhaps she'd have time to get her life back on track. And maybe she could give Grant a hand up in the process. She closed her fingers over the keys.

"Or even develop the building into condos on the waterfront. I bet you'd get a nice price for each sale. Go take a look. We can handle the paperwork later. Give you a few days to get settled and decide you've come home for good. You've had a tough time. But talk about kismet, huh?" He grinned.

The tiny hairs on the back of her neck lifted. She hated to think she was at the mercy of fate. With the curse hounding her, nothing worked in her favor. Tonight, she had a place to stay that wouldn't cost her a dime. Before she ran off with grand ideas for the future, she needed a break to catch her breath. Could she trust that the change in her luck would hold? She followed the rules and still got kicked when she was down. Her natural skepticism was on high alert. She leaned forward. "Mr. Baird, is there something I should know?"

"Nothing more than what I've told you. The town only prospers with a Maguire in residence. The address is written on the keys. If you have any problems, you know how to reach me?"

She nodded.

"Excellent. We'll be in touch." He slid out of the booth and ambled away. "Order whatever you please. I told them to add it to my tab."

"Thanks," she murmured to his quickly retreating figure. Two unsettling encounters in less than twenty minutes overwhelmed her. But she'd stay and eat, taking the break from facing her property. She shivered, worrying about what she might find. As long as she had a bed and a roof, she'd adapt. Was one boring day too much to ask?

* * *

Grant climbed the steps of the brownstone and continued through the open front door. Scanning the directory of the county courthouse, he found the department for business licenses. His sneakers squeaked against the tile floor with each stride.

He never thought he'd be filing incorporation paperwork again. In the midst of the buyout, he had fought with lawyers over contract language and getting his staff the best deal possible. He had had enough legalese to last the rest of his lifetime by the end of negotiations. He'd have laughed and taken the bet against starting something all over again within a decade. He would have been out quite a bit of money.

Not planning meant never playing clairvoyant. Because beginning from scratch wasn't the most unbelievable part of his day. He bestowed that title on his restaurant run-in.

An hour ago, he wouldn't have imagined running into Peanut again. He was grateful that he'd been given a second chance for closure with the one who got away. He wouldn't squander the opportunity.

She looked more or less the same. Her face was a little thinner, and her hair a little lighter. But otherwise, she was the brunette he remembered. Determined as ever. He raked his hand over his beard, checking for any crumbs.

She'd narrowed her gaze, focusing in on his facial hair. He looked quite a bit different from the last time he'd seen her. Until the encounter, he'd forgotten about the beard. Did she like his relaxed look? She'd been a pressed and starched sort of person. The only coed in college that used an iron. Judging by her appearance today, in a sundress, she had relaxed her stiff style. The slightly informal outfit softened her.

The wariness in her gaze had reassured him she remained true to her natural skepticism. Years ago, she had prepared for worst-case scenarios. When nothing bad happened, however, she hadn't relaxed her guard. Had life—or another man—taught her any different?

He couldn't think about that. For years, he'd

nurtured a secret dream. He'd never told a soul for fear of how ridiculous he'd look. One more smile. One more conversation. One last goodbye. At the restaurant, he'd been presented with that very opportunity. He hadn't thanked her for her encouragement and tough love all those years ago. Seeing her, he only had more questions. He wasn't satisfied with saying goodbye. He'd have to find a chance at another hello.

He passed three closed doors. A low hum of conversation filtered down the corridor. He continued towards the noise. The hall terminated at a counter with stanchions cordoning off a waiting area. He walked through the ropes, following the invisible queue, and stood at the counter.

"Hello, how may I help you?" A woman with a jet-black perm straight from the eighties asked.

"Good morning, I've come to file a business license. I was told you'd be able to help me." He spotted the name plaque next to a computer monitor. "Judy."

"I can certainly try. What is the business you are opening, Mr.?"

"Reem. Grant Reem."

Her jaw dropped, and her blue eyes widened.

He sucked in a sharp breath. It was the usual reaction he got when giving his name. Although, most business news outlets preferred to include his middle initial when mentioning him. Grant D. Reem had a certain cache. He was likened to a genie capable of empowering everyone he met by making their wildest wishes a reality.

Building his company from the ground up, his story lent itself to the American ideal of starting with nothing.

But that wasn't entirely true in his case. He'd had a lot of advantages to put him ahead.

While he took longer than expected to graduate college, he didn't have to worry about student loans. His parents saved to cover his education. When he told them of his plan, he was welcomed home and given the ability to spend a year working for himself for no pay. They had supported him every step of the way.

"Are you THE Grant Reem?" She narrowed her gaze. "The billionaire?"

He slipped a finger under the collar of his crew neck t-shirt. The faded, worn cotton cost him extra. He liked the softness of the fabric. Why did it squeeze like a vice? Maybe because her shock wasn't misplaced. He didn't dress in expensive, tailored clothing or spend hours being groomed. Neither would anyone expect to find a "top fifty under fifty" former CEO in the North Woods. He hadn't been lured by a million-dollar compound or place to park his private jet. He didn't need an exclusive country club or other amenities. He'd come because of sentimentality. "I don't really like to discuss finances."

She covered her mouth with both hands. "Of course, I'm so sorry, sir." She dropped her hands to the keyboard and started typing furiously. "I thought I recognized you."

The glimmer in her eye hinted at familiarity with his flashy magazine appearance in a "tech's hottest up-and-comers" spread a few years ago. She didn't meet his gaze, focusing on her screen with intent. He wasn't sure if she saved herself or him from blushing.

The news periodical had conducted a standard interview. For the first time, however, he'd been asked for a photo shoot, too. He had regretted the choice to pose ever since. The photographer had convinced him to unbutton his shirt and roll up his sleeves. Grant had been directed to lean in a doorway and asked to smolder, whatever that meant. Strangers acted like they had seen him naked. He'd had no idea a Bay Area business magazine article could go viral.

"What sort of business are you starting? Will you need help?" She smiled. "My son is just out of college. He's a smart boy. A self-starter. He'd be an asset."

Grant nodded. Once people deduced his identity, he prepared for the onslaught of requests. Strangers asked for favors with no hesitation. Fortune favored the bold or at least enticed acquaintances to make demands.

While he didn't appreciate the financial asks from unknown people, he had rewarded those who supported and encouraged him. He'd started philanthropy work through a foundation run by his mom. He wanted to lift up the next generation of doers. But he was never prepared for the spontaneous asks after saying hello for the first time. "Tourism and hospitality." He hoped the vague answer would dissuade her.

"You're in luck." Her grin broadened, stretching from ear to ear.

He gulped.

"My Josh majored in hospitality."

Of course he did. Since first hitting the news with his successful company, Grant had been bombarded with eager candidates ready for any employment opportunity.

Matchmaking mamas had evolved from setting up marriages to procuring careers for their children.

"He could be a manager. What do you think? I'm sure you'll have generous starting salaries and healthcare packages."

He cleared his throat. "At the moment, I'm starting small. Just myself and my boat. Tours of Loon Lake, Lake Superior, and the Apostle Islands. Nothing to manage besides my time." He forced a chuckle.

Judy frowned. "Oh. Sure. Okay." She turned away.

The metal-on-metal squeal of a drawer opening made him cringe.

He didn't mind being ignored. He kept returning to Molly. Her greeting was remarkable for how unexpected and normal the tone. He never thought he'd see her again. But if he did? He might have dreamed of her apologizing for berating him in college and then ghosting. Maybe she'd have begged for forgiveness.

But the real Peanut would never behave like that.

She acted like she hadn't spared him a thought. Maybe she hadn't. He smiled. Something about her ignorance of his lifestyle and wealth lightened him. She treated him the same with no special favors. Now he had to find a way to bump into her again. He couldn't risk fate.

Judy extended a pile of forms through the opening on the counter. "Here are all the forms required. If you need any sort of help, you can call my number. I circled it at the top."

Grant grabbed the stack of forms. He lifted his gaze and smiled at the older woman. He appreciated her position, wanting to help her son. Both his parents did the same. Dad had supported the app idea first but talked Mom on board. Without his family, he wouldn't have made a name for himself. "Thank you."

"My son is an excellent sailor, too. He knows these waters. Don't mistake the Great Lakes for being kind to beginners. Some of the most famous shipwrecks happened here. The deep water is as turbulent as the rough seas."

"I'll keep that in mind," Grant replied.

The front doors opened, and a crowd of people rushed inside. Voices carried through the halls. Flashes of light popped. The wave of noise traveled down the corridor towards one of the courtrooms.

Grant caught a glimpse of a man in orange shuffling forward between uniformed police officers. "What's that about?" he asked Judy, pointing over his shoulder.

"The preliminary hearing for the state against the Prims." Judy's eyes widened. "Wait a minute." She glanced at her notepad. "You're starting a tour company in Loon Lake, right?"

He nodded, his throat tightening and cutting off a reply.

"Did you find a gap in the market after their arrests? Or did you buy them out?" Her gaze narrowed.

She was shrewd. He'd give her that. And he had to remember life in a close-knit community meant nothing was truly secret if it was shared with another person. His acquisition would probably remain a hot topic of discussion for months.

"What am I saying?" She chuckled. "You're a savvy

businessman. You won't get involved with something shady and risk your reputation. And you've set yourself up to avoid being called for jury duty."

He forced a laugh and clutched the papers. "Thanks again." He strode away while he could. He had a hard time reconciling the small community he'd known and loved since childhood being a breeding ground for criminal masterminds.

Evil lurked anywhere.

She was correct that he was smart enough to avoid any underhanded dealings. His purchase was clear-cut. He had no association with the unfortunate previous owners.

A door opened, and the crowd dispersed, entering the room.

Grant neared the front entrance and took a deep breath. Ignorance wasn't always bliss. He reasoned he knew exactly enough to purchase the tour company. Learning more felt akin to gossiping. Or was he making a mistake by not digging too deep?

"A chill creeps over an otherwise sunny summer day," a deep voice said, carrying through the building as clear as if the man stood inches away.

Grant slowed his pace and spotted the man in a hoodie holding his phone to his mouth. The casual-clad figure didn't dress like a professional TV-ready journalist. "The Prims face their first appearances before a judge today. Will Steve accept all the blame? Join me as we unravel the messy web of lies and deceit every week on *The Sins of the Father*, available on your favorite podcast channels."

Grant definitely didn't want to get involved in that. He pushed outside and jogged down the steps, shrugging his shoulders and ducking his head. He didn't want to end up on the nightly news. Instead, he headed in the direction opposite the TV news cameras. He'd review the forms from the safety and comfort of the inn. He'd given himself a day off the boat. Maybe he could use it to his best advantage.

Chapter Three

Behind the wheel again, Molly turned off First Street. She followed the directions she'd been given. But she still couldn't make sense of the instructions. Every second in the car added to her fatigue. She was ready to be done with the road to nowhere.

Her smartphone didn't recognize the address written on the key. An internet search didn't pull up a company website but linked to the article on the town's historical society page. How could a business be the key to local prosperity with no information available? The town couldn't be dependent on it for its economy.

After she'd driven through town twice, she called Mr. Baird. His secretary told her to pull onto the dock at the last traffic light. At the intersection, she flashed her turn signal. "Here goes nothing."

She drove onto a concrete pier extending into the bay. She slowed the car and parked in front of a four-story building.

Staring at the ugly monolith, she scrunched her nose.

She'd seen similar prefab construction in some of the rural towns she had passed on her drive north. She wasn't sure what she expected of a sawmill. Maybe something small and historic. Mr. Baird called it old, giving her a vague picture of a waterwheel. Not this.

The sides of the building were covered in corrugated metal. White paint flaked off in sections, exposing rust and wood underneath. From the front, she spotted no windows. Under the worn roof, the only break in the sheeting was what looked like a garage door. Next to it, she spotted a smaller, solid panel door. She gawked, unsure how the property had the potential to be turned into condos without being razed. The location must be the sum of its value.

She hopped out of the car, shutting the door and locking the rental vehicle behind her. She scanned the lakeshore. A raised wooden boardwalk skirted the water's edge. Brightly painted shops faced the lake. The setup worked to connect society and nature in a pleasing way. She longed to stroll and enjoy the fresh air and cheerful company of the tourists.

On the opposite side of the lake, a Victorian building rose like an elegant landmark over the town. She remembered the Inn at Loon Lake from her initial digital survey of the town. She wasn't prepared for its grandeur in person. With a pair of turrets on either end, the inn almost touched the clouds and dominated the landscape. The white building shone like a beacon, calling to her.

If her credit card wasn't dangerously close to the limit before she bought her plane ticket, rented the car, and paid for the new wardrobe, she'd have been tempted to check in. At least she'd be guaranteed a bed in a habitable room. She warily eyed the sawmill again. She'd vowed to adapt as long as she could rest for the night. She'd find a way.

Should she nudge the insurance company with a friendly phone call? If she knew her reimbursement would kick in sometime soon, she'd splurge now. *Don't spend money you don't have.* Mom might be unreachable at the moment, but her advice carried on in Molly's subconscious.

Time to get going and focus on one step at a time.

She strolled along the side, heading towards the lake. The back of the building hovered over the edge of the water. A large, wooden water wheel protruded from the mill. It didn't move. Frowning at the missing rungs and damaged remnants, she'd guess the property hadn't been operational in years.

How could one person, not a corporation, turn this into a residential space? Any construction would require heavy-duty machinery, the sort only licensed operators handled. She understood the motivation. The view was spectacular. Past the edge of the mill, the lake stretched to the open water of the channel under a clear sky. A chill hung in the air. August meant shorter days but not the warmer temps she'd grown accustomed to after spending thirteen summers in Chicago.

The air felt lighter as she filled her lungs with big gulps of fresh oxygen. She breathed like she'd been trapped in the smoke-filled hallway of her building for days instead of minutes. Her raw throat still ached from that terrible escape. While she remained unsure of her unexpected windfall, she couldn't fault the timing.

"Hello? May I help you?"

With a jerk, Molly straightened at the haughty tone. Had she been loudly melodramatic? She shielded her gaze with one hand and squinted.

Kneeling next to the other corner of the building, a tall woman with her hair scraped back in a severe dark bun held a measuring tape against the building. Her hair was nearly black, so saturated the color almost looked navy blue against her pale skin. The woman retracted the measuring tape with a click and rose. She crossed her arms and arched a brow.

Molly pressed her lips together. The stranger was asking to help Molly on her own property? She couldn't deal with another hiccup this week and hated feeling like she had trespassed. She needed peace. With a wave, she smiled. The only way to approach the stranger would be to backtrack and walk around the building from the other side. "Hello. I'm Molly Maguire."

"Oh." The brunette flushed and tugged at her shirt cuffs.

The stoic woman didn't offer the effusive welcome Mr. Baird implied Molly would receive. Nor did she apologize for trespassing.

"He found you."

Apparently so. "Yes. Here I am." Molly held out both arms wide.

"Did you ask him to exhume the body?" The woman scrunched her nose and curled her upper lip.

"Of course I didn't." *The stranger knew about that?*

Did everyone in town? Sudden understanding flashed in her mind. No wonder the hostess acted so strangely. She must have imagined Molly was a gravedigger. "I did one of those mail DNA kits. Months ago. On a whim. For my mom." She had to stop rambling, but the sudden surge to prove her innocence against a grotesque claim was overwhelming. "I guess that's how he found me."

"Are you sure you didn't? Because you definitely have a lot to gain."

"I would never." Molly hated the defensive tone in her words, but the stranger pinned her against a wall with her blistering takedown. Drawing in a deep breath, Molly considered the situation. She still hadn't received a reason for the stranger's presence, and she didn't feel comfortable with the woman skulking about. Without windows, Molly would have no idea if anyone lurked outside the building. She hoped the garage door locked, and the front possessed a deadbolt. "May I ask what you're doing here?"

The woman widened her gaze and flared her nostrils.

Why was she offended? Molly didn't trespass on the stranger's property. "I'm not angry or going to press charges or anything."

The stranger snorted and pulled herself straighter. "Well, you wouldn't find much support if you tried a stunt like that." The woman sniggered.

Molly sucked in a sharp breath. The words whistled past her like fired arrows. Was the comment a threat? Or a statement? Weren't small towns supposed to be friendly and inviting?

"I'm Elise from the historical society." She tugged her

blazer over her pencil skirt. "I was in talks to develop the property as a museum slash event space. I didn't realize you'd been found."

"Oh." Molly wasn't prepared for the stranger to be so shockingly honest. The woman must be aware of the deadline for Molly's claim. Molly took another step closer to land and away from the deep water. "I found out about the property very recently."

"I'm guessing several hours ago?" Elise snorted and eyed Molly from head to toe. "Did you drive here as soon as you learned? You're quite lucky."

Molly shifted her weight from foot to foot. She'd argue the opposite but wouldn't waste energy with someone determined against her. No witty retort formed in response to the woman's bait. Molly was glad to be in control of her tongue again as she considered.

From what Mr. Baird had told her, her presence was in everyone's best interest. Bringing up the legend—*A Maguire in possession is prosperity for all*—to justify herself wasn't appropriate in light of how she was found. Was the town mad at her? The way Elise phrased her argument, Molly definitely embodied the role of villain.

Molly cleared her throat. "I'm still deciding what I'll do."

"Yeah, but you'll take it. Of course you will." Elise lifted both arms. "Why wouldn't you?"

Molly glanced at the building again. All she saw was a major headache. The roof was old and worn, exposing several layers of asphalt shingles in some sections. Some of the rusted areas of metal siding near the foundation looked suspiciously like the sort a critter caused while creating a home. She was here because she had no other option and hoped she'd sleep through the night without worrying for her safety.

Apparently, the townsfolk and lawyer saw the disheveled property differently. What wasn't she seeing? She turned to Elise, but the woman was gone.

Her departure was probably for the best. Molly didn't want a continued argument. Without all the facts, she operated from a disadvantage. She retraced her route around the building, narrowing her gaze at the wheel. Nothing stood out to her but perhaps she'd find the worth inside.

At the front, she pulled the key from her pocket and unlocked the door. Against the wall, she crept along inch by inch. Her fingers connected with a switch, and she flipped it. A low hum preceded the pop of electricity.

Artificial light filled the open space, nearly two stories tall, from a row of fluorescent lights overhead. Molly rubbed her eyes against the sharp change in brightness and studied the property. Giant saws protruded from the floor and lay discarded on tables. She knew nothing about the lumber business, but the tools looked worn and rusted. She'd guess the mill had last been operational during the early part of the twentieth century. At some point, the structure had been sealed in metal sheeting and a garage door had been added.

At the back of the main room, the wheel remained unmoving, although in better condition inside than out. What drew her gaze were the old beams that stretched the height of the building, supporting the walls. The solid timbers could account for the building's desirability, highlighting the craftsmanship of a bygone era. With a very healthy budget and a strong vision, the property could be restored to something unique and grand. This was the sort of project that needed someone with a big imagination and oodles of flexibility. Like Grant.

Of all the people she'd imagined encountering again one day, she had never included Grant. Should she call him and check in? She might be down on her luck, but he looked worse off with his holey t-shirt and scraggly hair. Sleeping on a boat sounded only slightly better than a car. He would be welcome to stay under the sawmill's roof. She'd better check out her living quarters before offering him assistance. She'd hate to put him on the spot to accept her charity and potentially end up worse than his current situation.

She strolled along the perimeter, hugging the edge of the wall. At the back, she found a spiral staircase. She could only hope her long lost relative had made some progress for living quarters upstairs. Maybe someone else followed a plan and actually came out ahead. Or—better yet—the curse had run its course.

* * *

Grant wasn't following Molly.

To do so, he needed specifics. Like where she was staying, what kind of car she was driving, or—most importantly—why she was here. He shook his head and studied the boardwalk under his feet. None really mattered.

If he narrowed his questions to the most pertinent,

he'd focus on her mode of transportation. He was rather surprised to see her in a locale that didn't offer publicly accessible buses to get around town. When she was in college, she didn't have a vehicle. She seemed content with him behind the wheel. It was the only control she knowingly gave up.

He remembered gladly spending hours driving for the chance to find time together in their schedules. While she was an early bird, taking her classes in the morning, he selected the latest classes possible. He'd pick her up after her last class and drive to the neighboring small town, forty minutes away, to drop her off at an art gallery for work. Then he'd return after her shift ended to bring her back to campus, content just being with her as she studied or spoke.

She was so clever and driven. He liked who he was in her company. She gave him a direction, both literally and figuratively. Losing her had upset where he thought his life was headed.

After leaving the courthouse, he could have returned to the boathouse or his room at the inn. What he thought might take a couple of days was accomplished in one afternoon. He'd taken the forms and driven to a coffee shop, working through the process quickly. He purchased priority mail and dropped the papers into the post.

When he drove out of the parking lot, he steered towards town, taking the scenic route to the inn. On a beautiful day, he didn't want to head back indoors. Instead, he enjoyed a leisurely stroll down the raised wooden walkway curving along the lakeshore. He hadn't realized how far his meandering had taken him until he glimpsed her hop out of the car and approach a dilapidated building on its own pier.

The old sawmill?

If curiosity led him to slow his pace, who could blame him? Over the years, he'd often thought about Peanut, wondering about her life. When his company first took off, he wanted to rub her nose in his accomplishments. If he'd followed some arbitrary plan, he'd have taken a low-level, nine-to-five. On the safe track to mid-level management, he would have lost all his creative energy and flow. He would not have had the runaway success that set him up for life.

But he'd have had her?

The question haunted him. In the first profitable year, the urge to gloat evaporated, leaving him with the certainty that if he convinced her to come on board his gaming company, he could reach new heights. His ego advised that she'd reach out to him. She never had.

He'd searched for her online and never found her. Had she preemptively blocked him on various sites? Or was she really that oblivious to the world of social media? For a photographer, the latter seemed unlikely.

Today, her shock was genuine. She hadn't tried to flatter or ask for a favor. She treated him the same way she had all those years ago. The polite but aloof interaction intoxicated him. He wanted more time in her company.

He scrubbed his face with both hands and scanned his locale again. The building looked like a warehouse. Stationed prominently on the lakeshore, the property wasn't a good spot for someone wanting to hide or lay low. Was she here to start over? Or was he misinter-preting their awkward encounter?

Heavy footsteps echoed off the boardwalk.

He spotted a familiar buttoned-up woman shaking her head and muttering as she rounded the building and barreled to the walkway. "Elise? Hello? Are you all right?"

The brunette halted and lifted her chin. "Why are you here? Are you helping her? Some sort of newcomer's brigade?" She pointed a thumb to the building.

"Sorry?" He frowned. He'd never seen her so angry and animated. In his typical interactions, he had encountered a reserved, cool woman. This version boiled over, steam escaping her ears.

"Are you involved with whatever is going on over there? Her convenient false identity?" She waggled a finger.

He was easily eight inches taller than the petite female. But her anger was ominous. He gulped.

"Because I will find out the truth. We are not losing on a lie."

He held out both palms. "I don't know what you're talking about. If there's a problem, maybe we should go talk to the authorities. I'm just a guy walking down the street."

"Oh, never mind. That property belongs to the town. Maguire or no, it's too late." Elise turned and stormed down the street.

He waited until she disappeared down the block. Then he released the sigh building in his chest. He faced the building and squinted. What was Molly involved with?

She's the heir.

The thought hit him like the slap of the chilly water on a windy day. Molly was the faceless entity striking so much fear into longtime locals. He was too shocked by the realization to do more than feel. Gratitude lingered in the warmth tingling through him. He never thought he'd see her again, and yet, they crossed paths in a totally random way. It had to be fate.

On the heels of luck, however, worry followed quickly.

Loon Lake was a special place. He never expected to settle in the community full time. And—for all intents and purposes—he still hadn't. Regardless of his permanent address, he couldn't shake his love for the town and his devotion to keeping it hale, hearty, and whole.

Everyone seemed set against an heir. The community spoke about the inevitability that a new owner would change the shoreline forever. No one wanted the solitary pier developed into a waterfront high-rise, but fear-based rumors couldn't be stopped. Gossip spread until it became accepted lore. Molly couldn't know the town was set against her, determined to stop any sort of development. If she did, she'd probably leave.

He wanted her here. But he wanted things to stay the same. How could he intervene to make that happen? Could he support both causes?

He knew better than to attempt a rescue. In the past, Molly had never appreciated any of his gallant gestures.

He'd given her his number on a sticky note and knew her location. He'd have to wait for her to find him.

Spinning, he strode towards the boardwalk only a few hundred yards away.

"Hey, stranger," a voice called.

Grant stopped in his tracks, scanning his surroundings. He'd reached the nineties-themed ice cream shop.

Scoops, There It Is was closing for the night. The owner, Zach Jenkins, waved to him and turned back to lock the door. "Did you get into it with Elise?"

"Was I loud?" Grant asked, cringing. He hated raising his voice to anyone, let alone a woman, and thought he'd kept himself in check. But his emotions regarding Molly might have got the better of him as he rallied to her defense.

Zach chuckled. "No. She stormed off past my store and kicked up the breeze. You look like you could use a treat. Unfortunately for you, I'm sold out."

With Zach's insistence on small-batch production, he often sold out of his inventory. "I'm fine," Grant bit out.

Zach crossed his arms over his chest.

"Okay, not fine," Grant relented. "But nothing ice cream can solve."

"I don't believe you. Ice cream fixes everything. Or at least it doesn't make a situation worse."

Grant had no way to refute it, and maybe Zach had a point to his logic. Showing up at Molly's doorstep with a pint might provide an opportunity. He'd offer the treat as a housewarming gift. She might invite him in. They could chat.

"But it's moot because I'm sold out. Don't worry,

though. Elise will turn her sights on someone else soon enough. The community is full of people falling short of her high demands."

"She's not mad at me. I was in the wrong place at the wrong time. An unsuspecting bystander that crossed her path." He wouldn't pretend—even to himself—that he was innocent. Molly's arrival brightened him more than he could have dreamed. He'd do anything to help her establish herself in town so she'd stay for good.

"Oh, well. Does that mean Baird found the heir?" Zach shuddered.

Grant shrugged. He'd offer no comment or say anything he couldn't recant if necessary. Somehow, the idea spread that Lily Maguire's eternal slumber was disturbed in the hunt for her heir. Grant couldn't trace the source, so he disregarded the notion.

Zach was sharp and wily. He'd been in a cold war against the inn and Christopher Lewis until Christopher's wife, Ashley, called for a ceasefire. Zach was at his best when he exercised his masterminding skills. Would he turn his attention to the sawmill? Or, more specifically, focus on Molly?

"Very interesting." Zach stroked his chin.

Grant disagreed. He'd come to Loon Lake seeking a peaceful second act and wanted the same for her. Whatever brought her here didn't matter. She shouldn't be held accountable for others' actions. If she needed a champion, she'd find one in him.

A cell phone chirped.

Zach slid the phone out of his pocket, smiling at the screen. "Nice chatting with you as always."

Grant tipped his head and continued on his trek to the inn. He'd accept his dismissal before he gave away any information.

Without planning his route, he had figuratively ended up at her door. He had to trust in the process and relinquish control of his destiny. Because maybe he'd been led to right where he was supposed to be. Again.

Movement caught in his peripheral vision as he neared the inn's lakeshore.

The boardwalk ended at the sand. A swimming section of the water was marked with buoys and rope. The ruins of a lighthouse sat like a blackened burn pit on a tiny island accessible via a rope bridge.

The lawn and beach were deserted. Had he seen a bird? Then he spotted the person.

Mr. Willie, the inn's curmudgeonly groundskeeper, toiled on the island. The man was as much a fixture of the landscape as the inn itself. He spoke in a harsh, clipped tone like he took offense to every conversation. And he remained always working in the background. Without him, the inn—and, by default, the town— would have collapsed. The older man stopped and stared.

With a wave, Grant turned to the building and found his way to the walking path around the side. He'd do well to follow Mr. Willie's example. Keep his head down and focus on his own tasks.

A hot shower, a good meal, and a warm bed were all he had space for in the near future. Tomorrow, he'd wake up and work on his new business again. He had enough to accomplish without adding Molly's dilapidated sawmill to the mix.

Chapter Four

Molly flailed her arms, slapping the surface of the icy water. Her skin tingled. She couldn't feel her legs. Oh no. Would she drown?

She couldn't see the shore. She'd fallen into the lake. Her legs were heavy and limp. Her efforts to tread water were pointless. Her knees wouldn't bend. She couldn't move her lower body. So much for years of swim lessons. She was trapped upright, bobbing and unable to save herself. This was the end. She slipped down, her shoulders under the surface, and her whole body jerked.

With a start, she opened her eyes. She'd been dreaming. She was lying on a full-size bed, staring at an unfamiliar ceiling. Her apartment had a popcorn finish, but she looked up at tiles. She scanned the room. The shadows cast by unfamiliar shapes offered no clues.

She pushed herself up to a seated position and drew in a deep breath. On her slow exhale, she remembered the events of the last few days. She didn't have an apartment anymore. She was lying in the studio apartment above the old sawmill. And she was soaked.

Squinting, she narrowed her gaze in the dark and patted the linens. The bed was drenched through the coverlet to the sheets. She untangled her limbs from the mess and hopped out of the bed.

"OUCH." Her knee connected with a sharp corner of the bedside table. She fumbled for the lamp and paused. Damp hands and electricity didn't mix.

She blinked, and her eyes adjusted to the dim light coming through the break in the curtains. The bed was soaked, water dripping from the drop panels in the ceiling.

From fire to water, what was next? Getting struck by lightning? She wasn't one to rail against fate. But couldn't she catch one break? Was the universe determined to bring her to her knees?

She picked her way from the bed to the windows and pulled back the curtains, illuminating the studio apartment somewhat thanks to a streetlight outside. When she had reached the top of the stairs hours earlier, she'd been relieved to find habitable living quarters. The space was open concept and roughly a thousand square feet. She preferred walls and privacy. But she was hardly in a position to get choosy.

Along the front of the building, a modern kitchen hugged the wall. In the corner, a full bathroom with a shower instead of a tub. With a couch in the center of the space, anchored on a rug with an entertainment center and TV, she felt almost comfortable.

She had decided against inviting Grant into the intimate space. He'd fill every inch available. If she told him he could sleep on the main floor, she would toss and turn, worrying about him and the giant, rusty saws.

But two steps forward and two steps back.

Now, the apartment was flooded with an inch of water. How had a leak sprung in the ceiling? A burst pipe? A sprinkler system? In the dark, she couldn't make out any overhead nozzles. She wasn't about to risk her safety by flipping on the power for confirmation.

At least she hadn't included Grant in her damp misery.

She crossed her arms and rubbed her wet shoulders. Pajamas clung to her clammy skin. She couldn't stay, but she wasn't sure what to do. If she called Mr. Baird, she didn't know how much assistance he could provide. Her welcome to town wasn't particularly warm, but she hoped the sprinkler hadn't activated in response to some sort of vandalism. *Old pipes burst.* She preferred that explanation even if she didn't know why pipes would be run through the ceiling and not the floor.

She spotted the wall clock. Ten o'clock. With luck, she'd catch a night manager at the inn and check in. She could figure out what to do next—and how to pay her maxed credit card bill—when she was dry and rested. She crossed to the closet in the corner of the room.

The walk-in was spared from the flood. Her aunt's clothes hung on double racks. Sensible shoes lined the floor. She'd have to go through and donate the woman's wardrobe. Was there really no one else in town closer to the woman? No wonder she'd been on the receiving end of such hostility. If her aunt left the mill to the town as a contingency, she must have had a reason. Why should Molly get in the middle of the civic arrangement? *Because I have nothing else.*

In the corner, her purse and banker's box sat on the floor next to her shopping bags of clothes. She quickly changed into jeans and a dry sweatshirt, dropping her wet pajamas to the ground. From the corner of her gaze, she spotted the edge of something between the trim and hardwood floor.

Kneeling on the wood, she slipped her hands into the space and tugged. After a few yanks, she pulled out a faded, manilla file folder. Why hide documents? Shouldn't important paperwork be secured in a fireproof box? Or a safety deposit box?

Water streamed nearby. She had to get going before she was soaked to the bone. Again. She ran through the apartment and turned every shut off valve she could find. The water slowed but didn't fully stop. Whatever pipe had burst, she hoped it would drain its source, too. If she had a flashlight, she'd head downstairs and investigate the first floor. Without enough illumination, however, the rusty tools scattered on the ground presented a real danger to her safety. She wasn't going to stay and be miserable here.

She grabbed her things off the ground and spotted a duffle bag on the shelf over the hanging rod. Jumping, she pulled the corner of the luggage. A wave of dust coated her face. Sneezing and blinking, she stuffed her belongings inside, folder included. With the suitcase and purse in one hand and her wet PJs on top of the box under her arm, she made her way out of the apartment, down the steps, and out to her rental car.

She drove to the inn and parked in the lot. She'd stopped sneezing and wiped the tears off her face. A glance in the rearview mirror assured her she was almost normal. She snorted and rolled her eyes. She left the wet clothes on the floor next to the banker's box and hopped out of the car.

Approaching the inn, she dragged up her gaze. The grand style was reminiscent of the nineteenth-century resorts she'd read about but never visited. She fidgeted with her sweatshirt hem. She couldn't change now. Maybe the night clerk wouldn't sneer at her casual wear.

She entered the building and sucked in a sharp breath. From the gleaming hardwoods to the polished paneling, she widened her gaze. The interior reflected a bygone time with velvet upholstered chairs and brass sconces; it felt like she'd stepped back in time. Carved wooden posts supported the recessed ceilings.

From the entrance, she spied windows overlooking the lake. Within the larger space, intimate seating areas invited visitors to relax and sit. She glimpsed brightly colored, patterned wallpaper and a tiled fireplace. A sigh built in her chest. She'd love to sink into softness. She'd already received a less-than-warm introduction to town. With her dusty bag, oversized sweatshirt, and dark jeans, she was out of place again.

She wiped the duffle and rubbed her palm against her thigh. She wouldn't back down from the first decision she'd made in what felt like a year. She'd go forward.

"May I help you?" A crisp voice asked.

She lifted her chin and met the gaze of a smiling woman behind the front desk. With minimal makeup and long hair, she looked college-age. With any luck, she wouldn't recognize Molly's last name and immediately deduce her purpose in town. She'd like one interaction with a member of the community that didn't involve an instant judgment and narrowed-eyed gaze. "Do you have any rooms available? I don't need anything fancy."

"Certainly. It's the end of the season, so we have a few vacancies." With a nod, she dashed her fingers over the keyboard. "Will you be staying one night? Or more?"

Good question. Molly bit the inside of her cheek. "Let's start with one." She pulled out her driver's license and credit card, handing both to the clerk. She rocked back on her heels. After the excitement of the past few days, she'd gladly spend the next week in a warm bed. But she might not have the chance, and she definitely didn't have the funds. She'd settle for a hot beverage. "Is the restaurant open? Or a coffee shop or something?"

The clerk returned her credit card and license, along with a receipt for signature. "The bar is. If you head across the lobby to the restaurant, you can't miss it. But it will close soon. Check-out is at eleven. Please stop by the desk before nine if you'd like to extend your stay." Molly signed the paper with a flourish and stuffed the card and license in her wallet.

The clerk slid the key card across the counter in a paper sleeve.

She dropped it into her purse and zipped the bag closed. While her life was at the mercy of Murphy's Law or a curse, she could take no chances. If everything happened in threes, she must be nearing the end of her bad luck. Or so she hoped. "Great. Thank you."

"If you need anything, please let me know. I'm Ashley Hale-Lewis, the owner."

A million questions tickled Molly's tongue. The owner? She'd have information about the sawmill and Molly's family. But could she dare ask?

Her encounters with the locals so far left Molly on edge. If she wasn't fawned over by the lawyer, she was feared by everyone else. She wanted what peace she could get this evening. Perhaps she should be grateful the woman didn't ask about her name.

"Have a good evening, and thank you for staying with us," Ashley said.

With a nod, Molly grabbed her bag off the floor and turned towards the restaurant across the lobby. A cup of coffee was cheap, exactly what she could afford. In the morning, she'd have to reassess the ridiculous plan to come here instead of going to her mom's empty house. She could still get out of this situation before anything else happened.

With the curse following her, perhaps she had better take old superstitions into more serious consideration. If bad things came in threes, she was either in the clear or dangerously close to the start of more tragedy.

Sitting at the bar of the inn's restaurant, Grant stared into the empty glass. Would ordering another caffeine and sugar-laden soda tempt fate? He wanted to get some sleep tonight. He should rest easy. He'd accomplished what he came to do. But he was on edge, tense, waiting and ready to see Molly again.

In a fight, he'd pick Molly any day of the week. She was scrappy and determined. Her self-deprecating, underdog attitude caught his attention at a turning point in his life. After wasting four years and making no progress towards his degree, he decided to get serious. And then he met her.

With determination, she had followed some sort of invisible path only she could see. She stuck so doggedly to the track, never veering. He'd wanted her to swerve and off-road with him for a while. She had always returned like a compass finding magnetic north. So why had she seemed lost?

"Another?"

He lifted his gaze to the bartender.

"We close in twenty." The man dried pint glasses with a rag.

Grant sighed and swirled the final dregs of cola and melted ice in the bottom of the glass. He was rude for keeping the bar open with his presence. But he felt worse about not showing up at the right moment to defend Molly and stop whatever conversation had happened.

After he had retreated to the inn, he grabbed a book and sunglasses and spent hours on the upper deck, facing her property. If something happened, he'd know. Right? He wouldn't burst in on her solitude unless he had reasonable cause. Like if someone started poking around the pier or another car parked at the door.

He couldn't stop his heart from hoping that they'd

crossed paths again for resolution. As much as he hated to admit his former corporate assistant was right that his personal life was stagnant in sacrifice to his career, the ever-wise Karen was almost close to the truth. He'd had a chance at something special and blew it. Until he understood what had gone wrong, he'd never consider risking his heart again. He liked to learn from his mistakes and improve. Now he finally had the chance to get a few answers. And then he'd move on. He vowed.

"We're almost closed."

Frowning, Grant stared at the man. Were five minutes unreasonable to make a decision? But the bartender gazed past him towards the entrance. Swiveling on the stool, Grant spotted her.

Wet hair hung to her shoulders, soaking a gray sweat-shirt. She gripped a worn, faded duffle bag. Purple shadows under her eyes shouted her exhaustion. A movie crew wouldn't be so heavy-handed in the cosmetics department. She looked like she had two black eyes.

Grant stood, kicking over the barstool in his haste to pull one out for her. Fragile. Vulnerable. He'd never seen her like this.

"Thank you," she murmured, dropping her bag. "I'm sorry. I know you're closing. But I've had a rough night. Is there any way I can get a hot tea? Or a decaf? Or something? Please?" Her voice cracked.

Grant turned towards the bartender and arched a brow.

The man flung his rag over his shoulder and nodded. "Be right back."

Molly sank onto the stool, dropping her arms to the solid counter and resting her head.

Grant righted his stool and scooted it next to hers. He faced her, angling his body towards hers and hovering his hand over his back like he'd catch her if she fell. Had she fallen?

"Are you okay?" He swallowed. Up close, she looked even worse. Had she been hurt? "What happened? Why are you soaking wet?"

She rubbed her red nose and sniffed. With a heavy sigh, she propped her elbow and rested her chin in a palm. She faced him. "It's been a week."

"It's not even Wednesday."

She shuddered and straightened. "Oh, don't remind me. I wish I could sleep for the next year."

He nodded like he understood. All he knew was he was treading on dangerous ground. Any comment on her appearance wasn't likely to be well-received. But he hated the melancholy hanging over her. Could he tease her back to normal? "And miss the chance at my charming company? I'm hurt."

She rolled her eyes. "Why are you here? How did you find this place? It seems rather strange we'd both end up in the middle of nowhere."

She didn't want to discuss her circumstances. Fine. He'd play by her rules. Maybe this was his real second chance at closure. She needed help. All those years ago, she'd guided him to higher ground. Now he could do the same. And then he could be happy for the rest of his life, knowing he'd repaid her. "As a kid, we vacationed here most summers."

"Really? It's so out of the way." Her tone was incredulous.

"Off the beaten path, sure. But a wonderful getaway. It's a small community, and you either love it or hate it."

"You moved here after college."

"No. A business opportunity arose very recently, and I came."

"The tour business, right?" she asked.

He grinned, lifting the corner of his mouth. She remembered. He wasn't sure if she'd listened at all or if she kept his number. But she had paid attention earlier in the day. He was melting the ice. With a hairdryer, maybe, but he was making some progress towards thawing her.

"Are you here on vacation?"

"I wish." She snorted. "If I tell you, you'll laugh at me."

"Why?"

"Because it's ridiculous. Unbelievable. Far-fetched."

He crossed his arms over his chest and narrowed his gaze. He'd never poked fun at her expense. Ever. But maybe she was worried turnabout was fair play. He arched a brow and held her gaze steady. "Tell me. I'm a good listener," he murmured.

Her expression softened, perhaps remembering she'd praised that particular character quality years ago.

"Oh, okay." She shook her head and straightened. "My apartment building burned down."

"Yikes. When? Last night? Are you okay?" He scanned her but saw no obvious injuries. Smoke inhalation was deadly. "Should I take you to a hospital?"

"No, no. I'm okay. The fire happened back in Chicago…" She tapped a finger to her chin. "Gosh, I guess that was yesterday. Like I said. These past two days are the longest week of my life."

"How bad was the fire?" He kept his voice low, not wanting to spark a panic with too much concern. She'd been funny like that, wanting his care but recoiling from any grand gesture.

"I escaped with a few things."

His stomach dropped. "That sounds…not great." *Not great?* He couldn't come up with something better to say to help her through a difficult time? He scrambled for a cohesive thought. "What happened next? You don't go from an apartment fire to getting out of town immediately." *Unless you started it.* He kept the joke to himself. She was too fragile for humor.

"I went straight to work and was fired for making personal calls on company time."

Personal calls? That didn't sound like her. Unless she had a boyfriend she needed to touch base with. Or a husband. He studied her left hand. No ring didn't mean a whole lot if she was woken up by an alarm with seconds to escape. Where was the man now? Why leave her on her own in a new town? "I'm missing something. Why are you," he pointed to the ground, "here?"

"Before I was fired, I had a visitor. A lawyer from Loon Lake. Leonard Baird. Apparently, I had a long-lost relative who died and left me property."

"The mill."

She narrowed her gaze and pressed her lips together.

He held up his hands. "Small town. I swear. I was

minding my own business, but word spreads, and I bumped into Elise."

Molly propped her elbow on the counter, resting her head in her hand. "I can't catch a break."

"Don't blame her. I'm bright. I can put together the context clues." He bumped her shoulder with his, not daring to offer more comfort than a friendly nudge.

"I'm being gossiped about, too? Did she tell you some draconian ghost story about me demanding the body be dug up?"

"No. Was she supposed to?"

Molly shuddered. "The lawyer tracked me through DNA. I mailed in a swab. Honestly, I wouldn't recommend those kits to anyone. More trouble than anything. Now I'm worried about what other revelations are waiting to jump out and upend my life."

A body was exhumed to claim an inheritance? He pressed his lips together. That sort of salacious tidbit would make anyone notorious in their community, no matter how large. In a small town like Loon Lake, however, it was enough of a scandal for a newcomer to never shake off. She'd be considered a necromancer, and her rundown sawmill home wouldn't change the image.

But he couldn't let her know that or she'd go into hiding. This random run-in must be fate. And he wouldn't push away a second chance. "Molly, it's me. I'm a little cleverer than the average guy on the street. I was a kid detective."

"Solving one case that you created hardly gives you the badge." She scrunched her nose and pursed her lips.

He grinned. She was fighting a laugh and had

dropped her downtrodden look. He was glad about that. As much as things had changed, at least something—his ability to lighten her mood—remained the same. "Am I right this time?"

"Yes. And speaking of cases." She hopped off the barstool and knelt on the ground. Unzipping the duffle, she rifled through the contents.

The bartender returned and dropped off a teapot, mug, sachets, and a sliced lemon.

She stood, holding a file. "Thank you."

The man nodded and exited through the swinging door again.

She handed Grant the file and sat on the stool. She dropped three slices of lemon into the mug and poured in hot water.

A burst of citrus released into the air.

He opened the file on the bar, glad for the distraction. He ran a finger along the tight, cursive scrawl of an unknown author. The ink left indentations on crisp, faded sheets of legal paper. "If you own a building, why are you here at the inn?"

She dunked a bag of black tea into the mug. "I woke up soaking wet. A pipe burst in the ceiling. Or the sprinkler system went off? I don't know. I think I turned off the water. Or, with my bad luck, as we speak, the building is filling up."

Her voice was nonchalant. He couldn't imagine she didn't care. The Peanut he knew kept everything in proper working order. Exhaustion must be overtaking her. He faced her. "Should we call someone?"

She shrugged. "I thought I'd reach out to the lawyer

in the morning. I am too tired to deal with whatever next steps he'll advise. I've had my fill of evacuations. Honestly, I just want my run of bad luck to end. I'm being chased by it."

"You believe in magic now? How much has changed?"

She sipped her tea, raising the mug with both hands.

He turned back to the file. Yep, he'd said the wrong thing again. In under ten minutes, he'd managed to lodge both feet in his mouth. "Is the building set up for living?"

"It was. Or at least the upstairs apartment was nice enough. Livable. It could have worked as a temporary home while I sorted through what to do." She set the drink on the counter. "I understand she wanted to convert the property into condos."

"Who told you that?" He clamped his hand over his mouth. He could have kicked himself. If he wanted to steer her towards community spirit, questioning her wasn't the way. What happened to thinking before speaking? He was off his game. "I'm sorry. I'm surprised. The mill is a landmark around here. Lily Maguire was a steward of history. I'd be shocked to learn that she wanted to develop the property so late in her life."

"Hmm. That's interesting." She wrinkled her brow and took another sip of her tea.

Silence settled between them.

He stared down at the bar. The polished surface reflected the lights overhead and a hazy image of his face. He looked anxious. Maybe he'd do better to follow her circumspect example. Clearly, she had no qualms about taking her time to consider her responses. He couldn't play games with her. He'd never hidden his thoughts—or his heart—from her scrutinizing view.

"I really have no firsthand knowledge of any concrete plans," Molly said at last. "I'm sorting through hearsay and opinions. I don't know if I'll be able to salvage anything out of the sawmill, much less develop the property. I found that file in a hidden spot in the closet. Please tell me it has instructions."

He studied the pages again. Nothing distinctive concerning construction or permits jumped off the page. "If you haven't uncovered a plan, what's yours?"

"I'm not sure," she murmured.

He widened his gaze. *How is that possible?* He didn't say the words aloud. Something about her was different: hesitant and halting where she'd been calm and confident. She asked for help, and he'd provide any assistance he could. She'd given him a chance.

"Maybe I will give the land to the town. Elise has big ideas for the use of the property." Molly traced the rim of the mug with a finger.

"Don't be fooled by the starched shirt and slicked-back hair. That's her professional uniform."

"Off the clock, I'll find her in sweatpants? If that's the case, I'll wait until I see her dressed down before I approach her again."

He chuckled, unable to picture Elise in anything fleece. "You're more likely to find Soupy, the Lake Superior monster, than to see Elise in a hoodie. Under normal circumstances, she's stoic. Never overly friendly, but she is respectful."

"I thought she was about to breathe fire."

"I'm sorry your first impression of her was poor. She's passionate about Loon Lake and working towards next year's big celebration of 125 years." While he'd had a similar initial encounter with the intense historian, he'd come to appreciate her drive. She was a valuable ally. He wanted Molly to be fully embraced and supported after her rough few days. Elise would be a key part of that acceptance.

He considered her earlier statement. "I can't believe you escaped a fire. You've been through a lot of trauma. Would you hand over your inheritance?" Would she leave? He wanted the status quo to include her. More importantly, he hated the idea of her destitution. She was the most capable—if also detrimentally careful—person he'd ever known.

"I didn't know about it until yesterday. Or was it this morning? A few days ago?" She rubbed her eyes and yawned. "I'm going through a lot. Maybe this is a know-when-to-fold-them moment."

He couldn't believe what he was hearing. She was smart and resourceful. She must have endured quite a lot in the past decade, to be felled by extenuating circumstances. Recent events sounded almost unbelievable. The statistical odds of losing two homes in two days had to be almost zero. *Unless someone is manipulating fate.* He couldn't outright accuse the small, angry woman he met outside the mill of breaking and entering and flooding the building. But he also couldn't ignore what seemed like blatant interference. Elise had a lot to gain by pushing Molly away.

"The girl that could take anything and make it a flash card can't come up with a plan?"

She flushed and reached for her tea. "You remember that? It had no application in my professional life, as it turns out."

He could never forget. Studying had been one of their top date activities. He'd learned more about fine art than he'd ever intended or needed because of the time he spent helping her. But every smile was worth the paper-cuts incurred along the way. "I actually have found use for your flash card system in my life."

She widened her eyes and sipped her tea in response.

"The first time I met some bigwig corporate types, I studied all of their names, hobbies, degrees, and like-nesses on index cards. I was completely prepared because of you."

"If you can figure out a way to make a study guide and save my future, please knock yourself out."

He waited for her to push for more information about his life, but she didn't. Frowning, he focused on the document and read the first page again. After a few attempts, he mastered deciphering the handwriting. He re-read the paragraph several times. "This is strange. It mentions a legend. *A Maguire in possession is prosperity for all.* If that's the case, I doubt Elise would want the mill."

"Oh, not that again. The lawyer said the same thing. He made it sound like I'd be some sort of savior if I came to town. Loon Lake prospers with a Maguire at the mill." She rolled her eyes. "I'm sure it's something super cheesy, like friendship and community are more valuable than gold." She snorted. "And I'm certain Elise won't let it stop her from a takeover."

The corner of his mouth tugged up. Molly was different than he remembered. The self-deprecation was a charming update to the type-A perfection that lived in his memory. "Yeah, okay, but this document very specifically mentions a cache of wealth with directions. Your prosperity could be real and tangible."

"What? How?" She leaned close. "Is it a map of buried treasure? I could use a few gold bars."

Her hot breath tickled his neck. He drew in a deep breath, inhaling the scent of her rose shampoo. He remembered the smell, hazy, happy moments lingered just out of reach. "Well, not literally. I don't see a dotted line ending in an x. But these numbers are latitude and longitude markers. We could enter them into my GPS unit and find the spot."

She stiffened and turned away, pouring more hot water into her mug. "I don't have time for something silly."

"Why not? You don't have anywhere to live. You don't have a job. What else do you have?"

"My pride?" Her voice cracked.

He was a jerk. His careless words slapped her. He wished he could take back the last five minutes. The universe provided him with a chance at redemption in the eyes of his dream girl. And he laughed in the face of fate. "I shouldn't have said that. I'm sorry. I was unfeeling."

She shook her head and flipped up her palm. "Can I

have the file? Sorry to drag you into my spiraling out-of-control life."

"I'm happy to follow. As it is, I'm sort of between things myself."

She drew back her chin.

She really didn't know about his success. For some reason, he liked her continued ignorance of his circumstances. It was freedom. Maybe he could offer a little bit of the same. "I have a boat. I can take a few days to help. You can call the lawyer and let him help coordinate the cleanup process."

"Will we be sleeping on deck? I don't have a pillow or sleeping bag with me."

"No, I have living quarters and bedding. Nothing grand. But I promise you'll be comfortable." He crossed his heart. "Come on, this sounds like fun. When's the last time you had an adventure?"

She lifted her chin. "Adventure or escapade?"

In her stormy blue eyes, he saw hurt and uncertainty. He hated it. He wanted to build her back up to the woman he'd known who spurred him on. Now he could return the favor. And if he spent a few days in her company again, all the better. He wasn't going to think anything could come of time together. After two years, he never convinced her of forever. How could two weeks or even two days prove otherwise? "Is there a difference?"

"One implies a plan. The other..." She shivered.

Everything depended on the correct answer. "We will embark on an adventure." He drew an x over his heart. "Promise."

"Okay." She stuck her hand out. "You're on."

He shook her hand. "I've always wanted to dig up buried treasure."

"I hate to disappoint you with the reality."

You could never let me down.

She had no clue how wrong she was. The real world encompassed the good, the bad, and the ugly. At her side, however, she'd made sense of it all and shone a light on a path he hadn't been able to see. Now was his chance to return the favor. In a complete twist of fate, in an unlikely location, they'd found each other again. He was along for the ride, no questions asked.

Chapter Five

Pounding echoed inside Molly's head. She shut her eyes tighter. She needed one more minute of sleep. One more minute to bask in peace. One more minute of bliss before she had to face reality.

Last night, she had shared too much with the easygoing ex who never pretended to understand her worldview. Nothing was ever a big deal in Grant's world. Which was great until it wasn't. Sometimes, a person had to care and had to commit. He'd never shown any real strong inclination for either. She'd saved herself a lot of heartbreak by breaking up with him and living on her own.

But they'd bumped into each other again and now were on a collision course to time together. She should have pushed back against working as a team on her treasure hunt. Her life was a mess and his didn't seem much better off. They weren't what either needed, no matter how much they both might want a distraction. He'd already agreed, and she couldn't back out without telling him in person. He would insist on helping, and he'd be right. She couldn't do it on her own. She sighed. She'd figure out how to keep the past in the past and forge a new friendship.

"Ma'am? Are you extending your stay? It's quarter after eleven." The muffled voice called through the door.

Molly sat up, rubbing the sleep from her eyes. She hadn't slept past eight in years. "No," she croaked. She cleared her throat of the groggy huskiness. "I'm checking out. I'm sorry."

"You have fifteen minutes before a late charge. I'm sliding the receipt under the door."

A piece of paper appeared on the carpet.

"Of course. I'm sorry. Thank you."

The footsteps backed away, retreating down the hall.

Pulling back the covers, Molly swung her feet to the ground and padded towards the door. She bent and picked up the paper. How much was her premature midlife crisis costing her?

She frowned. $0 charged to her credit card. Maybe worse than her free falling was being beholden to someone. But who? Mr. Baird? Would he charge her an hourly rate or a retainer if she needed him for every little thing?

She was an adult. She'd figure out a solution to her problem. Was it Grant? She gulped. He didn't have the means to treat her to anything. He struggled to launch his own business. Who else could be her mystery benefactor? Not Elise. Was an eavesdropping, superstitious local watching her? She shivered.

She didn't have the luxury of time to ponder. She showered in record time and quickly changed, brushed her teeth, and gathered her things. She swung her purse over her shoulder and held the duffle in her opposite hand. In this, at least, she was balanced.

Exiting the room, she strode through the hall and into the lobby. Flooded with natural light, the entrance was inviting. The seating areas in the nooks of the large space were cozy. She gazed towards the bay. A deck wrapped around the back of the building with chairs and tables. A few guests enjoyed coffee and the paper.

If she wasn't worried about another hostile reception, she might join them. The lake sparkled under the bright-blue sky. The green of the trees on the hills in the distance was vibrant. She'd love to capture the late morning with the camera tucked in her duffle bag.

She hadn't felt the urge to reach for her camera in years. Wasting film shooting the monotony of her desk job and dull commute wasn't appealing. But if she stepped outside, she'd stare at the sawmill. She needed to get a handle on what came next. Did the town really want the land for an event space? She couldn't see herself staying to work on the condo conversion project. But with the sudden building boom and demand for lumber, was her best option to repair and reopen the sawmill? She'd offer plenty of jobs, not that she had the first clue about how to run any business or the capital to take on the start-up costs.

Maybe I could find a partner?

She shuddered and turned, heading out the front door and crossing the parking lot. She didn't like someone paying for her room. How could she deal with a business partner who'd fund the endeavor? First things first, she'd have to dry out the building.

Popping the latch on the back of her rental car, she deposited the duffle in the trunk and shut the lid. She pulled open the driver's door and slid behind the wheel. She hadn't owned a car for years. She rarely ventured outside Cook County and couldn't justify the costs. But having her own transportation—even for a short time— was nice.

She reached for her bag and found her phone near the bottom. Swiping the screen, she pulled up her messages. She'd gotten a text from Grant.

Her heart pounded. Giving him her number again had been necessary in the current circumstances. She didn't have to like the rush of blood to her extremities, making her limbs tingle.

Falling for him at eighteen had been thrilling and inevitable. He was intuitive and understood her without ever questioning her. He accepted her. She had struggled to do the same for him.

GRANT: *Meet me at the boardwalk ice cream shop. Park your car at the sawmill.*

She exhaled. Good, she hadn't slowed him down. And she was glad she'd deleted his number all those years ago. Because when he entered the digits last night, she'd suddenly remembered the same phone number. Back then, she'd had him listed as Gorgeous Grant. She was glad *that* hadn't popped up on her screen.

She hovered her finger over the message and tapped the thumbs-up. He never tried to change her. Bumping into him now was a shock and maybe a chance to really right the past.

She could strike up a friendship, appreciate him for the man he'd become, and stop judging him by her standards. Following her path had landed her here: homeless, debt-ridden, and unemployed. If she was brave, she would have a fresh start.

In the upper corner of the screen, she spotted the clock flashing eleven thirty. She pulled up her recent calls and redialed Mr. Baird's number. The line rang twice and connected.

"Baird Law, Leonard Baird, speaking."

"Hi, Mr. Baird. It's Molly Maguire."

"Molly, my dear. How are you this fine day?"

She wrinkled her brow, frowning at the endearment from a near stranger. The only time she'd ever liked being referred to as dear or sweet was when Grant spoke to her. Nor could she agree with the lawyer's assessment of the morning. "I've been better."

"Well, I'm sorry to hear that. Are you having problems at the mill?"

She snorted. Her issues extended further than the property. But he wasn't likely to be able to help smooth her rough introduction to town. And she didn't want another run-in with Elise. "I ended up at the inn. I'm not sure what happened, but the upstairs apartment flooded."

"Oh my word, are you all right?"

He sounded sort of breathless. His immediate response was almost rehearsed. Imagining conspiracies? Maybe a treasure hunt was a bad idea. Perhaps giving in to flights of fancy unmoored her tenuous hold on the world. She gave herself a shake. "I am."

"Why didn't you call last night? I could have helped you. Is the water shut off? Is the mill underwater?"

His shock sounded genuine. He wasn't her mystery benefactor. She hoped she hadn't accidentally preyed on Grant. A credit card bill was easier than paying cash at the moment. She didn't know how, but she'd repay him if he had covered her room.

"My dear?" Mr. Baird asked.

Molly cleared her throat. "It was too late to reach out to you last night, and I didn't want to wake you. I don't know the current state of the building." She felt childish admitting it. Last night, her anxiety overrode her calm, and she had acted out of pure stress without forethought.

"Let me take care of you, my dear. You are my client. It is no bother whatsoever to do my job."

She pressed her lips together. She wasn't sure what she expected from him, but it wasn't quite this. She didn't really know the man. On their previous meetings, he'd been effusive in person. She shouldn't be shocked by the continued behavior over the phone. But she didn't have to like his manner. If he was putting on a show, he didn't need to play to the balcony. She was the only person in the audience. "I'm not sure that I fully turned off the water. I grabbed my stuff and left. I don't think I'll be able to stay in the building. I met up with an old fla —" She coughed. "A friend. I'm on my way to meet him. Do you think you could coordinate whatever needs to be done? I don't even know where to start."

"Of course, I can. I know everyone in town. I'll get the whole place dried and ready for you in a couple days. Plenty of time before you need to sign the papers."

"Great. Should I drop the keys off at your office? I'm heading out of town."

"No need. I have an extra set."

She dropped her jaw. Was that normal? Thankfully, she had no experience with lawyers. If he was the executor of the estate, was he entitled to free reign of the full property? She could ask Mom. In three more days, the cruise would be in port again. "Will you let me know any updates?"

"Leave it all to me."

"Great. Thanks, Mr. Baird. I'll be close if you need me."

"Wonderful. Have a great day. My apologies again." He ended the call.

She pulled the phone off her ear. If she stayed, she'd change the locks. With the property so accessible to the public, she wasn't sure how many copies of keys lurked in the town. At least the building didn't house anything valuable.

Since I grabbed the map.

She was probably ridiculous for sharing the file with Grant and entertaining the thought she could find treasure. But she had nowhere to go and nothing better to do. Why not set off on an adventure with her ex? *Because I might include him in the curse?*

She needed to forget about *that* encounter for another decade and a half. First things first, she had a destination. She turned the key into the ignition and pulled out of the lot, heading to her water-logged inheritance. After the first few days of her week, what else could go wrong?

* * *

Grant stretched his legs in front of him, crossing at the ankles. On a slat bench outside of *Scoops, There It Is*, he had a view of the bustling row of shops hugging the lakeshore. He'd know the second she arrived. He shifted on the hard seat; his muscles ached, and his mouth watered.

With an insatiable sweet tooth, he craved ice cream. He could eat a fully loaded banana split and still want more. Despite the temptation, he vowed to wait for her arrival before stepping inside. Under a clear sky, he soaked in his surroundings, studying the tourists and residents. Everyone smiled. It was hard not to. The community was nestled on verdant hills, every lot with a view of the lake. Harsh winters meant only the hardiest souls settled full time in the area. In the summer, however, the population bursts to life.

His phone vibrated in his back pocket. Shifting forward, he frowned as he retrieved the phone and spotted his former assistant's name. "Good morning, Karen," he greeted.

"Isn't it almost afternoon for you?" Karen retorted.

"You're right, of course. Time differences and all of that," he replied smoothly. "But I'm sure you aren't touching base just to hear me say you're right."

"You'd be surprised. Always feels good to get a win, no matter how small."

He chuckled.

"Do you have a moment?"

He glanced at his watch. He had ten minutes left. Molly would arrive soon. "Sure. I can spare a little time. What's up?"

"We need you at the upcoming board meeting."

Grant exhaled a heavy, weary sigh. He hated having this conversation. He'd been gone for a year and was finally easing into his next big project. He didn't want to get swept up in corporate politics. "I don't want to get on a plane and fly out to California right now."

"Can we put you up at a nice hotel in a bigger town so you'll have reliable internet? You could be on screen. We need you there."

He studied the boardwalk, willing Molly to appear and excuse him from this call. The girl he remembered was up and at 'em first thing in the morning. The woman, however, was different. "I can't drive to another town right now. I'm needed here."

"I'll make the arrangements. You won't need to worry about anything. But we need you. I need you," Karen pleaded. "Growth has been stagnant. We've had a lot of turnover with the culture change."

Grant pinched the bridge of his nose, hating what his former assistant's tone implied. He'd do anything in his power to protect his former employees. But he worried about Molly, too. He couldn't stretch himself to the breaking point to save everyone. It was okay to do something for himself, too. The guilt settling low in his stomach disagreed. "I can do a video conference. But I have to stay here. Work out the details. Call the Inn at Loon Lake. I'm not coming back in a full-time capacity. I hope this isn't some sort of game to get me to return."

She sighed. "I know. But even in an advisory role, I'd appreciate it. We all would. Thanks. I'll keep you posted on the details."

"Thanks, bye." He ended the call. The compromise put a time limit on his ability to search for treasure with Molly. He'd have to be back for the board meeting in three days. Without knowing exactly what they were undertaking, he couldn't gauge if that was enough time or too little. He'd take as much as he got so he could get to know her again.

Last night, she'd looked exhausted to the point of pain. After hearing her calamities, he wasn't sure how he'd process the situations. He couldn't imagine experiencing so much upheaval in his life, let alone a couple of days.

He couldn't pepper her with questions about her perspective on them and their past. He'd have to wait, content in the present time together while he puzzled over the clues. Any kid detective worth their salt would be hard at work trying to solve the mystery. But a big part of Grant's hesitation came in what he'd do with the truth and what he'd risk to uncover it.

Though he knew she'd object, he headed to the front desk at six and paid for her room. It was a small thing for him to do. Keeping his action secret was intended to ease the emotional burden on both sides. She never accepted compliments or presents with much grace. He didn't particularly enjoy being thought of as nothing more than a wallet with legs. The hush-hush gift suited both better.

A rush of wind swept past.

"Hey, sorry to keep you waiting."

He turned towards her melodic voice. His Peanut had reappeared in his life. He should be more shocked. In truth, he knew fate brought them back. Could she finally see the value in trusting unseen forces? Faith was a difficult concept: seeing with the heart.

Shielding her gaze with one hand, she strode towards him.

He smiled and stood, dusting his palms on his jeans. He liked her shoulders-back power walk. Like she had a plan and was in control. Much better than fragile and cracked. She carried a duffle bag and wore a purse. But where was her camera?

"Is my car okay in the lot overnight?" She bit her lip.

He nodded. "You locked the car and hid your valuables?"

"Of course." She shrugged. "I don't have anything worth stealing anymore."

He hated the raw vulnerability in her tone. "You're all set?" He reached forward, grabbing her duffle's handle and brushing her fingers.

She stiffened.

At the base of her throat, her skin fluttered from shallow breathing. He should drop his hand. But he liked being close. And he liked the rare moment of catching her off guard. "Sorry. I'll warn you next time I'm chivalrous," he murmured.

She snorted and dropped her grip. "Please lead the

way. I trust you know where you're going?" She clasped the purse on her shoulder with both hands.

He smiled. "I do. First, we need ice cream." *And allies.*

"Should we have dropped off my bag? This is out of order. I woke up late. I'm inconveniencing you. I can't believe I'm talking you into helping me." She verbally spun out of control.

"I can carry this bag. It's no problem." He kept his voice even and calm, lifting the bag with one hand. He didn't want to delay any longer. He'd had enough time to digest all the information flung at him overnight. Against all odds and reasonable assumptions, they'd reunited here at his favorite place in the world.

He wanted her to stay, and she needed a better opinion of the community to entertain the idea. They each had a fresh start if only they had the courage to reach out and grab their chance with both hands. He'd hold on tight to his and pull her up with him if need be.

She raised an anxious gaze to his. "Are you certain my rental car is okay parked overnight? I don't know that I can take another catastrophe," she muttered.

"Where else would you have left if I hadn't suggested the mill?

She shrugged. "The inn?"

"I promise your car is safer at the mill. The inn is crowded. Lots of comings and goings. A thief could easily break in and steal it. No one would know until you got back. Here, it's on its own. If it disappears, someone will notice."

She puckered her lips. "I don't feel any better about my choice with your explanation."

"How about trusting that you've filled your bad luck quota for the year." He adjusted his grip on her bag. "There really is not much crime up here." He paused. Hadn't he purchased the bankrupt tour boat business after the owners were hauled off to prison? He didn't have the full details about what had transpired. As far as he encountered, no one let the actions make them suspicious or nervous. "Loon Lake isn't immune to petty theft, but you should be okay." He needed to stop talking before he made this worse. "What did you do about the flood?"

"Called the lawyer. I don't know what else to do." She sighed. "I'm still waiting to hear back from my insurance company about the fire. I suppose I'll never be able to secure a reasonable policy again."

He wasn't sure what to do next either. He wished he could somehow ease her troubles. He'd like to be helpful without simply throwing money at the problems. Having ready cash definitely eased tough situations. But he didn't think she'd accept his generosity without feeling guilty. And he didn't want to change the ease of their unexpected reunion. They weren't picking up where they left off. Thankfully. The end had been tense and stressful. This meetup was better. Older, wiser, and beat up by life, he was more careful with his words. She seemed to be the same. "Let's get ice cream. Then we'll walk to the boat and drop off your stuff. I already entered the coordinates into the GPS. Your treasure is located at the museum."

"How is that possible?"

He shrugged. "I don't know. I guess we'll find out."

She shuddered. "My bad luck continues. Elise runs the museum. She'll block me from even entering."

"No, she won't. She welcomes everyone inside. She's proud of the town's heritage." But another thought bothered him. If the treasure was inside the museum, she might have already discovered it. *Was that what Elise meant by it's too late?*

He didn't want to upset Molly with the revelation. If Elise had discovered a windfall, she'd have funded a bunch of town projects. But keeping this tidbit to himself felt like lying. "I need to tell you something. I ran into Elise in town the other night. She told me you're too late."

Molly exhaled a heavy breath and hunched. "Should we give up?"

He hated the almost instant capitulation. What had happened to his Peanut? The fierce, fearless female must be hidden somewhere inside. He'd help her uncover gold and herself. "No giving up. If she had the treasure, she'd have told you. Finders keepers rules. She'd want you to know you lost.

"Okay." Molly nibbled her bottom lip. "Maybe Elise was talking about the deadline. I have to claim the property by Sunday, or it reverts to the city."

She hadn't made up her mind to stay for good? He'd show her why she had stumbled onto the perfect place to call home.

"So we have to head into the lioness' den?" she asked.

"I don't suppose there is a way to get Elise off her property without raising her suspicions?"

"One problem at a time."

She shook her head, her chin trembling. "I can't do this." Crossing her arms over her chest, she rounded her back. She looked small.

"Why not, Peanut?"

She leaned back and pushed the sunglasses up to her hair. "This—" she wiggled her finger, circling herself, her suitcase, the boat "—isn't me. I'm not adventurous. I stick to the plan."

"Following your plan, you ended up here." He'd call it fate but didn't want to spook her. "When's the last time you took a chance? This is a fun diversion. You have a few days. Why not?"

"The last time I didn't plan was the summer I moved to London for an overseas program. And..." She dropped her jaw.

He frowned. "What?"

"I was cursed by a gypsy." She snapped her fingers. "This whole debacle must be the realization of whatever hex she put on me."

He pressed his lips together, stifling laughter. But he shook the bench with the internalized, deep rumble. How did the most rational person he'd ever known accept something inexplicable as fact? He couldn't make sense of it.

"Don't laugh. It's the best explanation I have." She wrinkled her brow. The corner of her mouth lifted. "I know it's ridiculous that I believe in something that defies logic."

"Were you or were you not the woman that ranted against magicians as tricksters? And now you want to put your faith in, essentially, magic?" he asked.

"Yes, I know. I still don't trust any person in a cape. But I can't shake this. Please, just don't try to make sense of it. I can't."

He crossed his heart. Gypsy curse? Who was he to correct her? She agreed to go on a treasure hunt. He might have the most fun he'd had in years. He wasn't going to be the voice of reason. That was her job. "Let's get a scoop for courage then."

He pulled open the door. Smooth R&B trilled through the entrance, luring all inside to a nineties-themed wonderland.

She glanced over her shoulder and smiled, pleasure lighting her from the inside out.

Her first day in town hadn't proved the warm introduction she deserved. He'd right her first impression and introduce her to the community. Everyone would greet her like an old friend. She belonged here. And—thankfully—so did he.

Chapter Six

Nineties R&B music spilled onto the boardwalk from the open door.

Molly glanced inside and did a double take. The bright fluorescent hues of the early part of the 1990s pulsated to the beat of the song. The interior was candy-coated nostalgia.

A man dressed in white overalls scooped ice cream behind the front counter.

"Come on in," Grant said.

He stood close, just past her shoulder. She could feel the warmth and encouragement of his breath on her neck. It was nice to feel the physical security of companionship after the rough start to the week.

He was dressed in the same rumpled clothes as the day before. Up close, she couldn't ignore the scraggly state of his too-long hair. He lived rough. A stop at an ice cream shop seemed a trivial indulgence for someone needing real help.

She shook her head. "Are you sure?" she asked under her breath, anxious for her words not to travel.

"Absolutely," he murmured. "Your interactions with Elise have been unfortunate. Loon Lake is a welcoming place, I promise you."

She nibbled her lip and nodded. Her hesitance had nothing to do with Elise and everything to do with him. She'd cover the cost. With her hotel room paid for by some mysterious benefactor, she could afford to treat Grant.

He grinned and held the door open with his back, allowing her to pass him on her way inside.

She stepped up to the counter, scanning the offerings in the freezer case. She felt his presence at her side before she let her senses otherwise detect him. Grant charged the very air around him with his optimistic energy. She'd forgotten about the magnetic pull she'd first experienced the day they met.

Now, she couldn't fight the gravitational tug to linger within his arm's reach.

Not that he'd touched her. She almost angled herself into his space, willing him to press a reassuring hand to her lower back or steer her by the elbow. Living in an urban center, she had avoided others. Yet, here, she almost threw herself into his path. It was ridiculous. *I need a hug.*

She wrapped her arms around her waist and leaned forward, studying the ice cream tubs with far too much interest.

"Yo! It's a fresh day to keep it real. Thanks for stopping in and gracing my store with your beautiful presence," the ice cream seller said. "What may I get you, miss? A scoop of rum raisin the roof?"

She lifted her chin and met a smiling face. With fine wrinkles around his eyes, he looked older than her. Why had he offered her rum raisin? Was she old? She must look as tired as she felt.

"I'm just teasing." The man winked. "I like to trot out that pun whenever I can."

She grinned back, unable to resist his flirtatiousness or the dimple flashing in his cheek. She'd never imagined finding someone dressed in a fluorescent neon shirt and bright-white overalls cute. But somehow, the man made the retro outfit attractive.

"Hey, Zach. This is Molly. Molly Maguire," Grant stretched out her last name.

Zach's eyes widened. He rubbed his palms on his apron, sticking the pewter scoop in the pocket of his uniform, and extended his hand over the glass-covered case. "You're very welcome here. It's a pleasure to meet you, Ms. Maguire. Or may I hope it's, Miss?"

Molly accepted his shake, matching his firm grip with one of her own. She giggled and rolled her eyes. "Thank you. Please call me, Molly."

Zach dropped his hand and crossed his arms over his chest. "I'm sorry for your loss."

Molly nearly collapsed from relief. If he knew about the postmortem activity, he wasn't judging her as the perpetrator behind the dig. She was grateful for the kindness in treating her like a normal person. "I appreciate that. To be honest, I didn't know my late aunt." She shrugged, uncomfortable with sympathy she hadn't earned. She'd stumbled into an inheritance. Had she robbed the town with her good fortune? *My luck hasn't been all that golden.*

"Neither did I," Zach said. "It's nice to have some more young people in town. Are you moving into the mill?"

She opened her mouth and glanced at Grant, unsure how much or what she could share. Would her words be reported back to Elise? Would her intention become twisted to serve another narrative?

"She's still deciding," Grant said.

She shut her mouth, surprised at her relief. She didn't enjoy others speaking for her, but in this instance, she was glad. He stepped up and helped, guessing her needs by a single look. Again, warmth spread through her; this time she curled her toes in her slip-ons. She hadn't realized how much she longed for a feeling of safety until today. How strange.

"Hmm," Zach rubbed his jaw. "Shall I interpret the loaded silence to mean that you've met Elise?" He darted his gaze between Molly and Grant.

Molly stiffened. "Yes."

"Give her a second chance. She's got a good heart. Most people around here do," Zach said.

"What do you know about the treasure?" Grant asked.

Molly's eyes bugged out of her head. So much for subtlety. She hoped Grant's trust in this man wasn't misplaced.

Zach drew back his chin and dropped his arms,

shaking his head. "That is a sensitive issue. Don't bring it up."

"Why?" Molly asked. *Is it real?* She needed it so much that her throat clogged with emotions.

"It started as a marketing ploy decades ago and brought about the destruction of the inn's lighthouse earlier this summer." Zach darted his gaze from side to side. "Rumor is the spot is haunted. I haven't witnessed anything. But anything to do with the building is a sensitive subject around here, especially at the inn."

His words held a finality. She wanted to glance at Grant and judge his expression. Instead, she nodded at Zach. Whatever treasure Zach mentioned wasn't the same as hers. Should she ask specifically about the Maguire legend? Now she knew to stay clear of the lighthouse, glad for the heads-up about ghosts. She wouldn't bring more bad vibes into her life. "Okay, noted."

The door opened, and the whoosh of air rushing into the room drew everyone's attention.

A man carrying a box in both arms entered and closed the door with his foot. "Hey, Zach. Is now a good time?"

"Sure is," Zach walked to the end of the counter, clearing a space near the cash register. "Seth, you remember Grant. Let me introduce Molly Maguire."

Seth approached the cash register and set down his box, wiping his palms on his pants and holding out a hand.

Molly halved the distance between them and shook. "Hi."

"Pleasure to meet you. Officially. I'm Seth Boyd. I've

been wondering when we'd get the chance to meet. I've heard a lot about you. Elise told me you moved into the mill," Seth said with a smile.

His manner was open and guileless. Could he be genuine? "Oh, are you friends with Elise?" Molly asked.

Seth's cheeks turned pink. "Of course. We're all friends here."

"What merch did you bring today?" Zach asked, interrupting the increasingly awkward exchange. "Seth stocks the non-dairy items for sale."

"I finished your slap bracelets and stickers." Seth pulled a handful of bright-pink bracelets and white-and-neon circles out of a box and handed everyone one of each.

Molly grabbed hers with a grateful—if awkward—smile. She was accepted as part of the community without any hesitation? Could she trust their kindness today when she'd been met with such skepticism yesterday?

The slap of a bracelet smacking against skin snapped her out of her reverie.

"Gag me with a spoon," Grant said, reading the bracelet on his wrist.

She scrunched her nose and studied the flattened bracelet, spotting the white-lettered slogan. It didn't quite work for her.

"It's a great slogan, right?" Zach asked. "Very on brand. Combining nostalgia, slang, and puns has been harder than you might imagine."

She could believe that if a restaurant used a reference to choking as a catchphrase. "I like your stickers," Molly offered. Above a trio of ice cream scoops with kawaii-style faces, the phrase *full phat ice cream* was written in neon colors.

"Told you so," Seth said, beaming.

"Did you draw the characters?" Molly asked, choosing to focus on something positive for the moment. "Are you an artist?"

Seth turned pink. "I run the print shop. I doodle here and there."

"You're very talented."

"But you don't like the slogan on the bracelets?" Zach asked.

She bit the inside of her cheek. Yesterday, she hadn't deserved the cold welcome. But her behavior right now was giving her what she deserved. She should have kept her reaction to herself. "I appreciate the nineties reference. I'm not sure you want to give customers the impression that they'll gag at your store."

Zach crossed his arms over his chest.

"What about..." She stalled, trying to remember everything she'd gleaned from old sitcom reruns. "*All that and a scoop of chocolate chip?*"

Seth rubbed his chin. "Hmm. Maybe that's a good shirt or another sticker? It's a little long for the slap bracelets."

"Agreed," Zach said. "Thanks for the idea. I like it. How many bracelets did you make?"

"Only a couple hundred. I brought a big box to carry something else I want your opinion on." Seth reached inside and retrieved a gray athletic sock. "Soupy prototypes." He set the sock on the counter.

Zach grinned. "It's great."

Molly pressed her lips together. Was it great? She studied the men's sock and now spotted the googly eyes and felt flippers. What was it supposed to be? It looked like a charcoal lump with protrusions.

"Soupy is the Lake Superior monster and Seth's passion project," Grant said. "He had an encounter in his childhood with an extraordinary beast. He's spent the better part of his life searching for proof of its existence."

"Oh, very cool," Molly replied, glad for the assistance. Not that the monster was descriptive enough to fill in the blanks of the object on the counter.

"Ashley Hale-Lewis at the inn gave me the idea to branch into the children's story arena. With a book, I'll need stuffed animals. I'm still working on the details, but I'm loving this initial design."

"Yeah, wow. It's got a lot of work in it." Molly stalled the best way she could, false platitudes. She didn't believe in tearing people down but, at the moment, struggled with how to raise this man up. Was Soupy a snake? A dolphin? She couldn't tell.

"Soupy is a mosasaur," Grant added. "Seth first spotted him years ago while ice fishing, and over the past few years, he has really been working seriously to make observations and record his data."

"Sightings are up three hundred percent," Zach said.

Double of zero remains zero. Molly balled her hands at her sides. She had no reason to balk. She had plenty of questions. An introduction didn't feel like the right time and place for incredulity. "Very cool."

"Yes, it is. And I'm glad to hear Ashley's been encouraging. We've all been glad to have Ashley back in charge of the inn," Zach said.

His tone hinted at a significance over her head. Would she ever be included in the town's inner circle? Was acceptance earned or given?

"We're heading out onto the lake. I'll stay alert for any strange happenings out there," Grant said.

"Thanks, that's a big help. I'll be out on the water again soon, too. I'm still working on mapping out the Timber Triangle," Seth said.

"Like the Bermuda Triangle?" Grant asked.

Molly wasn't sure how much more of the supernatural she could handle.

"Sort of," Seth said. "We haven't lost any airplanes or anything, but it's a section of Lake Superior that has weird effects on equipment."

"Where is it located?" Grant asked.

"Just past the channel leading into Loon Lake, specifically to the east. I've been working on my search out there. Remember, I'm happy to create a Soupy sighting tour once you really get going," Seth said.

"I'm definitely taking you up on that," Grant replied.

His tone was genuine. Molly was glad Grant's kindness remained unwavering.

"Very strange readings out there. Storms pop up without warning." Seth waggled his eyebrows. "Be careful."

"If you need anything, please let us know," Zach added. "I can watch out for the sawmill while you're gone. It's close enough I barely have to leave my store to spy on it."

"I won't bother you with surveillance. I've got my lawyer, Mr. Baird, keeping an eye out for me," Molly said.

"Leonard Baird? He's been dealing with a lot lately. Marriage troubles," Zach added with a significant look.

Molly had no response. Were there truly no secrets in this town? She supposed having another person watching out for her wasn't a bad thing, and Zach was nothing but friendly. "In that case, another set of eyes wouldn't hurt. I'd appreciate your help. Thanks for offering."

"We'd better head out while the weather is clear," Grant said.

Molly was glad for the interruption in the awkward conversation.

"Better not let us keep you. Seth and I can talk for hours once we get started. Can I get you ice cream to go?" Zach asked. "Sorry we got so sidetracked in here. It's on the house to thank you for your great idea."

Grant shot her an expectant look.

Molly was touched by the gesture. But she couldn't fall victim to the warmth and familiarity in the unspoken communication between herself and Grant. Or she'd be powerless to fight a resurgence of feelings.

Nothing could happen between them. Neither was in any position for the distraction of a romance. They each had life troubles to sort through, particularly their respective precarious living situations. A reconnection wouldn't be a fling.

The impromptu stop was rather illuminating. Luckily, she didn't have to embarrass him by paying. "That's really kind. And totally unnecessary."

"Not at all," Zach said, reaching for the metal scoop. "Coming up with nineties-themed marketing materials and slogans is harder than you think. I've been trying to make *gag me with a spoon* work for years, but you're right; it sends the wrong message."

She agreed and, by the length of his answer, understood he wasn't going to let her pay. "Well, thank you. Two scoops of cookie dough, please."

"Same for me," Grant said.

The words were simple and obvious. His agreement with her order felt like an endearment. Like they'd gone back to those days when he said yes to every one of her suggestions and ideas.

She needed to get a grip. Fast. Before she fell hard for him all over again. Because being the center of his attention and adoration had been like a drug. She'd needed more than a good time to live. When the time had come to wean herself off him, she'd gone cold turkey and barely survived. She couldn't live through saying goodbye to him—romantically—again.

* * *

The only hiccup in Grant's plan so far was her luggage. The duffle didn't have wheels, so he volunteered to carry the bag. He'd tried to wear the bag like a backpack, but the straps were too close together. He wanted to tease that she made sure he'd kept his hands occupied. But she remained a little defeated and down. A joke wouldn't serve him.

He switched hands, flexing his cramped fingers. She'd lost everything and yet had managed to buy enough to weigh the cheap bag down. The seams stretched to the breaking point. They'd reached the end of the boardwalk and continued on the path winding along the shore to the inn.

"Another scoop?" Molly asked.

He licked his lips. "Yes, please."

She matched his pace and spooned a generous serving of cookie dough ice cream into his mouth. She had finished her ice cream before they'd reached the fudge and taffy shop.

While he hadn't considered the logistics of how he'd eat the ice cream and be a gentleman, he couldn't be mad at the results. He appreciated her feeding him. It was thoughtful and nice.

The delicious treat almost excused the flirtatious proprietor. Grant had heard rumors about Zach's lothario reputation. Supposedly, Zach was a Midwest Don Juan, hunting his prey among the inn's guests. With no love lost between Zach and Christopher, Grant had assumed the reports were overblown. Until Grant witnessed Zach's behavior firsthand. The man was too charming for anyone's good, flirting with Molly in front of Grant.

Grant had been sorely tempted to put his arm around her shoulders. She was not a notch in anyone's bedpost. She was some lucky person's endgame. At one time, he'd imagined himself in that lucky role. Instead of making a jealous and demanding claim on her, he'd settled for shooting a hard look at Zach and explaining her residential status until he backed off.

"One more scoop? You're almost done," she said.

"Sure." He nodded, ignoring his tight throat. The moment was almost engineered to perfection. He'd hate to give up the chance for continued, unexpected intimacy.

She stuffed the last bite in his mouth and—as he chewed—strolled to a trash can to toss the container. "I'm not sure if it's the ambiance or the fresh air, but I think that's the best ice cream I've ever had."

He nodded. "Zach uses cream from a local dairy and his family's recipes. The ice cream is small-batch production because that's all he can do by himself. He has no interest in growing his company. When he's sold out for the day, he closes up. It happens a lot."

"Good for him. He was nice." She frowned, her voice halting.

"Shouldn't he be?" Grant asked. As the proprietor of a shop serving sugar, Zach sold smiles.

"I guess I wasn't sure how I'd be treated by the locals after meeting Elise." Molly shrugged. "Yesterday was a very long twenty-four hours. I swear this week has been the most tragic decade of my life."

He felt a pang of regret on her behalf but wouldn't deny her experience. She was right. She'd endured more through the past week than most folks dealt with over a lifetime.

Time had slowed since the treasure hunt began. Either that, or he'd somehow stretched every minute to last twice as long. Or maybe, in not taking a single second for granted, he became hyper-aware of each one.

"How's my beard? Any chocolate chips stuck in it?" he asked.

She narrowed her gaze. "Nope, you're good. Do you often get food smeared there?" She waved a hand over her chin in a gesture reminiscent of a street corner magician.

"Not very often. I suppose I'd have more trouble if I regularly ate soup, but—"

"Soup is not a meal," she interrupted, repeating what he'd said to her too many times to count. "I remember."

He liked the little quick sidelong glances she threw his way. Falling for her had been easy the first time. He would crash into her again without a moment's hesitation. With her girl-next-door looks and charm, she was simultaneously down-to-earth and sophisticated. He'd been convinced she had all the answers in life. Back then, she'd believed the same. The flashes of her former self with the present woman transfixed him.

"How much further to the boathouse?" she asked.

"Only a little bit more." He strolled forward.

She quickly fell into step at his side, clasping her hands behind her back. "I can carry my bag if you want."

"No, I'm fine."

They reached the edge of the inn's beach and headed up to the grass, continuing across the lawn was far preferable to trudging through sand.

She leaned close. "Was that the lighthouse?" She pointed to a small island connected by a wooden bridge.

A charred pile of bricks stood next to flats of new

building material, still tightly wrapped in protective plastic.

"I suppose so. It's strange to see it destroyed. I grew up fascinated by the structure, imagining it as a perfect hideaway."

"Every kid wants a fort," she teased.

"True." He sighed. "I had no idea about the treasure thing. I'm glad Zach told us."

"Me too," she said significantly. "I'd hate for anyone to think we're colluding with whatever happened there. Our treasure didn't point to the island."

Our treasure. The two words were like and endearment. *Our* was quickly becoming his favorite pronoun.

"Do you know the details of what transpired?" she asked.

"I was contacted by the owner of the inn with a business opportunity because the tour business went bankrupt, and the proprietors landed in jail. I guess they believed in the story about treasure at the lighthouse and nearly killed someone. Actually, there were three attempts made on the life of the same person, although only one was targeted. They destroyed the lighthouse in the process."

"Yikes. This seems like such a nice place."

"It is," he said.

He was surprised she didn't have more questions. Wasn't she interested in his new business? She seemed to stop herself before getting too far into any conversation. He enjoyed the ease in her company. He didn't feel like he had the word billionaire tattooed across his forehead.

But she wasn't curious about him at all? He wanted to know everything about her.

He warred with sharing more to entice her to ask questions, like explaining that he'd stumbled onto a court proceeding for the father-son criminals and overheard a podcaster recording an episode. Restraint won over indulgence. With too much information, she might turn and leave town now, never to return. "For what it's worth, I don't believe it's haunted."

"What?" She scrunched up her face. "The rubble over there?" She pointed to the former lighthouse.

He nodded, switching the grip on her bag's handle.

"The residents of Loon Lake seem to really lean into the supernatural. I'm not going to question anyone about their beliefs."

Her tone was hesitant. Did she wonder if her gypsy curse would find local support? She wouldn't be laughed out of town if she did share it with others.

They reached the forest separating the inn from the boathouse and stepped on pine needles and twigs.

"Be careful. I haven't had a chance to cut a proper path here yet. I haven't had much time to do anything," he admitted. "You should find my tracks back and forth without too much effort."

"Ashley Hale-Lewis doesn't mind you trespassing here? She contacted you about the business venture?"

"Well, not specifically. I was on a short list of trusted folks that could be counted on to take over a business immediately." He smiled.

Molly's face was hard and serious, carved stone.

"To answer your other question, Ashley has been

quite gracious about letting me pass through the grounds. I haven't been arrested or shot yet. I'm sort of a guest." How did Molly know the name of the innkeeper? Why specifically mention one person? He remembered Zach's mention at the ice cream shop. Molly was razor-sharp and never missed a beat. Grant was glad to know she hadn't changed in that regard. "Have you spoken to her?"

"I only met her briefly yesterday when I checked in. But from your description, she sounds lovely."

If he didn't know any better, he'd think Molly was fishing for information about his dating history. He didn't mind. He'd had no significant relationship since their breakup. Like he'd been in a holding pattern, waiting for her. "She is very kind. But she didn't contact me about the business. Her husband did."

"Oh." Molly dropped her shoulders an inch.

Was this the moment to ask about her recent past? He didn't want confirmation of how many dates she'd been on or the names of her boyfriends. Filling in the gaps in his imagination, however, might be more painful.

"You really have the town's support," she said. "Are you going to take that guy up on specialty tours?"

He hated feeling he'd missed a moment to share. He wouldn't push his luck. "I'm thinking about it. Crypto-zoology is an emerging sector of the travel industry. And Seth is a good guy."

"He seems very passionate about his lake monster." Her voice pitched high.

"You don't believe him?"

She paused to shoot him an incredulous stare.

Grant chuckled and kept moving. "You believe in a curse, and you're setting out on a treasure hunt."

"True." She kept her gaze focused on her feet.

"I'm supporting you. Why can't I offer the same to a friend? Why are you judging me?"

"I don't mean any offense." She sighed. "It's not that I don't want to support him. I guess I draw the line for believability at prehistoric creatures that very clearly went extinct in the fossil record."

"I understand. I guess I don't see the harm in encouraging Seth. Neither does anyone else. He's convinced a monster lives in the lake. No one has been killed on the open water. It's rather harmless and sort of fun."

She nodded but didn't lift her gaze. "Are you laughing at him?"

"Never. Friends don't have to see the world in the same way to get along or show each other respect. And while Soupy hasn't caught on yet, I'm sure it's only a matter of time. Seth is endearing and charming. He's the sort of person everyone wants to root for. Maybe a legend will boost the economy. I wouldn't mind capitalizing on it, especially if it encourages Seth. Win-win for sure."

Molly didn't react beyond a stiff smile.

You're the sort of person others root for, too.

He hated seeing her so broken. She helped him save himself. He wanted to do the same for her. Their treasure hunt would—more likely than not—be a bust. He was rather counting on it. She'd dismissively brought up the idea that friendship was the prize all along. He wanted more for her. "You've had a few setbacks. Let's go get you a win."

She smiled.

"Did you bring sunglasses? And a hair tie?"

She nodded and pulled the purse off her shoulder. Rummaging inside, she retrieved both. She pulled her hair into a messy ponytail and covered her blue eyes with oversized dark lenses. "Is this okay?"

"Perfect. You'll need both once we get out on the water." He hoped the treasure hunt went further than one stop so that they could spend more time together. "And here we are." He waved to the boathouse and continued forward, fighting the urge to study her face as she surveyed his new venture.

She hadn't asked many questions about how he'd come to Loon Lake or why. She seemed to process every revelation slowly and on her own terms. Had she followed his career? He hoped so. He wanted her pride in his accomplishments. He needed her positive affirmation.

Chapter Seven

Molly followed Grant. The action, while unusual, was sort of relaxing. She didn't have to think or worry or anticipate. Instead, she studied and absorbed. She hadn't traveled with any preconceived ideas about the North Woods. And yet, at every turn, she was surprised.

Loon Lake was cheerful and bustling. Shops and restaurants had doors flung open, with visitors flowing in and out like a stream. The rest of the locals were far more welcoming than Elise. Grant had had the idea to meet up for ice cream. She was glad for the chance to make a couple new acquaintances.

She didn't have a plan. And it was sort of nice. If she stopped glancing at all her worldly goods held in her ex's arms, she could almost imagine she was on vacation. Trying to ignore the man at her side, however, was the challenge. Under the warm sunshine, she shouldn't notice the heat rolling off him or how he relaxed his gait to match hers. Their hands didn't quite touch. The air in the inches of space between them vibrated. She crossed her arms over her chest, gripping tight.

A far better use of her time would be quizzing him about what he knew of the town. He'd seemed genuinely shocked to learn about the supposed treasure on the inn's property. Somehow, it was connected to his new business. She could ask about that—like how he got funding to start a brand-new career and why—but she didn't want to upset the relative balance.

Grant touched her elbow. "We're here. Come on."

She pressed her lips together, ignoring the warm spot on her arm from his feather-light grip.

He smiled and stood, grabbing the duffle bag.

His grin still had toe-curling properties. His constant good cheer wasn't infectious enough to banish her natural skepticism. But she liked it anyway. He really believed everything would work out and that he shouldn't worry about a plan. She just wanted control. But the tighter she gripped, the more she seemed to lose.

She turned away from him to scan *here*. A structure sat on the edge of the lake. The building needed a paint job. The faded blue paint was chipped, and the siding was worn. The effect was almost like camouflage as they exited the forest onto overlong grass, the building melting into the sky and lake.

"Not much to look at now. I'm starting small. I have big plans. The innkeepers have ideas, too. They've floated the idea of a dinner-cruise partnership. Loon Lake has a lot of potential. So does this business."

How could he remain so positive in the face of such sadness? A bird flew out of a hole in the roof. He might as well pour the money he borrowed—probably at an exorbitant rate—into the icy water. She almost wished a little of his blind optimism would rub off on her.

"Come inside. We can drop off your bag. The museum isn't far. We can walk there and then come back for the boat." He leaned close. "We've walked nearly four miles. Only one to go."

He didn't have a car. She nibbled the inside of her cheek. She'd find out just how well letting the universe provide worked. "I'm not delicate. I can handle a walk."

"I remember."

Heat crept up her cheeks. She wasn't prepared for any hint of their history. He hadn't even referenced their romance, and still, she blushed.

She'd stop reading into every comment and just appreciate having a familiar face in an uncertain moment.

"This is a nice location," she said, eager to break the tense silence.

He turned and smiled. "What you expected?"

"I had no preconceived ideas." She scrunched her nose. "For once."

"Please continue to save your judgment," he said. "I'm only getting started."

"I'll try." She smiled.

He opened the man door next to a rolling metal panel and strode inside, flipping a switch.

She entered behind him, blinking as she darted her gaze through the darkened interior space. The ramshackle condition of worn boats lifted out of the water was almost picture-perfect. The sunlight streaming in through a row of windows overlooking the lake cast a dappled glow on the battered and bruised hulls. Her stomach clenched. The boathouse was in rough shape. How much money had he sunk into this? She worried over her situation, but it was nothing compared to this. Still, she couldn't fight the urge to frame the scene. Something about the decay was beautiful.

She lifted her hands and squinted as she studied the scene through the space between her fingers.

"Would you want to take some photos?" he asked. "I'd love to update the marketing material. I'm getting ahead of myself, I know. But I would hate to miss a chance to book an appointment with a talented photographer."

She met his gaze and shrugged. "I haven't used my camera for a long time. I'm not in demand. I'm not much of anything."

"Why not?" He arched an eyebrow. "Gypsy curse?"

She smiled. His conspiratorial look loosened the tight coil she got in her stomach every time she thought about her photography. "I wouldn't have thought you'd be so flippant about it. Are you or are you not currently engaged in a treasure hunt?" She turned his words back on him.

"True. I have a hard time picturing the how and why you received the ire of a gypsy."

"I was grabbing a bite to eat when a woman walked in off the street and accosted me. It took five minutes for the wait staff to remove her."

"Peanut, I guess it's a had-to-be-there story?"

She lifted her shoulder. Maybe it was. At that point, they'd split a year earlier. She kept seeing him everywhere.

She almost felt like he had been there. In the corner of her gaze, she spotted a flash of color. Stiffening, she turned towards the open door. She frowned.

No one passed by or cast a shadow. For all she knew, she heard the bird returning or some other creature who'd taken up residence in the wreck of a building. She couldn't shake the horrible, spine-tingling sensation of being watched.

Raising a hand to her neck, she smoothed down the hairs. The skin-crawling sensation was completely unwarranted.

"Here we are," he called, his voice echoing in the space.

She lifted her gaze and rubbed her eyes.

He boarded a sleek vessel.

She hadn't spotted the boat from the entrance. The massive and broken tour boats obscured the dock closest to the water. She wasn't sure she trusted her eyes.

She walked down the dock slowly, careful of her steps. She felt like she was in a dream. She didn't need to crash back to earth.

The rest of the building fit her understanding of him. Patched together with a mix of old and new. But this? Highly polished chrome over a pristine fiberglass body, the boat looked fresh out of a showroom.

She strode down the dock, studying the boat in the lift, hovering over the water. The bow had recessed cushioned seating. She scanned the immaculate upholstery and spotted a blanket and pillow. She gulped. Were these the sleeping arrangements? Definitely drier and cheaper than her alternatives. But she couldn't curl up with her ex. She lifted her chin, ready to object and apologize for wasting his time.

He disappeared.

She retraced her steps and carefully climbed aboard. Dropping her purse to the floor, she narrowed her gaze. The interior held a cockpit, seating, a sink, and a small refrigerator. And a door.

The door opened.

He reappeared.

"Oh good, you climbed on. I'll give you the cabin so you can have privacy."

She widened her gaze, glimpsing a washroom to one side and in the cabin opposite, the edge of a flat-screen TV. "You're rich?" She covered her mouth with both hands. And she was tactless.

"It's hardly a super yacht. But it suits my needs. I don't have a crew or anything. But I can live on board. Thought I'd give that a try this summer. Although to be fair, I've spent a lot of time at the inn."

The conspiratorial tone didn't line up. She could not relate to staying at a hotel on a whim and purchasing luxury vehicles and new businesses. Had they ever been equals? Their situations seesawed from have to have not and back again.

Only someone with wealth would be so unconcerned with discussing money or with a timeline for starting a business. If she had his means, she would do whatever she wanted. But had he earned the money or inherited it? She cared about the means of acquiring financial independence because it would again be a difference between them. She vowed to make the most of the opportunity to set herself up for success.

She'd accepted his offer, not knowing what to expect. In her wildest imagination, however, she couldn't picture his reality. Why was he helping her? Boredom? Was she pathetic for taking him up on his assistance? Was she a joke?

"I've done okay. When the owner of the inn called with an opportunity, I had the time and was ready for a new adventure."

"You're better than *okay*." She flushed. The words were simple and better reflected her shallow understanding of the moment than his truth. Now she understood his confidence in the future. He must have funds to spare for resurrecting a business and probably floating it financially for a few years until it turned a profit. The universe had looked out for him. She'd be jealous if she wasn't shocked his plans worked.

Why him? She hated the thought. It betrayed his kindness. For her own sake and his, she should call off the farce and leave. Whatever she found, she'd never be on his level. She could go back to Chicago and get a job.

"Look, I can see the wheels spinning." He held up both hands. "I love an adventure. I'm totally game. No strings attached."

Am I? She darted her gaze to the side. Maybe she hadn't experienced the feeling of being watched. Perhaps her sense of self-preservation pieced together the clues of his reality before she did and urged her escape. She wasn't good at trusting her instincts. "You don't have to help me," she said. "I don't want to take up your time. It's valuable." *I'm sure I can't pay your hourly fee.* She wasn't sure she knew enough numbers to count that high. Every surface gleamed. In every direction she turned, she swore she heard a cash register ringing up an astronomical tally as she mentally calculated the value of her surroundings.

"I haven't started the tour business yet. My lawyers and financial planners are working through a lot of details. The typical, boring, bureaucratic stuff and all of the licenses, etcetera, for a commercial enterprise. I have plenty of time to help an old friend. I want to."

An old friend? She nodded. Friendship sounded nice. Wanting more was ridiculous. She shoved all reconciliation ideas aside now. He was a fully functioning, apparently successful, adult. And she was a mess. She wouldn't add gold-digger to her list of superlatives. Unless she needed a shovel to unearth the treasure and save herself from her current downward spiral.

She pulled her shoulders back and lifted her chin, more determined than ever. She might have crashed to the bottom. The only way to go was up. "Should we go?"

"Do you need a few minutes? Want to rest?"

She shook her head. Absolutely not. The only thing stalling would do was twist her stomach even tighter. "I'm fine. You said it's a mile to the museum? Let's get going."

She smiled and infused it with every ounce of cheer she could dig up. She understood now. She'd been the ultimate loser. But she'd come out ahead. She wasn't giving up without a fight.

* * *

Grant crunched gravel under the thin soles of his boat shoes. He should have changed into his sneakers. He so rarely had to traverse any terrain that he'd forgotten the importance of arch support and a solid sole. He'd pay for the oversight later.

Although, he'd argue he was already paying a steeper price than sore feet.

He studied the phone in his hands, scanning the screen as he followed the coordinates to the museum. The activity provided cover as he did his best to surreptitiously study her from the corner of his gaze whenever he could. His companion was quiet. She'd been cagey since she found his boat.

Why? Was she upset about his situation? He was ok. Sure, he had a lot of work ahead to get the business operational and even more to really transform the tour boats into something memorable for his guests. But he'd be fine, and he wanted the same for her.

"We're almost there," he said, glancing at her.

She nodded but didn't otherwise acknowledge him. She didn't turn her head or offer a pleasant, if placating, smile.

Money changes people. He'd received the warning early in his success. While he'd argue his finances enabled him to be his truest self, unencumbered by the worry and struggle of day-to-day living too many people suffered, he'd witnessed how his money changed others' perceptions of him.

He'd made a game of guessing others' emotions regarding him. Jealousy and scorn were perhaps the most common. With Molly, he discovered something else. Embarrassment.

By any measure, she'd had a rough week. How long ago had her troubles started? Did she suffer the consequences of compounding interest adding more trauma to each moment? He wanted to know. He had to fix things for her.

Loon Lake promised him a fresh start. He'd make sure she got the same. The treasure was a great start. And maybe they'd find closure in their relationship and pick up where they'd left off with their friendship. Until he saw her, he didn't realize how she soothed an ache in his soul. He wasn't lonely. Or he hadn't thought of himself as lonely. But her company cheered him, and he hoped to do the same for her at a moment when she needed a shoulder to cry on the most.

A branch snapped.

"What's that?" she hissed.

"Probably a squirrel."

"What if it's a person?" Her voice trembled.

"We'd still be okay." He itched to reach for her hand to squeeze her fingers and calm her. Her hands were always cold. Warming her up had been a key part of his role as a boyfriend. Could he be caring as a friend? "The only person who would be out here is Mr. Willie. He's the groundskeeper at the inn. Trust me, he keeps to himself. He won't talk about us skulking around, and he won't interrogate us either."

"How can you be sure?"

"Because he doesn't want anyone asking questions of him."

They reached the last rise and began their descent to the log cabin on the lakeshore. The road forked, continuing past the museum to join up again with the main, paved state highway running through the region and the other path leading to a curving drive around the front of the building.

The front door opened, and a group of chattering people spilled out.

"Thank you for stopping by," Elise called over the din.

Grant widened his gaze, grabbing his aviator sunglasses from his shirt collar and hiding his eyes. He pulled Molly behind him. Her breath was hot on his neck. Before he could let himself worry about manhandling her or gaining Elise's notice, he was saved.

Tires crunched on the road.

He stepped off the gravel and onto the grass, tugging Molly.

The car pulled up to the front of the museum and parked, the engine running.

"Hello, I've come to escort you to our meeting and a late lunch," Seth shouted over the noise.

Molly yanked on Grant's shirt.

He turned.

Seth? She mouthed, eyes wide.

Grant shrugged. He was equally surprised by the pairing. More, however, he was relieved the shock seemed to snap her out of her awkward behavior around him.

A car door slammed.

He whirled around to spot the car pulling away, Elise riding shotgun. He shielded Molly from view until the car disappeared. "That was good timing. I don't think she noticed us."

She blew out a sigh. "Will the museum be closed? Are the doors locked? I feel like Elise is the person with an elaborate security setup."

"She probably would be. But Loon Lake isn't like that. The town runs on the honor system. The door will be unlocked until five. If anyone goes in while she's gone, they'll leave their admission fee on the front desk." He stiffened. Maybe Loon Lake shouldn't be so trusting. Perhaps the events earlier in the summer should be enough to warn locals against their open-door policy.

"Okay. Let's get going before she comes back." Molly strode ahead with purpose.

He smiled, glad for the return to normal in the interactions. As he neared the front door, however, he paused. His skin prickled, and he fought a shudder. Was he being watched?

He scanned the open landscape and didn't spot anything or anyone besides the retreating tour group. He was being overly sensitive after she explained her recent string of bad luck. He wasn't one to believe in anything other than hard work. And he wouldn't start now.

Strolling in through the front door, he slid a crisp twenty into the jug on the front counter then studied his phone again, making his way into the main display room. According to the GPS, he stood on the spot. But he saw nothing. Against a wall, displaying photos of the region's logging history, he was on firm ground. No x marked the exact position. He bounced on his feet. Under the soles, he felt no give. The industrial carpeting covered what must be a solid subfloor.

For a historic log cabin, the interior was remarkably updated. He sort of expected to find old floorboards. He came prepared to pry up a loose plank and find the treasure in a dusty, forgotten recess. Instead, he entered a quaint museum finished with drywall and updated electrical. Luckily, the staff didn't have the means for a full-fledged security and camera system.

Too bad. He'd been counting on engaging in some sort of handy task. He wanted to help and get back to the comfortable companionship that vanished when she saw his boat and asked if he was rich.

Cringing, he shook his head and strolled the perimeter of the room again. He hoped his earlier deflection wasn't too obvious but effective enough to stop her from asking again. Her blunt ask was refreshingly direct. Everyone he met probably made assumptions about his wealth based on what was said and written. But no one came out and put him on the spot.

He was comfortable. But he'd struggled for so many years, getting his business launched and supporting the loyal employees dedicating their lives to his vision, he didn't often think about the monetary rewards he reaped.

He didn't like the change in her expression. He wanted neither censure nor adoration. Being with her again was a return to a slower pace. And he didn't have to constantly explain or defend himself. He liked the unexpected second chance to be friends again. He wasn't going to let something as paltry as financial security change the dynamic.

"Anything?"

He spun around.

She stood a few feet away, frowning in front of a row of logs.

The display showed the process of taking wood from trunk to lumber. The examples supplied by her family's former business.

He shook his head. "I haven't been to this museum since I was a kid. I don't remember it being quite so finished." He shrugged.

"Are you disappointed? Were you hoping for more of a struggle? Did you think we'd be taking a crowbar to the floor?"

"Well...yeah." He ran a hand through his hair. "Going on a treasure hunt conveys a certain thematic flair."

She rolled her eyes. "Someone's watched too many movies. We don't even know what the treasure is."

"Wah-wah. Why bring down the mood?"

"I don't want you raising your hopes," she murmured.

Mine or yours? He wasn't interested in the haul. He liked the adventure and time together. "But you don't think it's real?"

"I don't want to cause damage to the building if it's a hoax."

"Maybe we're helping. If your treasure is here, won't you donate some back to the museum?"

"Well, sure. But I'm not expecting a chest of gold.

Whatever it is could be trash. I'm not counting on a chest full of booty."

He stared at her hard.

She met his gaze with a steady one of her own. If he'd initiated a staring contest, he'd forgotten until this moment her sheer determination to never lose. "There weren't pirates up here. Did you not read any of the plaques? This is a land of indigenous people and fur trappers. We're not on the road to El Dorado."

He liked the inner strength and steel he glimpsed. He preferred her this way and liked her return to form. He did the gentlemanly thing and broke away first. "Not with that attitude, we're not," he muttered.

"I didn't tell you specifically what the lawyer told me at the first meeting. As long as a Maguire owns the mill, the town is golden." She lifted one shoulder.

"And I can't interpret the gold as literal?" He widened his gaze.

"Am I a fool?" She nibbled her bottom lip.

She never was. He didn't enjoy seeing her down. But he liked the push to spontaneity. "Of course not." He raised his phone and refreshed the screen with the locator app. He retraced his steps to the spot. "This should be it."

She stood close, peering over his shoulder. "Nothing's here?"

"Looks like a dead end." He kicked the bottom of the wall, and his toe stuck. He'd pushed in a piece of trim. He glanced at her. "Oops."

"What are you doing?" she hissed, looking over her shoulder and back again. "Get your foot out of there."

"I can't," he murmured. "Help."

She sank to her knees and grabbed his ankle with both hands.

She was cute. But no way could her tiny fingers release him from the wall. And he wasn't sure he wanted her touching him. Anywhere. He swallowed the lump in his throat. Hands-off was the only way he could proceed as just friends. "Maybe you should be lookout or go make a diversion. I'll slip out of my shoe."

"She just left. We have plenty of time." She grunted. "And I almost have it." She gripped both hands around his ankle and tugged. On the third yank, she freed him and fell backward on her behind with a thud.

He bent and extended his hand. Then, remembering the incident at the dock, he corrected himself. He coughed. "May I help you up?"

"I'm fine, thank you." She rolled forward onto her knees and stilled, staring at the trim.

He didn't have a toolkit with him. He scanned the surroundings. Between the two of them, they managed to lift the heavy, carved chair in the corner and place it in front of their accidental vandalism. "Come on, we can get out of here before anyone notices." Or they were caught.

He'd write a generous check to cover damages. With any luck, he'd be able to do so before Elise discovered their handiwork.

Molly turned her face. "We have to take this piece. It's carved with more numbers."

"Wait. What? It is?" He knelt on the ground at her side. "Really?"

Shoulder to shoulder, she handed him the section of trim. "I found the first clue underneath trim. This has to be the next."

"We can't take it." He scanned the room.

Elise must have a stash of papers and crayons for school groups at the ready. He'd made a rubbing. But he couldn't find anything.

"We can't stay any longer," Molly said.

"Didn't you just tell me we had nothing but time?" He arched a brow.

She pursed her lips. The twitch in her cheek gave away her amusement at the good-natured ribbing.

This back-and-forth teasing was them at their best, recalling all their playful moments a lifetime ago. He'd never understood how they went from laughing together to breaking up so swiftly. Neither of them had cheated on the other. He never looked at anyone else around her.

"Let's go. Please?" She tucked the trim under her arm.

"Okay, hold on. I have an idea that doesn't involve theft." He pulled up his phone's camera app and motioned for her to hand over the piece. He snapped a few photos. In the album, he zoomed in. He could just make out the numbers. "These photos are good enough. Put it back, and we'll get going. We might have a lot of ground to cover." He handed her the trim.

Again, their fingers brushed. He held his breath. He hadn't spent their years apart daydreaming about her or fantasizing about what they could have had. Because he didn't believe in wasting time doing that. But her reappearance was a wake-up call. He liked who he was around her. Maybe she felt the same?

He stood, slipped the phone into his back pocket, and held out his hand.

She finished securing the trim to the wall, dusted her hands on her pants, and glanced up. She put her hand in his.

He tugged her to her feet. He wouldn't rush their time together, but he wouldn't delay either. She was off her game, and swooping in at a moment of weakness would only lead to regrets. On her side. He wouldn't retract a thing. But he owed her space and a clear understanding of friendship and nothing more. "Come on, it's a beautiful day to tour the lake. Wild goose chase or not, let's go have some fun."

Chapter Eight

Have some fun? Molly reapplied the sunscreen on her pale arms and throat. Sitting on the cushioned bow of the boat, she had a clear view of the lake ahead of her, stretching far into the horizon. Despite the scenery, she was trapped in her own head. She kept replaying his comment from the museum. What did he mean?

When she first boarded the boat, she had promised herself she would stop trying to predict the next scenario and ready her response. Hadn't she learned in the past few days that she could prepare all she wanted, but life happened without regard for a person's strict parameters? She owed both of them a better mood. He eagerly joined in her folly with a sunny smile.

He tapped in the coordinates.

"Where are we going?"

He shook his head. "Don't focus on that. Sit up front and soak in the view."

She grumbled, scrunching her nose.

"Enjoy the ride."

She rolled her eyes. "Can I help with getting the boat into the water or something?"

He frowned. "Do you have experience?"

She shook her head, her cheeks heating.

He chuckled. "No worries, first mate. This is all automated."

As if on cue, he pressed a button, and the boat lurched as it lowered into the water. Mechanical whirring continued as the engine started. The low hum was almost soothing.

He steered the boat away from the dock and opened the rolling door leading to the water.

She did as directed and sat on the front, out of the way. The first rush of air from the lake was a surprise. She shivered. Once the boat was out on the open water, however, she started to burn.

With no obstruction or overhead screen, there was plenty of opportunity for her light skin to sizzle. She'd never been the baby oil and burn sort. She knew her limitations and respected every invisible boundary line.

Steering the boat from the cockpit, Grant was positioned behind her.

She turned to watch the door to the boathouse close as Grant remained focused on the water ahead. In this instance, he had a plan and was in control of the passage to the destination. She wished she was.

She wanted answers. She'd settle for how many clues led to the treasure. With each minute in his company, she relaxed a little more.

And what was at the end? Where would the trip

lead? She hated the nagging worry that if trash to one was treasure to the other, then the same held true in reverse. Because then she'd roped him into nonsense and wasted his time. She remembered how he sparked joy and lightness in her heart. She didn't want him to feel used. She wanted to end on good terms.

The boat was the only vehicle on the stretch of quiet water, slicing through the surface like a heated knife through cold butter. At the mouth of the channel, the boat turned north into Lake Superior. Here the water was rough, the boat occasionally hitting the wakes of other vessels.

She glanced east in the direction Seth had warned her about. The water looked no different from any other stretch of lake. With no shoreline, it was uninteresting. Perhaps she was too much of a lake novice to decipher the subtle changes. Instead, she faced forward and enjoyed the view.

After a while, she spotted a town on the shore. With chain hotels and several streets of red-brick buildings, the town was practically a metropolis compared to Loon Lake. She waved at the people on passing boats, her cheeks stretching tight with the first real smile she'd had in days.

The rush of fresh air exhilarated her. She shut her eyes and turned her face to the sun, breathing deeply. She was at peace. For at least a little time, she was safe.

The boat continued north. She shielded her gaze with a hand to study the passing scenery. Hills rose and fell, the green setting almost like a folkloric American painting by Grandma Moses. They came upon another town, this one dotted with grand Victorian structures up the hillside. Across the lake, she spotted an almost flat island.

Ferries crossed in opposite directions, and a few sailboats glided across the water's surface with masts unfurled.

"That's Madeline Island," he called and pointed. "Bayfield is across the bay."

She turned and cupped her hands around her mouth. "Are we stopping here?"

"No." He shook his head. "We're going further."

He navigated towards an island.

Instead of a forested shoreline, she spotted rocks and caves. The landscape was extreme, from high ground to water with no gentle undulation between. She shivered. She'd hate to be stranded here.

The icy lake was deep. Swimming would be torture. Although she could probably use a cold shower, she refused to test the lake's water temperature with her limbs.

He slowed the boat and stopped several yards away.

A mechanical whirring from the port side preceded the clinking of unfurling chain links. She scrambled to her hands and knees, inching towards the port side to observe the anchor as it hit the bottom.

He powered off the engine. "We're here."

She faced him. "Where? I don't see anything beyond trees."

"We're on Devil's Island. And, you can't see it from here, but there is a lighthouse up there. I'm ninety-nine percent sure the sea caves are our destination."

She surveyed the seemingly pristine island again. It was almost a land from another time. She couldn't believe she hadn't known about such a beautiful spot. "I've heard all about Door County and Mackinac but never this place. I can't believe I haven't."

"From Chicago, this stretch of Lake Superior is a bit of a haul. But worth it. A hidden gem. The towns aren't commercialized, and it's designated a protected national lakeshore. It hasn't changed much since I came here as a kid."

He held a can of aerosol spray, shut his eyes, and liberally doused himself.

Bug repellant wafted in the air. She scrunched her nose. The acrid smell burned her nostrils. "Mosquitoes on the water? Don't they get blown off course?"

"No, much worse than mosquitoes. Black flies that can bite through jeans." He circled his wrist. "Come on back and spray yourself. We can talk strategy for the next clue."

She squeezed through the opening and stepped back into the covered cock pit. Straightening, she grabbed the can of spray, shut her eyes, and held the trigger. She opened her eyes and frowned. She'd gotten some on her mouth. She smacked her lips.

"Here." He extended a water bottle.

"Thanks." She uncapped the drink and took a long swig. Swallowing, she set the water to the side and folded her arms over her chest. "So, where are we going?"

He pointed to the caves on the island's coast. "At the moment, I'm not fully equipped. I don't have a kayak or dinghy. But I have plenty of life jackets and pool noodles."

She shuddered. "I have to get in the water? I don't have a bathing suit."

"I've got you covered. I have extra rash guards and board shorts."

She frowned. Served her right for even thinking up a new no-go that would be immediately shot out of the sky by whatever twisted scheme brought her to the North Woods in the first place.

"I don't want to get in the water any more than you do. But we're on an adventure. We have to commit."

She widened her gaze. He said the C-word without hesitation. She turned away.

Under normal circumstances, she'd give up here at the hard part. Playing life safe landed her in her current predicament. She had to swerve off her normal course.

"Do you think every stop is going to involve potential hypothermia exposure?"

"I'm not sure." He grinned and ran a hand through his hair. "Okay, I tell you what, I'll explore this one on my own. But wherever the next stop, you have to join me." He extended his hand.

She reached for him and shook. "Deal." His palm was warm, and his grip firm. But the touch was knee-buckling. If she let go of his hand, she might collapse to the floor.

A shrill chime rang.

She dropped her hand and turned. On the floor, she'd dropped her purse. The sound came from her bag.

She hadn't received a call for a few days. She'd almost forgotten the sharp ringtone.

"I'm going below to change."

With a nod, she stepped out of his path and grabbed her purse. Fumbling inside, she retrieved her cell. An unknown number flashed on the screen. She answered the call. "Hello? Molly Maguire, speaking."

"Ms. Maguire, good afternoon. This is Sheila York, calling from your insurer. How are you today?"

Molly scrunched her nose. The words were delivered in monotone. Was Sheila a pre-recorded voice or a living person?

"Ma'am? Ms. Maguire?"

Molly cleared her throat. "Good afternoon, Sheila. Yes, I'm fine."

"We're glad to hear. And you're suffering no lasting health effects from the building fire?"

Again, no real emotion lingered behind the dry tone. "I'm okay."

"Good. The fire investigator has completed their work."

"Oh?" She tucked her free, clammy palm under her armpit.

"Yes, ma'am. The fire was an act of arson. And as such, your coverage is declined."

"What?" Molly dropped to the nearby seat, grateful for the cushion and support. Someone set the fire? She was chilled to her bones. Was she the target? It was a ludicrous thought. But after several days of bad luck, she couldn't dismiss it out of hand. Was the universe—or someone—out to get her? She pinched the bridge of her nose and took in a sharp breath. Until her run-in with Elise, she hadn't thought she made enough of an impact on another person to have a full-fledged enemy. The petite woman wasn't even a true nemesis. They had one meeting and stood on opposite sides to no fault of the other. *As long as she doesn't blame me for the destruction to the museum.*

On the boardwalk and again at the boat house, she had the sensation of being watched. If she assumed she was a target, she'd lose more than her physical comforts. Paranoia was no way to live the rest of her life. "Can you please repeat what you just said?"

"We will not be sending you payment. The fire was deliberate."

"But...I didn't set the fire." She hated the slow build-up of tension behind her eyes. How could she make an insurance company that dealt in black and white come to her vision? "I live in a building with twenty units. It could have been anyone or no one. Some stranger could have done this. And I won't get my money? I've never missed a payment to you."

"We are aware. If you read your policy carefully, you will see the stipulation about our payouts. In the event of arson, we are not required to reimburse."

She needed the money. She couldn't live in the flooded building on the lake of a town that hated her. If she got back to Chicago, she could find another job. Her two weeks' severance wouldn't cover a security deposit.

"Ma'am? Did you hear me? You should expect a call from local law enforcement. They'll conduct interviews," the agent said.

She shivered. For that to happen, she needed to get back. She needed to cover travel expenses and another apartment and still have enough to feed herself.

"You sure you don't want to come?" Grant asked.

She turned towards the doorway leading below deck. Once again, she felt her icy limbs thaw. He had some kind of calming superpower. His nearness relaxed her. With him, she thought she had a chance. Everything might be okay. As long as they were together. Was that trusting him or the universe?

Dressed in a long-sleeved rash guard and board shorts, he held a pool noodle and mouthed *Sorry*.

She nodded and held up a finger.

"Ms. Maguire? Is there anything else?"

She shook her head.

"Ma'am?"

"No," Molly croaked. "Thank you." She hung up the call and dropped the cell into the purse on the ground.

"You okay?" He tipped his head to the side.

"I'm fine." *I have to be*. No one was coming to save her. She'd have to save herself. She desperately needed a win. The treasure had to be real and valuable. Or she didn't know what she'd do. "I'll stay onboard this stop. But shout out what you find or if you need backup."

He saluted her and crossed to the stern. Hopping over the back seat to the swim platform, he disappeared with a splash. "Woooooooohhhh."

She smiled. Nothing was going her way. But she still couldn't stay upset around him. She wasn't sure if she wanted a swift, resolute end or if she wanted the hunt to continue indefinitely.

* * *

The icy plunge stole his breath. Grant bobbed in the water for a second, his brain seized with the overwhelming physical sensation of frigid cold. He bicycled his legs and started the blood pumping again. With his arms, he cut figure eights in the water.

He reached for the noodle he'd left on the swim platform, tucked it under his arms, and paddled to the caves. He had to do this for her. It would be more fun if she joined in. But the stricken look on her face told him to back off and not push. She agreed to get in the water at the next stop.

I really hope the treasure isn't here.

He wanted to keep going. He wanted to wipe away the frown from her phone call. Who had she spoken with? What could have ruined her day so thoroughly, so fast?

Kicking his legs, he relied on muscle memory from years of swim lessons to carry him through. The longer he stayed in the water, the less he could control his appendages. He relaxed into trusting himself. He could do this because he'd done it a hundred times before.

He wished he could instill some of that faith into her. When he had walked in on her call, he'd been devastated. Her skin was an awful shade of pale green. She was hunched forward, curling her body inward. He wouldn't pry. When she was ready, she'd share. He trusted her.

Swimming closer, flies circled his head and shoulders. The angry beasts landed and bit. He winced. The bug spray had washed off as soon as he'd plunged. Only a swim shirt provided a thin layer of protection. Nothing covered his face, neck, or ears. He had to move fast.

The sandstone caves were formed by glaciers cutting across the land in the ice age. Dramatic and seemingly endless, an explorer could get lost in the various recesses or turned around in the dead ends. A seventeenth-century oceangoing buccaneer couldn't have dreamt of a better place to stash booty.

Grant had the advantage. The latitude and longitude gave him an exact point. He picked up speed and entered the cave. His kicking echoed off every stone.

Over the centuries, the waves had sanded down the rough edges, leaving scattered, even, polished surfaces. Approaching a flat outcropping, he paddled to the large, smooth stone and pulled himself up. He set his noodle to the side and drew in several deep breaths.

The island boasted a lighthouse and had a dock for boats to use. But then he'd have had an even longer swim. The sea caves were only accessible from the water. He needed a kayak. If he wasn't worried a joke about her owing him would pierce and wound her tender heart, he'd have teased her.

He scrubbed both hands over his face and sighed. He'd take nothing from her. She was so broken. He'd focus on his task and show her his commitment. Those remained his objectives. He scooted up the rock, avoiding the slippery sections of algae and analyzed the stones set against the natural wall.

Batting away the loose top layer of smaller pebbles, he methodically lifted and flipped every stone from left to right. He had no notion of how long the clue or treasure had been left in situ. But it was clear this wasn't the final stop.

Midway across the nine-foot-wide wall, he reached for a stone. Instead of solid rock, however, he gripped a plastic imitation. He smiled. Growing up, he had a fake rock like this next to his front door, holding the key. He flipped the stone and spotted a plastic sandwich bag stuffed inside.

The creator of the treasure hunt must have been the mysterious aunt. Had she known family could be tracked down? Or was the exercise purely about faith? Her descendant could use a little belief in herself and the world at large. The entire endeavor offered Molly a second chance. He was glad to be part of it.

Holding the rock tight, he wrapped the noodle around his torso and tucked it under his armpits. He slid down the outcropping and held the hand gripping the clue out of the water.

Flies swarmed, chomping on his arm. Each bite was like the puncture of a needle. Not sharp enough to draw blood, but rapid and piercing enough for constant pain. With each kick, he propelled through the water. He stared at his destination. The icy temperatures numbed his skin until he couldn't feel his submerged extremities. The body parts exposed to the air burned.

Finally, he reached the boat, pulled himself up the swim platform, and climbed over the stern. Grabbing a towel, he dried his face and neck, leaving the terrycloth hanging over his shoulders, another layer against the black flies. "I found it."

She didn't respond.

He lifted his chin and widened his gaze.

Sitting nearby, she slapped herself.

"The bug spray didn't work? I'm sorry."

"It's okay." Her arms and legs were covered in angry welts. "Can we get out of here?"

"Do you want some allergy medicine first?" He'd been focused on his situation, forgetting her. He crossed to the cockpit, grabbing the first aid kit and rifling inside for the single dose packet. He ripped open the package and handed the pink pills with a fresh water bottle from the small refrigerator nearby.

She accepted both and took the medicine, gulping down the water. "Thanks." She leaned back against the seat, pressing the cold plastic against her skin. "What did you find?"

He retraced his steps to the stern and grabbed the fake rock. "Another clue, I'm afraid."

"Good." She swatted at the flies. "I'd hate to be accused of getting out of our agreement through trickery."

He arched a brow. "You promise you'll get in the water?"

"If need requires it, yes."

He pulled the bag from the hollow underside and entered the coordinates into the GPS. "Well, looks like you will get your chance. Our next stop is Raspberry Island. They have a public dock, but it's pretty busy. Tour companies use it regularly for its access to the lighthouse. We need a little subterfuge for our secret treasure hunt so we'll have to weigh anchor off shore and swim."

"I really have to swim?" She wrinkled her nose.

"The other option is I carry you to shore." He wouldn't mind holding her close again. "You know I'll take every chivalrous opportunity presented."

She blushed.

Her face matched the hives blooming on her arms. How she wasn't scratching herself raw remained a mystery. "If you want to go below, I left out another rash guard and trunks for you. We'll reach our destination soon."

"Great." She smiled and turned, slipping from view.

He turned on the engine, pulled up the anchor, and steered the boat around the northern tip of the island, heading southwest. With the whip of the wind, the flies were blown off the boat. Good riddance. Every creature existed for a purpose. Grant couldn't identify much beyond annoyance in the life's work of a black fly.

Several yards off, he spotted a speedboat. Raising a hand as he passed, he waved.

The sole occupant of the boat, an indistinguishable person dressed in a hoodie, jeans, and a ball cap, held a pair of binoculars and didn't wave back. A sour taste filled Grant's mouth.

Was it his imagination, or did the other boat angle towards his vessel? Why? First, the encounter at the courthouse, and now, this odd occurrence; his hackles were officially raised. He was on alert. His brain sought rationality. He'd grown used to Midwest friendliness. Any action that didn't include a kind word or a broad smile rubbed him wrong.

He shook off the worry and navigated towards his favorite of the islands, Raspberry Island. Skirting Bear

Island, he spotted more boats. He kept one hand on the wheel, and with the other, he waved and smiled in greeting.

Passing the lighthouse, he sighed. She was missing a great scenic opportunity. The passing landscapes were picture-perfect in every direction. He'd love to see the scenery through her eyes. Her photos had always touched his heart. She captured the ordinary with a tender reverence that elevated the commonplace to the divine.

He'd have to give her the option before they headed to the next stop. He continued on and pulled into a cove on the south side of the island. Dropping anchor, he cut the engine and pocketed the keys. He retrieved the life jackets and set out towels to warm in the sun.

"At least I won't run into anyone I know here."

He turned towards the cockpit and smiled, extending a life jacket. "You look great."

She slipped into the vest, buckling the straps. "At least the icy water might soothe my itchy skin."

"I concur." He nodded. "Once you submerge, you won't be able to feel a thing." He handed her a pool noodle, grabbed the other, and climbed over the stern.

She followed, standing on the swim platform.

The boat bobbed in the wake of a passing vessel.

The water lapped over the teak, splashing up to mid-calf.

She winced.

"On the count of three. One, two, th—"

She jumped into the lake. "AAAHHHH."

"Three." He grinned and leaped in after her.

Chapter Nine

He wasn't wrong. She couldn't feel a thing.

Molly hoped she was kicking and paddling. She wasn't entirely sure. Losing sensation in her limbs was an odd thing. When she first hit the water, she felt like she'd been hit in the ribs. The air emptied from her lungs. Her body took control. Luckily.

She neared the shore and swam onto the rocky beach. Only when she sat on the pebbles, tiny stones digging into her skin, did she remember her allergic reaction to the awful flies. No wonder their last stop earned the moniker Devil's Island. The flying insects were evil. She extended both arms and studied her limbs. The icy swim cooled her burning skin.

He walked onto the shore and settled next to her, leaning back on his palms.

How did he make every excursion look so uncomplicated and easy? He hadn't worn a life jacket but cut through the water like a shark in the warm Caribbean.

She bent her knees and hugged her arms around her legs. "Just a little note." She turned her face towards him. "If you're serious about launching a tour business, you might want to look into a drier way to ferry to various points of interest."

He grinned. "Good note."

"Are you serious about your new role?"

"You've seen the boathouse and my current inventory of vessels. It's an investment. Do you doubt me?"

"Not your loyalty or your dedication. The town will be lucky to have you."

Would she feel lucky to have him? *Don't go there.* They weren't reuniting for good. Their run-in had a purpose. She just couldn't quite figure it out at the moment.

"While I'll concede your boats don't look particularly seaworthy, I have to imagine they'd be better than this."

"Fair point. I'm still waiting on the delivery of my inflatable boat for personal ferrying. I will have tour vessels ready to go by next spring. He pushed off the ground and stood, extending his hand. "Can I help you up? We have a bit of a hike from here to the lighthouse."

She gritted her back molars to stop her teeth chattering. "I'll follow you. But I have to make something clear. I don't think I can commit more vandalism on a historic property today. We're already trespassing. By the time we finish, our faces might be plastered on wanted posters all over town."

He rolled his eyes. "This isn't the Old West. You aren't an outlaw, and we aren't heading inside. I believe the point is near the well. We should be able to reach it without destruction. And if it makes you feel better, we are well within our rights to use these trails and anchor the boat here."

She scanned the empty shoreline. She couldn't shake the feeling of being watched. If she voiced the feeling, would she be laughed at? She didn't mind his playful, never serious demeanor. Except when she did. When something was important, like the future, she couldn't roll with his good humor. "After the museum, I'm on edge. Will we be conspicuous?"

"Only one way to find out." He shook his hand.

She accepted his help to stand. If she was still numb, she wouldn't feel the warmth of his hands. But still, a tension vibrated in the soft touch. Back on her feet, she dropped his hand and rubbed her palms together. "Do we leave the noodles here? Can we walk to the lighthouse without shoes?" She couldn't be surprised he wasn't prepared. But why wasn't she?

"It's a wooden plank boardwalk through the forest. Once at the edge of the property, we'll walk on the manicured lawn. We won't be allowed inside the lighthouse. Dripping on the antiques is frowned upon. But we'll be okay outside. We won't be that noticeable."

She crossed her arms over her chest and hugged herself. The soaking rash guard clung to her skin, chilling her even more than her worries. She didn't want the hunt to end, but she had questions about the whole point. Who was her distant aunt? Why had she devised the scheme? If the treasure was real, why hadn't she retrieved it to fund the condo conversion? Was that even her goal?

He bent, reaching for the swim noodles.

Molly hated that she was constantly on alert, tracking his every movement. She kept noticing things she wanted to forget. Like how the corners of his eyes crinkled when he smiled or the stretch of a shirt over his muscled shoulders. Remembering his kindness didn't help establish the distance she had to keep. She'd gotten so far off the track to success. Any detour threatened her future for good.

He strode towards the edge of the tree line and dropped the noodles. With a glance over his shoulder, he met her gaze and tipped his head.

She nodded and strode forward onto the wooden boardwalk behind him. She kept her chin pinned to her chest, studying every step for potential hazards. With everything going wrong, she couldn't add a sprained ankle to the mix. Or maybe she was being shoved in another direction?

She lifted her chin and widened her gaze. She'd stepped foot into a forest out of a child's imagination. Dappled light filtered through the green leaves. The ground was covered with ferns. If fairies existed, they'd make a home here. She exhaled and rolled her neck.

He stopped and turned. "Are you hurt?"

"I'm fine." She lifted a shaky arm and pointed. "It's beautiful."

He grinned and resumed his stroll. "The green is so much brighter here, isn't it?" He called over his shoulder.

She nodded and followed. The air was lighter and the sun warmer, too. If she had the chance, she could unwind and release every last worry. She shut her eyes and stumbled. Jerking upright, she frowned. Nope, she wasn't the sort to enjoy relaxation. She focused on the planks.

The path wound around the landscape, skirting streams and cutting through the forest. The thin streaks of sunlight weren't enough to dry the wet trunks and rash guard. At the end of the walkway, however, she was no longer dripping lake water. Her last few steps left no footprint.

"And here we are." He extended both arms.

She sighed and crossed the threshold of the lawn. Soft grass padded the soles of her feet. The blades were like brushed velvet after the rocky beach and rough wood. She stopped and scanned the surroundings.

The rectangular lawn extended past the front of the Victorian lighthouse. The white tower rose high into the sky from the center of a two-story, American Queen Anne, wooden home. A few outbuildings dotted the yard. She didn't want to waste time searching every structure, and she really didn't want to desecrate another historic property.

Several yards away, along the back edge of the lawn, she spotted a stone well sticking up out of the ground. Maybe she'd get a little bit of a break and could find the next clue there. She'd start in the open at least, before attempting to enter the other buildings. She stepped forward.

He held out his arm, catching her in the ribs. "Not yet," he whispered, tilting his head towards the back of the lighthouse.

A park ranger addressed a group of ten tourists. The well-rehearsed speech hummed at a low tone.

Straining, Molly couldn't make out a word the woman said. She studied the visitors aiming cell phones towards and away from themselves. A cell flashed with a bright light. The likelihood of herself or Grant appearing in any of the self-focused images was slim. Still, she wanted to escape quickly. She hadn't felt watched since entering the forest. She wouldn't lean into paranoia willingly.

The door opened, rusty hinges squealing. After a few more minutes, the door shut with a thud.

"Okay, now's our chance." He dropped his hand. "Once they get to the top of the lighthouse, they'll see us."

She craned her neck and shielded her gaze with one hand. She'd like to come back and see the view. She met his gaze and nodded.

He strode across the yard with shoulders back and chin lifted.

Anyone would think he belonged.

She took a step forward, and her right knee buckled. She collapsed to the ground.

"Are you okay?"

Pushing against the patch of dirt she landed in, she stared at the hand he offered her.

Needing to get back on her feet in the most literal way, she couldn't accept his help. She had to do this on her own. She stood and wiped her palms on her thighs. *Heel toe, heel toe.* She rolled her feet with deliberate effort. The few hundred feet to the well might as well have been a few thousand. Her heartbeat thudded, and she shivered. She held her arms at her side, imagining her limbs weighted with iron, and crossed.

"The first two clues were in trim, right?" He looked into the well, not turning towards her or the lighthouse.

"Correct."

"Stands to reason, the second set of two will both be fake rocks."

She frowned and stepped back. Naturally colored stones of gray, red, and black formed the visible section of the well. If something was out of place, wouldn't the rangers have noticed and fixed the error long ago?

Resting her palms on the edge, she absorbed the warmth of the rocks from the sun. She absorbed the heat, holding her hands out like she stood before a campfire. She licked her lips. Any chance she could convince him to set up a beach bonfire and make s'mores?

"Are you looking?"

She frowned and stepped forward. Her shin hit the well. She sucked in a sharp breath and glanced at the protruding stone. The rock was almost shiny, not nearly as matte as the others. She glanced over her shoulders. No one stood nearby. She knelt and studied the stone. With her fingers, she gently tilted the rock backward and forward. It popped out and into her hands. "This is it," she whispered. She turned the plastic stone over and found a sandwich bag containing paper stuffed inside.

Carefully setting the rock back into its position, she stood and opened the sandwich bag. She reached inside for the scrap of paper and squinted. Sun hit the white sheet with blinding brightness. "N 46°41'57.6", W 90°33'14.4"

He held out his hand. "I have a pocket. I can hold onto the clue."

She nodded and reached forward.

A gust of wind caught the sheet.

In her clammy grip, she couldn't hold tight. She watched in slow-mo. She might as well have been a TV viewer for all the impact she had to stop it.

The paper fell into the well, disappearing from view.

Heat crept up her neck and cheeks. Her skin itched. Her shin throbbed. She was a mess. And she was dragging him down with her. "I'm sorry." She croaked.

He shook his head. "N 46°41'57.6", W 90°33'14.4?"

She sniffed and wiped her eyes. He remembered? "I'm glad the curse hasn't grabbed hold of you."

He wiggled a finger. "N 46°41'57.6", W 90°33'14.4"

He'd already said that. She knit her brow together. What was he playing at? She scratched her arm through the long-sleeved rash guard.

He turned and waved to the path. "N 46°41'57.6", W 90°33'14.4"

He developed a rhythm. She wouldn't insert herself and confuse him. She asked for help. She couldn't dictate the terms. Stepping foot onto the path, she shivered. Was someone watching? She glanced up at the lighthouse tower and around the lawn. No one was near. She dropped her chin to her chest and monitored her steps. If she didn't keep herself in check, she was in for real trouble.

* * *

"N 46°41'57.6", W 90°33'14.4" Grant recited his new mantra and pulled himself up onto the swim platform. A splash of water covered the teak, darkening the wood. The force of his action rocked the boat. "N 46°41'57.6", W 90°33'14.4"

He locked his knees, holding steady as the movement slowed. Water dripped onto the slats, streaming down his body. He observed the phenomenon, not feeling the chill. Either he'd gone numb, or he'd adjusted to the temperature.

Molly swam to the edge of the boat. She didn't gracefully slice through the water with even strokes, head submerged and legs outstretched. She slapped the surface, splashing herself. Her face contorted into a frozen grimace. The expression was half shock and half desperation.

He sank to his knees and extended a hand.

She reached for him.

In one solid movement, he pulled her onto the boat as if he'd plucked a piece of lint off his sleeve.

Onboard, her teeth chattered, her lips were blue, and her icy hands were wrinkled. She was right. He needed a better way to get clients to shore.

"N 46°41'57.6", W 90°33'14.4" He dropped his hand and climbed over the stern. He crossed to the cockpit. Retrieving the key from his zipper pocket, he unlocked the compartment near the wheel and grabbed his GPS. As he typed in the points, he fell silent. Grateful for the reprieve from the self-inflicted catchy song.

She remained in place behind the stern, fumbling with the buckles on the life jacket.

In a few long strides, he reached her. "Let me help." He extended his hands and froze. "I promised I'd ask before I acted like a gentleman again. May I be of assistance?"

She nodded, her chin quivering and shudders wracking her body.

He made quick work of unsnapping the closures.

She slithered out of the life vest. The jacket hit the teak swim platform with a plop.

He bent and lifted the bench cushion, grabbing two dry towels. He handed one to her, brushing against her cold fingers but not lingering.

She wrapped the terrycloth around her body, tucking the ends under her armpits. "Aren't you cold? Getting into the water the first time was tough. Somehow, it felt even icier on the second swim."

He stared down, surprised to find another towel still in his hands. With his focus on her, mesmerized by the way she secured the fabric without any clips, he'd forgotten about the chill. He dried his face roughly and scrubbed his arms and chest. When he lifted his gaze, he caught her staring.

"Thanks." She gulped. "For the towel."

He smiled, glad to know he wasn't the only one aware of the other. "You don't owe me any gratitude."

She shook her head. "Of course I do."

She'd slipped back into distress mode. He hated her at a disadvantage. "I'm serious," he said, softening his tone. "I'm enjoying the diversion." He slung his towel over his back and folded his arms over his chest. "Sorry I was a broken record about the points. I didn't want to forget."

"If I hadn't stupidly lost the paper," she muttered.

"You can't control the weather." He narrowed his gaze. Something shifted in her. Was it regret? He didn't want her to feel beholden to him or to worry that he'd take away too much from their unlikely reunion.

Being with her again was better than he'd have imagined. Good things couldn't last forever. Not without reckoning of the past and real change for the future.

"You're right. No man can exert power over the elements," she said. "But it is proof of the curse."

He pressed his lips together. A laugh built deep in his belly. He rocked back and forth, shaking the boat.

She puckered her lips like she knew what was coming. Then she giggled.

He threw back his head and released the chuckle. Straightening, he wiped tears from his eyes. "I'm sorry to laugh. But really with the curse?"

She shrugged and looked at the ground. "Well, yeah."

"Random coincidence and bad luck aren't scientific fact, Peanut."

She shook her head.

Building her up and restoring her confidence proved harder than he'd first thought. He had hope. For her. For him. For them. "I successfully won a battle against the gypsy." He flattened a hand over his heart. "I remembered. Stick with me. I'm the antidote."

She rolled her eyes but lifted the corner of her mouth.

"I'm not sure how much good that'll do us, however," he added.

"Why?"

"The point isn't on land this time. We might have reached the end of the trail. It's off Chequamegon Point, with no island nearby. Past the mouth of our channel."

She gripped her upper arms, shifting her weight from foot to foot.

"We'll be heading towards Seth's Timber Triangle," Grant said, emphasizing each word. "We've been warned, and with our concerns about curses..."

"Do you suppose we'll catch a glimpse of the infamous Soupy?" She waggled her eyebrows.

"Wouldn't that be the greatest discovery of all?"

She held his smile with one of her own, her whole face brightening.

He loved her like this most of all. Teasing. Flirting. Once upon a time, he'd imagined himself the foil to her perfect plan and exactly who she didn't know she needed. After all the years apart, he hadn't realized he'd held his breath, waiting for a chance to see her again.

She broke away from his gaze, untucking a corner of the towel and wiping her face. "I suppose I can't discount the lake monster now that this treasure might really be real."

"Very fair." He retreated to the storage bench and grabbed another towel, extending it to her.

"I'd feel bad if we did spot Soupy." She flipped her hair forward, quickly fashioning a turban from the towel. "Seth is so nice, and I definitely owe him one for showing up at the museum and distracting Elise. He should be the one to find the lake monster if it really exists."

"Right place, right time. Can't argue with the universe today."

She sighed and scrunched her nose. "I really have wasted your time. I can't help but feel like the treasure is going to be something worthless."

None of this has been worthless. Neither did he want it to end. "I'm along for the adventure and not the loot. That's all yours."

"Even now that it's turned into an escapade?"

He smiled.

A cloud blocked the sun.

Raising his hand, he shielded his gaze. Daylight lingered longer in summer. Sudden storms were also bound to spring up. The darker clouds gathering overhead might signal a full-fledged disturbance or a passing downpour. Either way, a decision had to be made. Continue on or stop for the night? Should he insist on stopping at Madeline Island to refuel? Would she decide to call the whole thing off if given the choice? He had to let her make the decision. He hoped she'd want to keep going.

"I was going to suggest we circle back to Madeline and stop for food. But I have a small grill and the essentials," he said.

She arched an eyebrow. "Define *essentials*."

"Hot dogs, chips, and s'mores."

She licked her lips. "Yum. I'm in."

"Do you want to go below and change first? I'll straighten up here."

"Yes. And seriously though, thank you. I wouldn't have followed through on this out-of-the-box trip if you hadn't been here."

He was glad. Once upon a time, he hadn't been the best boyfriend. It wasn't by design. As a slacker twenty-three-year-old, he had convinced himself the over-achieving eighteen-year-old was his salvation. Because the logic was perfectly reasonable given his matriarchal upbringing. If his mom was iron, then his grandma was steel. Without the guiding force of one of the two women who made most of his choices with their heli-copter sort of love, he floundered. Molly appeared like an answer to a question he forgot to ask.

Instead, he'd brought her down. She wasn't the boss of him. She was learning how to take care of herself. Why should she have been responsible for his future? He screwed up. When she disappeared, she made her feelings clear. He didn't try to find her.

Now, he could prove who he really was. He wanted to show her he was the guy she must have thought she'd seen to give him a chance to begin with. No regrets now or ever. "You'd have been fine. The curse can't chase you forever, right? And some cultures believe evil spirits can't follow over the water. We'll lose your bad luck. Give destiny and fate a chance."

Smiling, she strode to the front of the boat and disap-peared below deck.

Watching her go, he sighed. He didn't want the trip to end so soon. But how could he stall without being too obvious? He scrubbed both hands over his face and rolled his neck. Something caught in the corner of his gaze. He turned and faced the shore. Squinting, he couldn't see anything in the tree line. From the water, the forest was a solid mass of darkness.

He raised a hand to smooth down the hairs on the back of his neck. He wouldn't tell her about his suspicions. But it was almost time to maybe be a little more forthcoming about his life. She was spiraling in shambles. He could step up and help her. Would she accept? If he bought his way into her life, would he find peace or always question her loyalty?

If he didn't admit the true depths of his feelings now, he'd never get another chance. Fate could only do so much. He had to step forward of his own free will.

Chapter Ten

Molly held the oversized hoodie to her face, sniffing the collar. He had used the same body wash in college. A musk and cedar scent absorbed into the fleece. When she changed, she had spotted the sweatshirt on a hook next to another. Her outlet shopping spree had been remarkably short-sighted. She had purchased only one pair of jeans and no long-sleeved shirts. He wouldn't mind if she borrowed the piece of clothing. Grant was generous in every way. His good nature was his most endearing quality.

She slipped the hoodie over her head and wiggled into it. The sleeves extended several inches past her hands. The hem hung below her bottom. She was wrapped in warmth and memories. He made her feel safe. That was part of the problem. Years ago, she could have stuck with him forever, mindlessly bobbing along at his side. Where would that have gotten them?

He did well enough without her to start a new business at forty on his own with no loans. That was impressive. Maybe a tour company wasn't exactly taking the world by storm or building a major corporation, but he was living on his own terms. She envied that. Following some elusive and ever-changing path to success led her to rope him into a wild goose chase. Hugging herself, she pretended for a second that his arms wrapped her tight in a safe embrace. She was glad to have said her fear aloud, even if she wasn't sure he entirely believed her.

She definitely didn't believe there would be a curse if she didn't stay in Loon Lake. Elise must not either, or she wouldn't have been so unwelcoming. Of course, Elise was seemingly out of step with the rest of the superstitious citizens.

The treasure was probably nothing. Molly might be desperate enough to need a chest full of gold, but she doubted she'd discover a valuable find. In truth, she expected to find a note explaining the whole point of the journey was the friendships made along the way. She wouldn't regret spending time with him. But she didn't want him to feel deceived.

Thump thump thump

"Coming," she called.

Was he in that much of a rush to change? She never remembered him as pushy.

Thump thump thump

With a sigh, she crossed to the door and yanked it open.

To nothing. She'd heard a sound. She wasn't imagining it. But had she misjudged the direction of the noise? Was it coming from the submerged hull? Then it would be an animal. The creature would have to be large. *Soupy?*

Frowning, she slid sideways out of the cabin. She needed distance from a lake monster. No extraordinary encounters today. Not happening. Climbing the stairs, she spotted Grant near the back.

He turned. "All dry?"

She nodded. Above deck, she noticed how the waves hit the boat from the wake of another vessel on the water with a dull thud. Good. Not a lake monster. Because she did not believe in Soupy.

He studied her from head to toe, smiling as he conducted a slow appraisal. "You look good in my sweatshirt."

The tip of the corner of his mouth nearly buckled her knees. Every time. Even as an adult. Even half-hidden by his beard, which was probably really scratchy when kissing, the expression still tugged at her. *Kissing?* Her aching skin burned. At least the hood provided a shield to hide her obvious blush. She studied the cuffs, rolling the sleeves back to shorten to her wrists. "Yep. You want to change?"

He stepped towards her. Staring at the ground, she glimpsed his feet moving near. She jumped, knocking back the hood, and lifted her gaze. His hands reached out and grabbed her shoulders.

"Sorry, you're in the way."

"Oh, right." She raised a shaky hand to smooth a tendril of hair behind her ear and stepped to the side. "I'll go up front."

He nodded and padded past, down the steps, to his cabin.

She exhaled a heavy sigh. Crossing to the back, she studied the cushioned bench, looking for hinges. On the end, she spotted the latch and lifted the seat, grabbing another towel. She strolled to the bow, crawling under the passthrough, and settled against the front, wrapping the towel around her like a blanket.

More clouds gathered, blocking the remnants of blue sky. She wasn't sure how many daylight hours were left this far north. She hated to delay but would let him make the decision if they needed to head back to shore and wait until the morning to resume the hunt.

She studied the tree line and shuddered. At least she wouldn't worry about being watched on open water. If she hadn't experienced the sudden chill from her server at the restaurant or the awkward run-in with Elise outside the mill, would she still fight the skin-crawling sensation now? She didn't want to tell him her fears. He already teased her over the curse. She accepted the jibes with a certain level of self-deprecation. She'd forgotten about the curse until everything started to go wrong, compounding the previous problem with even more issues.

She narrowed her gaze but didn't spot anything moving on the shore. Good.

"Ready to head out?"

She turned and flashed a thumbs-up.

He turned the engine over, pulled up the anchor, and steered out of the cove.

She cuddled up, bringing her knees closer, and

enjoyed the view. In the corner of her eye, movement caught her attention. She squinted at the area of the dark shadow. What was she doing? Looking over her shoulder? What did she imagine she'd heard below deck or seen following their boat? Soupy?

She chuckled and shook her head, snuggling into the sweatshirt.

Rounding the island, the boat passed other islands and visitors. A captain standing on a nearby vessel waved. She glanced over her shoulder and frowned.

He waved back.

She lifted her hand to her shoulder and awkwardly offered a greeting. Did he know the other occupants?

The next time it happened, a few minutes later, she watched him from the corner of her gaze.

Again, he smiled and waved.

She followed his lead, glad the distance could hide her tight grin. Grant lived life with a sunny-side-up personality she barely understood. She assumed most scenarios started as worst-case. On the occasions she wasn't proved correct, she rationalized it was a one-off. She was rarely wrong. She'd hardened more than she realized until exposure to his eternal optimism. With him, she could drop a smidge of her skepticism.

He navigated the boat through a channel.

Up ahead, she spotted the mainland and a ferry cruising through the lake.

He steered around Madeline, between it and another island. He slowed the boat and stopped near the shore of the other island. Dropping the anchor, he shut off the engine. "Are you hungry?"

She nodded and scurried to the back. For the next half hour, she followed directions, helping where she could. She did her best not to offer any unsolicited opinions. He was a fully functioning adult. He didn't need micromanagement.

But she almost wished he did. She was a mess. He retained his fun with a hint of gravitas. He was more appealing than ever. They were heading in opposite directions. After sliding two hot dogs onto two plates, he directed her towards the bench on the stern. She bit into the hot dog and moaned. Roasted sausage never tasted so good.

He laughed.

She swallowed the bit and giggled, too. "My compliments to the chef."

"I'll take it." He smiled. "Sorry I don't have condiments."

She shook her head. "I'm just glad you had food. I'd hate to stall you with a stop on Madeline Island. I'm sure you want to be done." She stuffed the hot dog into her mouth, halting any further obvious lies. Of course she wouldn't. She chewed and swallowed. "Unless you think we need to wait until tomorrow? Better light?"

He shrugged. "I'm not sure how much of a difference that makes. The big issue is equipment. I have snorkel gear. But if it's in a deep spot, we're out of luck. I'm no scuba diver."

"Me either. I'm sort of thinking it has to be somewhere shallow."

"Why?" He tipped his head to the side.

"It has to be somehow related to lumber, right? That was the business."

He rubbed a hand over his chin. "Like a sunken delivery?"

She wasn't sure. Her hunch might be wrong. She'd questioned herself more in the past few days than in the previous thirty-five years. She shrugged.

"Makes sense. You're probably spot-on. What will you do with it?"

"I have no clue. If it really is valuable, I need the money. But how much value could there be?" And how much could it cost her to deploy a team to retrieve it? Prohibitive costs had to factor into why the timber remained undisturbed.

"Potentially a lot. One of the businesses in Ashland sells reclaimed wood. It's used for all sorts of projects, from cutting boards to installation in buildings and homes. There are a lot of possibilities for commercial application. You'd be in a growing industry."

"If Elise has talked to any of those businesspeople, I doubt they'd want to partner with me. I don't know how else to approach the situation. I need expert help." She stuffed the last bite of hot dog into her mouth.

For a few minutes, she was content to finish chewing in silence. As much as Molly wanted to paint Elise as a villain, Molly couldn't. A distant relative offered Molly a life preserver for the choppy waters ahead. Molly and her great-aunt would never know each other. But her great-aunt had known Elise. Molly was grateful for the unexpected blessing but acknowledged she received her gift at someone else's expense.

"Would you stay?"

His tone was soft, tender. He tugged at her heart. "I have no reason not to. Except the town hates me."

"Despite what she thinks, Elise isn't an elected official representing the whole community. Mayor Burt holds the job for his final term. She's the tourism board and not local immigration."

Molly snorted.

"A first impression isn't always the best indicator. You need a redo."

She waved a hand at him. "Yeah, looks like I've been off for the last thirteen years."

He frowned.

"I don't need to know the details about your life to be sure I was wrong. I'm sorry for underestimating you. Not that you should care about my assessment."

"But I do." He reached a hand for hers and squeezed. "Thank you."

She stared at their clasped hands. Why did he offer such an overwhelming sense of security? Why had he always felt like home?

She gave some supernatural forces—like the curse—her serious attention. And others—like attraction—she relegated to the periphery. Did it even matter? He had the world at his feet. He shouldn't want her.

Before long, he'd wake up and realize how much better off he was without her. She'd only drag him down. He'd leave. The realization triggered her self-preservation instinct.

She pulled her hand back and reached for her second

hot dog. "Better finish this so we can get on to the main course. S'mores."

He grinned. "You've got it."

She stuffed the hot dog into her mouth. If she chewed loud enough, she could override the little voice in her head urging her for more. To do something. Say something. To apologize. To keep him forever.

She didn't know a lot, but she was sure she'd drag him down. That was nothing she wanted a part of. Wherever she went next, she'd pull herself back up. Without a white knight riding to the rescue.

* * *

From his position at the grill on the stern, the portable appliance mounted on the chrome railing, Grant stood on the swim platform. He had a clear view of the bright phone screen near the wheel. Anchored off Michigan Island, in the channel between it and Madeline, he returned to cell phone range. He left the phone on silent. But hadn't thought to flip the device face down on the dash. Now, the screen flashed with the logo of his company and a familiar number. His former assistant.

With a sigh, he studied the metal skewers hovering over the grill. He held one in each hand. The double prongs allowed him to roast four marshmallows at a time. Or eight, if he wasn't trying to give the impression of civility.

From the corner of his gaze, the screen flashed again. He hated the assumed accessibility inherent in cell phones. He felt trapped, tethered to the device. What happened to leaving messages? During his career, he always returned a call within one business day. In his retirement, he relaxed his rule. Besides, he knew what Karen was calling about. She must have finished arrangements for him to use a room at the inn for a video conference into the board meeting. He was not catching a flight to the West Coast this week or any time in the near future if he could help it.

This was the absolute worst time for him to leave.

Near the front, Molly retrieved the chocolate from the refrigerator. She crossed to the makeshift dining room and prepped the graham crackers.

As the day dragged on, he worried. By not disclosing the truth of his situation, he did both of them a disservice. And—if he was really being honest—he'd admit her project appealed to the business side of his brain. If her hunch was correct, she had a unique opportunity. He wouldn't mind flexing his negotiating muscles again. After the year-plus of working out his buy-out package, he rather enjoyed the discourse.

He studied marshmallows, careful not to touch the sticky surface to the grates. It wasn't as efficient as a microwave or as much fun as roasting over a big fire, but the grill toasted the marshmallows to a golden color.

He didn't want her mad. In only a few hours onboard, he couldn't remember why he thought he wanted to be on his boat alone. He wouldn't settle for just anyone's company. He liked hers. Her slightly grumpy, skeptical demeanor hadn't softened. Earning her good opinion was still a sought-after prize.

Would he lose with the truth? Would she walk away for good? If someone else told her, maybe. "All done."

"Great. You mind if I assemble?"

He shook his head. He liked giving her some semblance of control. He learned long ago that he only had his reactions to the world at large. Turning, he held still.

She reached for the skewers.

He handed them over and turned off the grill.

Using the graham crackers, she slid the marshmallows off one at a time.

A boat passed by. The wake rocked theirs. Water splashed on his bare feet.

Still, he raised a hand in greeting. He knew enough to change into shorts and a sweatshirt. He liked her in his other fleece. With his hand in the air, he frowned.

The other boater didn't return the greeting. Odd. And was that the same boat he'd spotted with the binoculars on Devil's Island?

"Do I need to be polite and wait for you before I eat this?"

He turned and grinned.

She held a s'more inches from her mouth.

He climbed over the bench cushion. "Not on my account." He strode to the cockpit, flipped his phone face down, and grabbed the towel he left on the driver's seat. It was still damp, but he didn't care. He just needed to wipe off most of the water and the icky feeling.

If he wasn't already suspending a certain amount of disbelief, embarking on a good old-fashioned search, he would shake off the suspicious feelings about not getting a wave back on the water. The other boater was never quite discernible. He couldn't tell if the figure was a man or a woman or anything distinguishable. Dressed in dark colors and a hoodie covering their head, the person could have been anyone. Including just a random, unrelated local enjoying a spectacular day out on the water.

Elise? He hated thinking it. He had only had a dozen or so encounters with her, and she was always dressed in her slicked-back style. He wouldn't recognize her in jeans. But she was his number one suspect for not returning a friendly greeting. He had no idea what her motive would be.

He returned to the stern and grabbed his plate. He bit into the first s'more. Chocolate oozed out of the back, along with sticky, melted marshmallow. He chewed and licked his fingers.

Perched on the edge of the cushion, she ate with much more dignity. Taking small bites, she hadn't disturbed the precarious position of the different elements stacked on each other.

He should have guessed. She was a master of the block stacking game, removing the tiny rectangular pieces at the bottom with no disruption to the integrity of the rest. He finished his s'more in a couple more bites and made quick work of the second. Chewing almost blocked out his internal dialogue.

She'd said she'd be disappointed if the hunt ended in nothing. For him, the past day had held more value than the amount in his bank account. But he wasn't struggling. And she was. He wouldn't diminish her needs with a few pretty words. She wanted success. Ever since he met her, he watched her chase something she couldn't define or explain. Without setting goals, she did little more than hope. She'd chased it. "I'll put away the grill, and we can head to the treasure."

"Oh, sure." She swallowed and smiled, reaching for her second s'more. "As long as you're sure you won't be disappointed about a pile of sticks." She scrunched her nose.

He smiled. He liked the wrinkles forming between her brows. He was remembering how much he'd forgotten about her and how she made him feel. He wanted some reciprocation. "Of course I won't be disappointed. And I promise, I don't mind." *Now or never.* "I could help you if you wanted. If the treasure is timber, I can approach the company with you. I have experience dealing with contracts and less than enthused partners."

"Really?" She covered her mouth with a hand as she chewed her second s'more.

He nodded. "I'm not just the charming cad."

She blushed. "I'm sorry if I gave you the impression that I thought so little of you."

He shook his head and smoothed his beard. His fingers stuck in the marshmallow debris left behind. "The beard kind of gives off a vibe?"

She nodded and finished chewing.

"And it's a hazard for s'mores," he said.

She giggled.

He reached for a napkin and wiped what he could. Once he got back to dryland and stable flooring, he'd shave. "I grew it out recently. I lived next to my grandpa's nursing home. After he passed, I came here. I stopped shaving when I moved. I've gotten used to having facial hair. But I haven't been eating many s'mores."

"Wow." She wiped her mouth. "I don't know what to say. I'm sorry is so...lame."

"Yeah," he said softly.

"What a gift, too," she whispered. "The time you spent with him was precious, and he slipped away with a loved one nearby. I can't imagine a better passing."

He nodded. When she found her words, she managed to perfectly verbalize what lay in his heart. "Thanks. I had the opportunity to be with him, and I'll cherish every single day. That's what matters. Family and love. Nothing else."

She crossed her arms over her chest. "If you have the ability, sure. You were privileged to be able to do it."

She said privilege with an edge. Like he'd freeloaded on someone else. As much as he enjoyed her ignorance of his financial situation, he couldn't let it continue. "You're right. I had the means. I sold my gaming company to a major conglomerate almost a year ago. I retired. And then my grandpa got sick. Everything happens for a reason. The timing was right."

She narrowed her gaze. "Like, retired for good? You don't have to get another job to pay for food and housing and healthcare?"

He nodded.

Shaking her head, she dropped her chin. "I've really dragged you into my nonsense. I'm—"

He reached out a hand and grabbed her shoulder. "Whatever you're about to say, please don't."

She lifted her face. She pressed her lips together, flaring her nostrils.

"But maybe answer another burning question." He dropped his hand off her shoulder. "What happened to us?"

Her cheeks flushed, and she shook her head.

"What? I can take it. I wouldn't have asked if I couldn't hear your opinion."

She exhaled a shaky breath. "It's so ridiculous now in light of," she waved her arms around, "all this."

He frowned, twisting his head from one side to the other to scan the open water. "The lake?"

"No, the boat. And your success. I..." She faced him fully, her face hardening. "I loved you. A lot. But we weren't on the same page. You were always on the couch at your apartment. Always ready whenever I called."

"Being reliable was a bad thing?" He'd never considered his devotion to her as such. But he could see where he might have been suffocating her. They never looked at other people because they spent all their time together.

"No but letting me call all of the shots was. I hated nagging you."

He frowned, wracking his brain for those last moments. She had been his North Star, and the longer they'd been together the more he depended on her guidance. In many ways, he'd been lost at sea before finding her to navigate his way home. "I never felt like you were nagging me. I wanted to do whatever you wanted. You liked being in charge, and I was happy to listen."

She reached for his hand and squeezed. "It was a lot to feel like the center of someone's world when I was trying to figure out who I was and what I wanted," she murmured.

She slipped out of the touch and rubbed her hands together.

With hindsight, he could understand how he'd let her lead and seemed lazy for doing so. They definitely weren't equals in the end. But could they be on the same page now? Everything had shifted in their power dynamics. "You could have talked to me."

"You had no ambition besides taking everything one day at a time. No plan or goals. I didn't know what to say back then. I thought you were holding me back." She sniggered. "Turns out it was the reverse, huh? Without me weighing you down, you soared."

"That's not true."

She shot him an incredulous look.

He ached to hold her in his arms again, but that wasn't what she needed or wanted. She'd given him the answer he'd asked for but was only left with her own questions.

"For a long time, I was a slacker," Grant admitted.

Her expression softened, tight lines relaxing.

"Your initial impression wasn't wrong," he said. "But you still gave me a chance all those years ago. And honestly? I started to think about myself differently. Because of you. I took chances, and along the way, I had a big payout. I don't pretend I'm some harrowing rags-to-riches story. I had a lot of luck and help." *In large part, I owe you*. At the start, he'd imagined making it big would catch her attention and bring her back into his orbit. It hadn't, but he hadn't stopped. Maybe their woes were due to timing and nothing more. And yet, they'd found each other again. A second chance.

"Why didn't you say something sooner?" she whispered.

"Because you are the first person in a long time who doesn't treat me differently or expect something from me. I don't have to question your motivations."

She nodded. "I get it." She shivered, tucking her feet underneath her. "I must seem really pathetic. That my life is in complete shambles."

Everything happens for a reason. "You're not pathetic. Far from it," he said, his voice thick with emotion.

He had had plenty of soul-searching moments over the years. He'd been lost more often than found. But he trusted that the path he'd trod had a purpose. And he was glad he ended up reuniting with her, accepting the good and the bad along the way to the destination. "Of course not. I've had more fun in the last day than the last year. I was working round the clock to ensure the best deal for my employees. Until I stepped back to be with my grandpa, I didn't get to just unwind. I had a good three months. I've been getting antsy on the water. Starting the new tour business was to give myself a purpose. But then you needed help. And this has been a gift."

"And you'd really help me negotiate about the timber? If that is what it is?"

It's good practice, dust off the cobwebs before I have to make an appearance. He wanted to delay his return as long as possible. He knew more than just Karen viewed his retirement as a sabbatical. And maybe, before bumping into Molly, those doubters would have ultimately been proved correct. But then she returned. And he saw a whole new path for himself. "Let's go get your treasure."

"Thank you. I'm almost embarrassed by how much I need this win."

"I've been there. Plenty of times."

"You have?" She tilted her head to the side. "I can't see you feeling anxious or uncertain or desperate."

All that and a scoop of chocolate chip. The sassy retort popped into his brain. At another time, she'd appreciate the tease. Right now, she was painfully vulnerable, telling him raw truths maybe she hadn't admitted to herself.

He wanted to be her safe zone. "Trusting the universe is more about accepting that I don't have all the answers and vowing to learn through the process. I trust every choice is taking me closer to where I need to go even if I have no real idea of the destination."

She drew in a sharp breath. "Wow. That's...beautiful."

So are you. He ached for her pride in his actions. He had no guarantees. He'd simply savor their time together, one step at a time.

Chapter Eleven

With a full belly and clear conscience, Molly leaned against the cushioned seat up front and snuggled in the hoodie, fighting her droopy eyelids. She didn't have to worry about giving Grant the wrong impression, which was great. He knew the treasure was a long shot, and if they found it, she might not even be able to retrieve it. Luckily, he wasn't depending on her to come through and fund his new business. He had that fully under control. He even had a potential solution so she could utilize what she thought they might find.

And maybe she'd done some good in explaining their breakup. The end hadn't been premeditated on her part. She hadn't been mature enough to set boundaries for herself or understand what she didn't want. In one sharp moment all those years ago, she had realized she couldn't stay. But now they were different people, and the dynamic had completely changed. Wants and needs aligned.

The only hitch in what should be her happiness was her.

She nibbled her lip. She wasn't sure what she wanted anymore. Over the past few hours, her newfound resolve to ignore her feelings for him had weakened. Her defensive lines hadn't crumbled. Yet... It was more like she had dropped the wall around her heart. She had no barriers left. Falling for him again would be easy. Like nineties-romantic-comedy simple. Stumble into his arms and kiss him.

She wasn't some wide-eyed innocent. She read the heat in his gaze. Her body quivered with dormant memories. She wasn't an ice queen immune to her desires. Only a tiny bit of sanity stopped her. If she pursued him, in present circumstances, she'd be a gold digger. Timing was always their issue.

The boat cut through the water. The wind whipped past her cheeks.

She wrapped her arms around herself. Under the hoodie, her skin ached. Raw and dry, she could add sunburn to her list of woes. What sections of skin had been spared from the flies weren't pain-free.

Physical pain wasn't enough to distract her thoughts. She'd been wrong, and he'd been right. But he wasn't rubbing her face in her failure. He wanted to help. Could she let him? She wanted to, but she hated the feeling she'd used him. She never wanted to drain anyone. But here she was. Demanding. Needing. She gulped. Begging.

She scanned the horizon. The water met the sky with no other landmass or bobbing vessel to ruin the illusion. She dropped her shoulders but couldn't quite relax.

A gnawing pain plagued her from the inside. She had plenty of reasons for the quickly forming ulcer in her stomach lining but couldn't shake the most illogical. Since starting the hunt, she hated the uneasy sensation of eyes on her every move. Out on the open water, no one lurked nearby. She couldn't forget her paranoia so easily with the freedom. Had Elise truly been the person following her?

Was she so desperate for the property she'd have snuck into the building to mess with the pipes? Molly couldn't shake the worry that every accident of the past week wasn't coincidence but orchestration. Had Elise—or some crony—started the fire at her apartment to try to wipe out the heir apparent?

Molly shivered. She hadn't enjoyed the first impression on her property, but accusing someone of arson with deadly intent was too much. Elise couldn't disappear. In a small town, everyone was conspicuous. Every action was noticed.

Molly did not look forward to being interviewed by police. Although, maybe she'd get plenty of practice. She'd have to face the authorities twice. Once to file a report for the flooded sawmill and again in Chicago.

Would her sudden departure show guilt? She'd have to discuss the situation and her options with Mr. Baird. If she had learned anything from TV, she knew she needed to lawyer up. A fast-talking detective would make her head spin.

The boat cut through the wake, making the only ripple on the otherwise smooth surface.

She shook off the worry of being watched. With no shoreline or other vessel visible, they were well and truly alone. Now, she could totally shift the blame for any discomfort she felt onto herself.

If she had made a move before learning he was secretly wealthy, she wouldn't feel so off balance. She should have kissed him when she had the chance. At any point, she could have pounced.

But making the first move was never her style. So, she waited. And now the realization of her feelings came too late. He'd probably dated any number of women who were more than she could ever be. More interesting, more beautiful, more pulled together, more sophisticated.

She was just herself. A woman who thought she knew how to live her life at eighteen and spent every year since getting knocked down.

The sky was awash in splashes of pink and orange. If she turned, she'd see the sun dip behind Grant. Twilight would illuminate him, casting shadows on his chiseled features and highlighting his angular jaw. His beard couldn't hide his dramatic cheekbones. Was the beard soft to the touch? Did it tickle?

She faced forward, choosing ignorance over torture. The view was no less dramatic, featuring an ombre fade starting at the water line from light blue to dark purple. The sun was setting. Fast. Time was running out.

The boat slowed to a stop.

The roar of the wind and engine replaced with the gentle tapping of water against the hull.

They arrived.

Her pulse pounded at the base of her throat. She unrolled the cuffs of the sweatshirt, covering her clammy hands. Whatever she found determined her next step. If she discovered something, she could redeem herself. To the townsfolk, to herself, and to him. With her own financial means, she could start a new path.

"Hey, I'm dropping the anchor. Stay clear," he shouted.

She flashed a thumbs-up.

The whirring of the mechanics as the anchor lowered had become the soundtrack of her day. The boat rocked side to side as the waves from its wake dissipated.

Her thoughts roared in her head louder than the surroundings. Converting the building into condos wasn't in consideration. She'd hate to mar the landscape of Loon Lake. What about Elise's idea to convert the mill into an event space? After Molly shored up the living quarters, she could invest in a better exterior structure than rusted sheets of corrugated metal. She'd restore the water wheel and add windows overlooking the lake? She could transform the main level into a multiuse space. Almost like a modern gallery in Chicago. Could she take up photography again and display her work?

On her own terms, she wouldn't feel like a failure. Or a fraud. If she ran her own gallery, she could decide whether or not she was any good. Putting her work out there at all might be too far a stretch. But on her own merits, she could be his equal. And then he wouldn't have to worry about her reasons for wanting to pursue something again. She could take chances. If the treasure was what she needed and wanted.

The anchor chain halted.

"Okay. We're all set," he called. "Do you see anything?"

First, she had to look.

Now or never.

She scooted towards the front of the boat and leaned over the chrome railing.

Under the fading sun, she had a clear view. The lake wasn't as deep in this spot as expected. Several hundred meters below, she spotted it. A neatly stacked pile of timber. Like it had been placed and was waiting for her. Only a pretty ribbon was missing to gift wrap her future.

The treasure was real. Until this moment, she hadn't taken an easy breath. She gripped the chrome railing tight, afraid she'd fly up or slip down. Her entire being was light and boneless.

She slowly turned her head to the side and met his gaze. She lifted the corners of her mouth as far as possible, a broad grin that stretched her skin taut and probably gave her crazy eyes. But this was it. Everything she could ever want. All she didn't know she needed. Pulled together, assembled, and waiting. And all she had to do was be brave enough to reach out. "It's...here."

He smiled. "I'm coming up, hold on." He ducked and slipped through the slim opening.

She scooted to the side. This was it. She was back on top. She could approach him without any worries about seeming ulterior motives. She drew in a deep breath.

He joined her and held onto the railing.

Pressed side by side, she felt heat rolling off him like the waves still hitting the hull. She held her breath, hyper-aware of his every inhale and exhale. The heady scent of freshwater, sweat, and sundried cotton wafted off him, a mixture that should be bottled and sold. *Desire.* From under her lashes, she studied him.

The muscled and tanned arms hinted at the man's outer strength. His physical trappings were no match for his inner resolve. She could lean on him physically and metaphorically. He'd catch her.

Oh, she wanted to tumble into his arms. She wanted to press every inch of herself against him. She wanted to feel protected and cherished. It could all be so easy.

The boat bobbed.

He leaned over, peering at the water.

She held onto the railing. If she gave in now, she'd never trust their relationship. She wanted a partnership. Not an unequal alliance that always left her off balance.

He sat back on his heels. "I'm so happy for you."

For us. She nodded. She dropped her gaze from his clear eyes to his full lips. Maybe his way was better. If she had stuck to her plan, regardless of the misgivings about how she'd been knocked off track, she wouldn't have been here. She wouldn't have bumped into him again. She licked her bottom lip.

Not yet. She frowned. If she were in his position, she wouldn't trust her. Until her future was secure, she'd still be throwing herself at him. The damsel in distress desperate for a savior. Kissing him wouldn't be solely an act of passion but tainted with a heavy helping of desolation. Romance remained suspicious.

Not yet, but soon. She had the rest of her life. Thanks to him and fate, she could take her time. "I think

I'm going to go below and grab my camera. Take some photos. The light is perfect."

He nodded.

She crawled past him and slipped back to the cockpit. Ducking, she descended the tight staircase to the main cabin. Focus on one step at a time. She couldn't rush ahead and grab, or she'd be greedy.

* * *

From his position on the bow, Grant was happy to sit back and watch her snap away.

Holding her camera, she turned towards the water.

Her face was obscured. He didn't need to see it to feel her happiness. The ease in her shoulders and the softening of her brow only reinforced the lightness now that her burden was gone.

In his mind, he pictured her smile again. When she turned her head and met his gaze, she grinned from cheek to cheek. The expression was honest, warm, and heartfelt. That's when he knew. They could be happy. If she let them. He wanted her to give him another chance with every cent in the bank.

In building his company, he learned the value of responsibility. He prized his employees' loyalty. And he was blessed to see them well rewarded. But he hadn't been happy. He hadn't been unhappy either. He had been in a sort of stasis. And then he had an opportunity to go in search of happiness.

At first, he pictured retirement as a long vacation. Golden days stretching into eternity. With no demands on his hours after a to-the-minute daily schedule, he'd found the freedom overwhelming. He hadn't been quite sure how he'd adapt. After years of rising at four thirty, he'd craved sleeping in only to find he didn't need an alarm to wake before the dawn. But he didn't have long to ponder how he'd fill his time.

Within days of his retirement, he had learned Grandpa's health was failing.

While Mom and Dad did their best to visit as often as they could, both still had jobs and responsibilities elsewhere. Mom had long been a social worker. And Dad prized his role at the new company. Grandpa had refused to move nearby, so Grant had moved to him. The compromise was a blessing.

Besides having the time together, hearing stories he had never heard before, reminiscing about the good old days, and enjoying being together, Grant had come to understand that happiness wasn't in seeking one's own pleasure. True joy came from giving to others. Being there for someone else in a quiet but meaningful way lightened the heart and filled a person's spirit with more love than anyone had a right to.

When he decided to move to Loon Lake, Grant had arrived in search of happiness again. He knew he wouldn't find it on his own. But this time, he thought he would find it in the old ghosts of his happy childhood. He felt an urge to come here. And now he knew why. She was here. She needed him. He could be happy for the rest of his life giving for her.

A bright flash startled him. He rubbed his eyes.

"Sorry, I should've warned you."

"It's OK. I'm just not much of a model."

She rolled her eyes.

He chuckled. Maybe if he shaved the beard, he'd be happy to pose for her. But he never liked being the center of attention or the focus of a camera. He'd rather shine light somewhere else. "What do you think you'll do?"

"You had a lot of good ideas. I could use someone who knows what questions to ask."

"I'm happy to help negotiate, brainstorm, whatever you need to get the logs."

"And after?" She lifted a shoulder. "Are you looking for a job?"

"Not quite." He scrubbed a corner of his eyes and dropped his hand. The tour business would keep him busy enough, and he didn't want to add any confusion to their association with each other. He'd keep professional and personal separate.

Earlier, before she left to get her camera, had she been about to kiss him? He wanted her to. One last kiss would satisfy him forever and help him move on. He'd realize his feelings for her had more to do with nostalgia and comfort. He'd be satisfied to know the passion had always been in his imagination.

Just one kiss was all he needed to get everything out of his system.

If he made the first move, he worried he'd be taking advantage of someone in a vulnerable position. He would never do that to anyone. But especially not to her. He valued her too much for her to think he took advantage of a weak moment.

"On second thought. Convince me." He stroked his

beard. Maybe taking her up on the opportunity was the better idea. His ethics surrounding appropriate behavior in the workplace would cool his continued ardor. "What's the pay? And the benefits?"

She blushed.

She turned almost as pink as the fading sky. He swallowed the bubble of amusement building in his chest. She was adorable. He liked making her blush.

She smoothed her hair behind her ears. "I'm afraid not much of either."

I doubt that.

She held out her hand. "I would really value your help as a partner. I'll pay what I can. I have to confess my career skills are limited to date entry."

"Really? Not project management? You love to boss people around. You'd be a natural."

She blushed deeper red and snuggled into the sweatshirt.

"Sorry, I'm not trying to put you on the spot. I'm surprised. This treasure is a real chance for you to start over, and I hope you'll include photography in your next chapter."

"Am I in over my head?" she asked, her voice subdued and soft. "I don't know how to run a company. I have no experience in leadership."

"None of us do until we get a chance. I'll help, and I won't take a cent. I was just teasing. But I'm glad to see everything coming together." He reached out and grabbed her hand. The air sizzled where their fingertips touched.

"Why?" she murmured and darted her tongue over her bottom lip.

With a gentle tug of his hand, he pulled her closer. Inches shortened to centimeters. The delicate skin at the base of her neck fluttered. He was equally flustered, his breath coming short and fast. "Because..." He traced the side of her face with the fingertips of his free hand, dragging his thumb over her bottom lip. "I lo—"

And then a fat drop of rain smacked their clasped hands. Turning his face heavenward, he frowned.

Angry, dark clouds gathered, ruining the last minutes of sunset and spoiling a moment he wouldn't reclaim. He'd have plenty of chances to kiss her. Right? For once, he wasn't so sure of the no plan. He worried she'd slip away like water through fingertips if he didn't tell her everything now. Who was he kidding thinking one kiss goodbye was all he needed? His heart wanted forever.

He opened his mouth. He had to tell her. He had to say it. Now. Who was he kidding? One kiss wouldn't be enough. Not with his heart beating along for her for years. At the restaurant, she had been a human defibrillator, jumpstarting his pulse. She needed to know. "Molly, I lov—"

Thunder cracked above their heads, so close it was deafening. Too close. He'd rail at the sky if it wasn't so foreboding. His stomach clenched. Once they were on dry land, he'd confess the strength of his feelings. How he'd never stopped loving her. But not right now. "Come on, quick, get below."

"What about you?"

"I'm right behind you. Go," he shouted.

With a tiny nod, she knelt and moved towards the cockpit.

He couldn't operate if he was worried about her. And he had to move. If he had lived hundreds of years ago, he'd have imagined their connection sparked the electricity sizzling in the air around them. He navigated his way to safety via the side of the boat. But it was the shortest route around to the cockpit.

With deliberate steps on the fiberglass, he strode forward and reached for the railing. His grip slipped on the chrome railings as he clung to the boat. Movement caught in his peripheral gaze. He froze. Near the bow, a dark shadow slithered through the water.

He couldn't gauge the depth as the raindrops slammed against him. Was it a fish just below the surface? Or something larger fathoms below? What was he seeing?

Awareness chilled him more than the rain. They weren't alone on the water. Rain pelted him, an unforgiving onslaught that didn't slow or dissipate. Lightning would strike soon. He couldn't stay there, exposed to the elements.

Neither could he leave.

Was it Soupy? Had the lake monster stirred up the storm? Grant had offered support for his friend's belief but hadn't put faith in the monster's existence. Now, he reassessed. Seth had described the large jaw full of serrated teeth. Was Grant about to fall into its path? Would he forever erase doubts about Seth's claims? How would Molly get to safety?

The terrible thoughts spurred Grant into action. His story would not end here. Neither would hers.

Drenched like he'd fallen overboard, he pulled himself into the cockpit.

She shivered and shuddered in place.

Fear immobilized her. Luckily for them both, he never gave up or gave in. He'd get them home. Only happy endings need apply.

Chapter Twelve

Clutching her camera to her chest, Molly scrambled to her knees and crawled through the opening to the cockpit. The vinyl cushions were slick from the first few drops. Her palms slid, and only sheer determination not to damage her camera kept her from slamming into the boat chin first. She didn't need to hear what he said to know she should move.

Keeping low was good. Because she couldn't make out much more than a few inches in front of her face. Her racing heartbeat pounded in her eardrums. An awful metallic taste filled her mouth.

Thunder cracked overhead.

If she wasn't on a boat in the middle of the water, she'd duck and prepare for a tree to land on top of her. For a minute after, the deep rumble shook her to her core. She felt the reverberation like a tuning fork. Under the canopy in the cockpit, rain fell sideways in large drops, skirting the cover and splattering her bare feet. She locked her trembling knees.

What should she do? Should she go into the cabin? Close the door? Was safety only below deck? What if the boat took on water? Should she stay above? How much danger were they in?

She had been so tantalizingly close to everything she wanted.

For a moment, she saw her heart's deepest desires waiting for her to lay claim. The treasure, the future, and the man. She'd felt electricity in the air. The sizzle and pop spurred her to lean forward. She was about to kiss him and seal her fate to a life of no plan, following his steps to success.

And then a storm unleashed on their heads.

He joined her in the cockpit, his feet hitting the deck with a thud. He'd come from around the side, swinging on the boat's exterior like a trapeze artist. Grant was braver than her. A splash accentuated his landing.

She stared open-mouthed and wide-eyed.

"Go below." He frowned

Her throat tightened. He looked fierce and frightened. If he was scared, he must know the full extent of their danger. She shivered, her teeth chattering. "Are you coming?"

He shook his head and moved to the controls. "I need to get us to land."

The chain clinked as he pulled up the anchor.

The rain increased, slapping the water and every surface. Lightning hadn't struck. Yet. But they bobbed in the middle of an angry lake. At the mercy of nature, they were nothing more than a toy. A higher power controlled them, like the curse. The water hadn't protected her from evil spirits. She'd felt an ominous presence throughout their journey. She couldn't abandon him.

"It's not safe up here." Her voice cracked. She widened her stance and pulled back her shoulders. "You have to come with me."

"I'll be fine. I'll get us to safety. You need to go."

Not without you. I can't leave you here. Her brain spun, but she couldn't get the words out of her mouth. None of her body parts worked. Only her mind operated at a high speed.

Thunder rumbled. Instead of a distinctive crash, however, the sound morphed into a constant, growling roar.

From the corner of her eye, she spotted a flash.

He turned his head. "GO. NOW."

She jumped. His sharp tone was a first. Since when did he yell? And at her? She spun and slammed her toe into the sidewall. Wincing, she descended the steps to the cabin and hopped onto the bed, tucking her legs underneath, her toes throbbing. She set her camera down carefully.

Lightning struck within thirty yards.

The boat rocked side to side. The waves lifted and lowered the hull.

Her stomach twisted, and her head ached. She shut her eyes and breathed through her nose. But the darkness made her nausea worse. The cabin had one slim window. With the movement and the pouring rain, she couldn't find an unmoving spot on the horizon outside.

Thump thump thump

Oh no, had the earlier noise been indicative of a

problem? If she had alerted him to it, could she have prevented this predicament? She'd forgotten all about it when he'd complimented her. Lust had led her astray. At least she hadn't told him she was worried they'd steered into Soupy's path. He wouldn't have to worry she'd lost all sense in addition to concern over their physical safety.

Thump thump thump

This was it. She took a deep, steadying breath, forcing herself to hold onto the air for as long as she could before exhaling. Could she gulp enough oxygen now to stave off drowning? If the curse was real, was the legend also true? Wouldn't the elements or spirits or monsters of Loon Lake want to keep the Maguire alive? If she had been more superstitious, would she have saved them? Did he have any salt below deck she could throw over her shoulder? Was she too far from the sawmill for otherworldly protection?

She needed a better plan. If she had one, however, she wouldn't be out here. She should have told him what she'd heard and the strange sense of being watched. Now, it was too late. If they'd been followed, their stalker was gone. The storm handled that piece of business more thoroughly than she could have.

She pinched the bridge of her nose. She'd tried to follow a well-worn path to success and found nothing. Instead, she chased a fantasy. For a few hours, she'd felt more alive than ever before.

She wanted more. A full life with love and freedom. Was the treasure merely a short cut? Was the storm a reminder she couldn't cheat her way forward? Or an opportunity for her to reconsider and take charge?

He didn't think of her as an equal. How could he? He was far above her in terms of everything. His life was truly well-lived.

For so long, she had thought herself two steps ahead of him. In truth, the roles were reversed. She couldn't blame him. At least they hadn't kissed. She hadn't embarrassed herself completely.

She reached for her camera and scrolled through the photos, smiling. While the ending wasn't what she wanted, she'd be glad for the day. Questions were answered. Her past found resolution. But she'd have to go forward alone. And maybe, the next time they crossed paths, timing would work in their favor.

The lights cut out.

The hum of the engine died.

The cabin door hit the wall with a thud.

She jumped and squinted towards the entrance.

Soaking wet, he stood in the doorway. Behind him, the sky illuminated.

Her eyes widened. "Get in, get in." She waved her hands.

He shut the door and sank onto the bench seat, panting.

"What happened?"

"The GPS is haywire. The fuel tank is empty. We're stranded here in the middle of a storm. I can't save us. I need to tell you that I—"

"It's the curse." Whatever apology he had, he could keep it to himself. She didn't want to hear about his regrets. She wasn't prepared for a bedside confessional. She'd rather blame a chance encounter with an old woman than face the truth about what he thought of her.

Because she had a bad enough opinion for the both of them.

* * *

In the cockpit, in the seconds before she moved, she had terrified him. What was she thinking? Why risk her life? Couldn't she appreciate he was trying to save her?

Grant couldn't do it all. He couldn't fight the GPS, pull up the anchor, turn the boat around, and protect her. She had to do her share. And in that moment, her part was getting below.

He knew she'd be livid. She was a doer. Passive wasn't her style. When first together, he'd been sort of awed by her constant forward progress. Something shifted in her. She bobbed in place.

He needed her to go. So, he yelled.

She disappeared from view as the anchor lifted.

He watched her until she closed the door below deck. He needed her safe.

He fiddled with the GPS, entering coordinates for Loon Lake. He'd passed the mouth of the channel but couldn't gauge how far away they'd sailed. Squinting, he looked through the windshield, but the driving rain reduced all visibility. In every direction, he saw only water.

A bolt of lightning touched the lake. For a second, he stared. The water illuminated where the light sparked. It was stunning. The gradient blues and grays of the water hinted at the very depths. And what had happened and continued was extremely dangerous. They could be electrocuted. The boat was at the mercy of the storm.

Rubbing his eyes, he stared again. Had he seen a shadow in the water? A large shape had lurked just in the corner of his sight. Without the added illumination, he only saw blackness, the horizon melting into the lake, the world entirely water.

What did he think? He'd spotted Soupy? He wasn't going to add paranoia to the very life-or-death situation he found himself in. His priorities did not include confirming an invented story. She was his number one.

He had to check on her. He needed to apologize. He had to kiss her, or he'd miss his chance. Forever. If everything ended tonight, he needed her to know how he felt.

He'd been a fool to push ahead and not call off the search. He pushed too far. He endangered both their lives because he couldn't say goodbye. His fear ruined her future.

Another thunderous crack shook him off his feet. He gripped the wheel tighter. The sound came too close to their location and with hardly a break between booms. Was she safe? He checked his navigation. The GPS screen turned black. He tried to rev the engine. The fuel tank read empty.

He gulped. He caused their demise for no good reason. *Go to her. Tell her how I feel. Now.*

Spurred by desperation, he abandoned his post and descended the steps. Standing in the doorway of the cabin, he didn't see her. His heart dropped to his stomach. Where had she gone?

"Get in, get in."

He squinted and spotted a tiny figure curled up on the bed at the front. He shut the door and sank onto the bench seat under the window, panting. Adrenaline pulsed through his veins. He studied his hands, clenching and unclenching his fingers. His stupid, ineffectual, useless hands.

"What happened?"

"The GPS is haywire. The fuel tank is empty." He hadn't checked the fuel tank after filling up a couple days ago. He should have topped off. If they'd stopped on Madeline Island for a proper meal, he could have parked at the fueling dock.

But he thought the hunt would start and end at the museum. The boat would be a floating inn. And he'd been having too much fun to ruin it with something so practical. He didn't have a plan. He let her down. She'd always assumed this would happen, hadn't she? He just couldn't believe the end came in such dramatic fashion. And seconds after he thought they could start over.

He lifted his gaze. Without lights, the cabin was dark. But he could see her. He'd always find her. His heart guided him to her like a compass pointed north. "We're stranded here in the middle of a storm."

The whites of her eyes flashed bright even without overhead illumination.

He had to unload the feelings on his heart. If the worst happened, he needed her to know. He'd fooled himself, imagining he could improve and find love with someone else after learning the mistakes he'd made wooing her. The terror on the water only confirmed what his heart had always known. Molly was the one for him. "I can't save us. I need to tell you that I—"

"It's the curse," she repeated, her voice barely above a whisper.

Again? He'd roll his eyes and brush it off if she didn't look so tiny and fragile. Her face was a ghostly white mask of fear. "That can't be your answer for everything."

"I know, I know." She sighed. "But I started taking photos and..." She snapped her fingers. "Don't blame yourself for my troubles."

"When did you stop taking pictures?"

"The morning after the curse."

His temples throbbed. He wanted to have a real conversation with her, and she pushed him away. He wanted her to know how he felt. She blocked him.

"It wasn't because of the curse. I really forgot about the whole incident until everything started going wrong this week. I don't believe in that stuff. At least, my rational mind doesn't want me to, but my heart vehemently disagrees. Because if it isn't a curse and if this is how my life was supposed to turn out?" She shuddered. "I can't argue with destiny and a higher power pulling the strings now. This is more than bad luck. This is...fate. I'm supposed to lose."

He disagreed. Why would she, of all people, be singled out for failure? He hated the defeat in her words. Fighting her wasn't helping his side. "Why use that one single moment as a marking point? You forgot about it for years. Why return to it now?"

"Because...with a chance to actually think and reflect, I can appreciate now what I've been avoiding for years.

That moment was the turning point in my life," she whispered. "Before, everything I did achieved a positive result. I put in the work, and I reaped the rewards. The semester in London changed my whole trajectory. It was a fine-arts-focused program, and it was rough. I wasn't good. Not like the others. They were so natural and confident. For the end-of-term project, I gave my all. I poured hours into my art. I was vulnerable with every shot. I had never given more of myself. And I was critiqued as a department store studio photographer. Not an artist. You can't make up for lack of talent with drive. After a while, you have to have a natural propensity and an eye. I didn't."

He cringed. He remembered her photos capturing joy and sunshine. He'd been charmed by her snaps of the hills and forests near their alma mater. For a person who espoused negativity on the regular, she found something different through the viewfinder. "What happened? Why did you give up?"

"No, I didn't give up." She bristled, sitting stiff and straight.

He bit the inside of his cheek.

"I should have," she murmured. "But I stuck to my plan. It was too late and too expensive to switch programs. I finished college. My bachelors in liberal arts got me interviews but never any job in my field. I worked at a few portrait studios for a while, but as malls started to close, I lost even those opportunities. I don't have connections. I'll be hired for entry-level roles forever." She shrugged. "I'll die in debt, collection agencies chasing an unsuspecting family member. Like how I'm trapped with a building and bad luck in a town that hates me. I thought if I followed all the steps, I'd be successful."

He had no words to soften her pain. Neither could he force her to listen to him. What she said had clearly burdened her. With each sentence, she lightened some of the load off herself, losing a few of the worry lines carved into her forehead like stone.

Love meant listening.

He cared more that she was heard than his will was done. In this moment, he could finally be present for her without demanding or expecting anything for himself. Being quiet mattered. "What does success mean?" he whispered.

"I'm not sure I know anymore." She sighed. "A full night's sleep without stress dreams about my finances sounds pretty amazing."

"Is that why you wanted the treasure? To cash in and clear your debts?"

"Sounds like a fantasy when you repeat my words back to me. Like buying lottery tickets as a retirement plan."

The boat heaved to one side before lurching back upright. He breathed through his nose. The stuffy air in the cabin choked him. But it was the safest place to be and provided the chance for this conversation.

"Honestly? I didn't think it was real. But what did I have to lose?" She sniggered. "Such a flippant thing to say. And ungrateful. Sure, I'm not living anyone's ideal life. But I am alive. Healthy. I've had a few setbacks, and I run off screaming. I'm ashamed."

He longed to pull her close and hold her tight, to tell

her she didn't need to apologize for her reactions, no matter how big or small. Everyone had the right to their feelings. No one needed to justify their existence in relation to others.

"I didn't value what I had. I don't think every problem is solved with money. Financial security is a start. What happens if I get sick? I couldn't add health-care debt. But none of that matters now. I put your life at risk for my folly. If we survive…"

"We'll survive." He delivered the words with certainty. He'd do everything in his power to at least save her. If his life ended now, he'd achieved a lot. Grandpa wanted him to find love. Grant had.

Only, he hadn't realized how much the real connection with Molly meant until he'd seen her again. He owed her an apology. He'd risked her life just for a few hours in her company. Back on land, if she wanted to split for good, he couldn't blame her. "What about pursuing photography?"

"I gave up on that dream years ago. I hadn't even thought about my camera until I grabbed it in the fire on instinct."

"I don't know what happened in London. And the only thing I know about legends, curses, and superstitions is that if it's real to you, you give it power to exist."

As the storm quieted some, the boat's rocking slowed. But the occasional roar of thunder continued. Expressing his love might be off the table, but he had plenty else to say.

"You are talented," he continued. "For what it's worth, a little self-confidence goes a long way. If you need me to believe in you, you've got my unwavering support. Your photography is special and beautiful. You're an artist."

"Thank you." She smiled. "That means quite a bit actually."

"Pursuing your passion is being successful. Even if the art you create is only for yourself, it's priceless."

She held his gaze with a teary-eyed stare of her own.

"What's your plan now?" He shouted over the latest crack of thunder.

"I have to decide what to do about the sawmill. Elise was right to want it. It looks ramshackle from the outside. The mismatch of siding lends a decrepit air. Inside, the structure is actually pretty nice. Or at least it has the potential to be a town destination." She gripped the seat, holding steady as waves pounded the hull with regained strength. "The original mill has huge unbroken timbers. That has to be valuable. And before the flood, the apartment upstairs was nice. To be honest, I don't think it could be condos. But it would make a nice venue for events. It still needs money to renovate the property."

The longer they talked, the less green her pallor. "Are you going to give them the property?"

"If I do, I have nowhere to go." She sniffed, rubbing a hand over her nose. "I actually like it here. I'm not sure how I could build a life for myself. What would I do? But even if I figured that out, I haven't made the best first impression. The town would never let me stay."

He didn't agree. She had to reach her own conclusions. He could tell her the truth, or he could show her. Actions always spoke louder than words. When he got back, he'd find a way to encourage her from the sidelines. "If you could, would you stay?"

"Sure."

"Maybe that's success. Living life on your terms."

"Then you're the richest person I know."

He chuckled. "I'm fighting against being dragged back. If I go, it'll be too easy to pick up and work around the clock again. I want something different." He paused and turned to glance over his shoulder. Through the window, he glimpsed dark. The boat stopped rocking. Straining, he couldn't hear the lashing rain or thunder. "I think the storm has passed."

She exhaled a heavy breath.

He turned towards her. He didn't need to ask what the sigh meant. She was no closer to her answers than she'd been before. He wanted to help her. But she'd push him away. How could he convince her to stay? Could he?

Chapter Thirteen

Molly needed air. The longer she stayed below deck with him, the more confused her thoughts about everything. Especially him. Why was he so good in a crisis? Why had he opened up so much? Why did he believe in her?

She had made herself more vulnerable than she had in years. He saw her. The prospect both terrified and exhilarated her. What would loving him now look like? How would she change? Could she?

The stagnant air stifled her.

"Is the rain over?" she asked. "Are you sure?"

"I don't hear anything. Storms move fast across the lake. We're probably out of the worst."

"Good. I've got to get out of here, or I'll be sick." She jumped off the bed and raced to the steps. In the tight space, she banged against both sides of the stairs. She didn't let a little throbbing pain radiating up her shin slow her progress. She climbed to the top and gulped the damp, fresh air.

Under the canopy in the cockpit, she couldn't see anything. With hands outstretched, she felt her way to the cushioned seat on the port side. The floor was cold. With the protection of the roof and windshield, the seat was mostly dry. She climbed onto the seat and tucked her legs underneath. A chill hung in the air. Dragging in a deep breath of clean, fresh air, she gave her eyes time to adjust to the sudden darkness.

The treasure was real. Soupy might materialize. Was her connection with Grant equally as tangible? He was better than she remembered. Unfortunately, she was such a mess. Since their breakup, they'd headed in opposite directions. While he'd taken the express elevator to the top, she'd trudged down a spiral staircase of failure.

Heavy steps echoed from the stairs.

"Hey, you feeling better?" Grant shined a flashlight on his face, highlighting the wrinkles.

"A bit. Fresh air helps."

"It does, doesn't it? I sleep better close to the water than anywhere else on Earth. I like the silence, too."

He sounded so normal. He didn't feel any of the discombobulation? No awkwardness? In the cabin, she couldn't run from the conversation. As the walls closed in, she realized she didn't want to. But what good would opening up do out here?

Their surroundings were silent, and the boat barely moved. From chaos to calm in seconds. She could hardly believe the storm had happened. Maybe she could act like her life wasn't in turmoil, too. Perhaps that was the secret to confidence. Faking. "And you get a break from your shareholders."

He frowned. "I don't follow."

"I'm teasing. Trying to defuse my own anxiety. My cell is totally out of range." She shook her head. "I didn't think America had any unconnected spots left."

"Just a few. Tough to get a tower in the middle of a lake."

He coughed. "I found you a flashlight, too."

"Thanks." She grabbed the flashlight and powered it on, shining the light on the ground to provide a break in the dark without blinding either of them. "Be honest. Are we really stranded out here?"

He nodded. "I'm sorry. I'm afraid we are."

"Don't apologize. This was my terrible idea." She needed action. She had to do something. "Do you have any more dry towels? Maybe we could clean up?"

"We can't stay out here. It's not safe. If you fall asleep, you might roll off the boat."

And Soupy would get me? "I'm not talking all night. I need a break from the hot air in the cabin. Unless you are hiding motion sickness pills, I don't think I can stay down there much longer."

"I don't have medicine. But I will get you towels. As long as you promise not to sleep."

With her index finger, she crossed her heart. "On my honor."

"Okay. Give me one sec." He descended the steps and returned with arms laden in a few minutes.

She grabbed a couple of plush towels and crawled through the opening to the bow. She mopped up what she could. The cushions were slightly damp and needed a day in the sun to properly dry. But at least she had space.

After a few minutes, he joined her with another stack of towels, pillows, and blankets. "This is the brightest spot on the boat. Mind if I join you?"

"Please." She reached for the stack, building a nest up front. She'd ignore how cozy the setup looked. She settled on her half, wrapping the blanket around her like a cocoon and laying back, head on the pillow. "Wow." Overhead, the clouds parted, revealing a full moon and a sky full of bright stars.

He laid down. "Almost makes the storm worth it."

She sighed. "Sure. Every moment has led here, to our current stranded-in-the-middle-of-the-lake catastrophe, but yes, it was worth it."

He bumped her shoulder. "You know what I mean."

And he didn't deserve her sassy retort. She softened her tense jaw. "I do."

Silence surrounded them. Every conversational break was met with the suffocating void. Did she confess everything on her heart?

She counted her inhalations and exhalations, measuring each breath. They kept circling near serious talk and then easing away. Was she glad for the reprieves he offered? Or frustrated?

"If you are serious about moving to Loon Lake full-time, you should know..." Grant began.

Another problem? She squirmed, adjusting the blanket.

"The dating pool is very limited," he finished solemnly.

"That's the dire warning?"

"I didn't say dire. Just giving you a friendly heads-up. It's not what you're used to in Chicago."

If he was fishing for information about her recent romantic entanglements, he needed better bait. Admitting the truth about her absolute lack of a social life wouldn't make her look better. She was bursting with curiosity to learn about his dating history. But maybe the truth would hurt.

They'd broken up forever ago. They'd only dated for a few years. They weren't the same people.

A connection flickered between them. A tiny ember sparked something more. And she wanted to add kindling to the flames, not douse it with water.

"Never mind," he said. "Forget I said anything."

"No, you've stunned me. Loon Lake is lousy with bachelors."

He laughed. "Lousy? Like infested? Where'd you hear that phrase? An old movie?"

She flushed. Guilty. She was glad her reaction was concealed by the night.

"Lousy with keeping them, maybe. Seth is pining for Elise."

"The ice queen? Really?" She couldn't believe Grant. The pairing made no sense. Why would sweet Seth be interested in the walking stonewall?

"It's true," he replied with confidence. "And Zach is only interested in flings with tourists. As soon as you settle down, you're off his list."

She had no interest in Zach. Too flirty for her taste. "He gives off the vibe that he sends a lot of unsolicited pictures."

"Spot on," Grant replied. "All that's really left are Lonnie, the senior citizen widower owner of the taffy shop, Mr. Willie, the inn's groundskeeper, and me."

She propped herself up on one elbow. "Only three choices, huh?"

"For the time being."

"If I don't act fast, some other bachelorette might swoop in and snatch up Lonnie?"

He chuckled. "Hey, Peanut. Not to bring you down, but I keep thinking. You want a step-by-step guide of what comes next? How to rebuild your life?"

"I don't know that I want that. What I lived before..." Her throat squeezed shut. How did she explain without sounding pathetic? How could she paint her past in a way that didn't make her totally beneath him? She swallowed the lump clogging her airway. She had to be honest with both of them. "What I had before isn't something I want to recreate. I was living but just sort of going through the motions. I was paying my bills and chasing my tail like a dog. It wasn't... I didn't take pride in my work or joy. I just did it and never got ahead."

"You had the misfortune to be born at the exact wrong moment for success. College became ridiculously overpriced. No one should take out a loan to pay for education. Even doctors can't afford freedom from their interest rates unless they specialize, and now we don't have enough general practitioners to take care of our citizens."

She widened her gaze. "You're pretty passionate about that."

"I guess I just continue to understand more and

more how opportunity isn't evenly spread. Some people are born without a chance."

She'd thought she had a shot.

He rested a hand on hers. "You aren't one of those people. You have talent. And right now, you have a big opportunity in front of you."

"If I'm brave enough to take it."

"You're stronger than you know. You're courageous, and you're hard-working. You've been knocked down. You'll get up."

She nodded. His hand warmed hers. For a second, she believed him. His matter-of-fact manner conveyed a confidence she desired. But what he didn't seem to get was that she had to do this on her own.

* * *

Under the stars, Grant almost wished he'd taken an astronomy class. He frowned. Actually, was that one of the courses he had failed so spectacularly during his first four years of undergrad?

He wouldn't worry about failures. Not now. When he survived the worst storm and came out on the other side next to her. Neither would he be dissuaded by her declaration. She'd always had a clear understanding of her immediate needs. He respected her boundaries. But, with time and patience, she could change her mind. He'd give her the grace and space to do exactly that.

He wouldn't push her away.

She pulled her hand back.

He didn't reach for it again. She needed space. He

hated the unspoken moments coming faster with the darkness. He worried about everything unsaid. He had to lighten the mood for himself if not for her. "I feel like we should play a game."

"How? We can't see anything."

"I'm not talking about a board game. How about truth or dare?" He had his first dare ready to go. Would kissing her spark another tempest? Was the electric charge between them too combustible for the earth?

"No way. No how. No truth or dare. No never have I ever. Nothing like that."

"Your other option for entertainment is *I spy*, and, given our current circumstances, that's not very effective either."

She chuckled. "Tell me a story."

"Me? You're the creative one."

"No, I haven't been creative in years. You have all the ideas for my next step." She sighed. "You've had to do a lot of brainstorming and imagining to build a business with international reach. You're brave."

While he respected her fierce independence, he wouldn't leave her with nothing. He never planned ahead. If he started now, however, he'd include her. She'd be his first priority. "Starting my company had nothing to do with courage."

"Really?"

The question was soft, almost breathless. Bravery couldn't match perseverance. "I wanted a better experience, so I created it. I started as my customer, and I ended there, too."

"But...was that it? Just passion and luck?"

She sounded disappointed. Distilling his entire career into a few sentences, he'd left out all the details and sanitized the endeavor. The sleepless nights spent developing the product. The nonstop hustle to secure placement. The rapid delivery and constant learning curves in an industry demanding dynamism. Everything was erased for a clever soundbite.

But passion and luck were important factors. She'd dismissed both like they weren't two of the most elusive and fundamental ingredients. Perhaps she couldn't face the truth that life required love in every aspect for a chance at success. But winning was never guaranteed, especially with a heart on the line.

"Oh, I'm so sorry. I sound dismissive when nothing about you deserves to be undervalued or undermined."

"It's okay," he said. "I get the sentiment. That I'm downplaying the process with an oversimplification. The passion would have kept everything small and manageable." He turned onto his side, propping his elbow and resting his head. The stars held nothing to her. "I wasn't set on controlling every aspect. Which was good. I couldn't be. As I brought on smart people, I realized the weight of the responsibility of being the boss."

She turned her head and met his gaze. "And what's that?"

"Respecting that they believed in me enough to stake their futures on mine."

She smiled.

The lopsided tilt tugged his heart. Would she have done the same? Gone all in if he'd asked her to marry him? Back then, forever had seemed impossible. He'd been living one day at a time. Not so much to espouse the motto of carpe diem but more because he wasn't sure future projections held anything but disappointment.

"What happened?" she asked.

"We scaled up and brought on more people. After several rounds of expansion and a massive launch, we got tons of attention. A conglomerate approached me about buying the company. I saw no other way. Financial opportunities for my staff meant more than me staying in command."

"You walked away? From what you loved?"

"It wasn't the same anymore. It had changed. By the time I sold the company, I wasn't part of what we did or what I created. I gave lectures and pep talks. I managed. I missed the day-to-day problem-solving and operation. My staff did well. Most stayed."

"And you came here to start over? Try something new?"

"I'm not afraid of the unknown. Life is change. This time, I chose to reinvent myself. The new business is small and manageable. A one-man operation that I have no intention of scaling." He chuckled. "Although, I probably will bring on more people. I can't predict the future, but I know I won't keep this as small as I started. Admittedly, the tour company idea needs work and requires at least a handful of employees. As my first customer, you've definitely pointed out a lot of flaws."

She shivered. "Like being forced to swim to shore?"

He laughed harder and pushed himself up to a seated position, looking down at her. "There have been some kinks pointed out."

"Some?" She arched a brow.

"Fine. I might need to sit down and totally reimagine the idea. The experience is lacking. I've got plenty of time to make things right." He hoped she heard the underlying promise. Bringing up their pasts had been a moment of madness. Jealousy had sparked at the idea of her pursuing someone else. But now that they'd sort of established an understanding, he wanted her to know he'd wait. He'd never push her.

She giggled. "Can you really go through the rest of your life semiretired? Won't you get bored?"

He wouldn't with her by his side. Every day would hold a promise of wonder and happiness. He'd found peace and contentment in his life before but saw now what was missing. Someone to share every moment, no matter how small.

"Will Loon Lake be enough?" she asked. "You built and ran a major corporation. You're still in demand."

With a dark night sky overhead and the cleanest air he'd breathed, he couldn't imagine willingly trading in his current situation. He didn't have great ambition anymore. But he understood her point, too. From overseeing a team and workforce to operating alone, he'd taken a huge shift.

"I don't know what I could offer the board," he said. "Their company owns so many different brands in a variety of industries. I found success in a gaming experience created by a user first and foremost. They do all sorts of marketing and studies. We were small, agile, and instinctive. But it's different. It's so focused on the bottom line and not the actual product. My employees are happy, so that's all I can ask. And then being with Grandpa." He shrugged. "I've found success in doing for others. But I'm not naive. I know I've had opportunities that enabled me to take chances. I want you to be successful, but it needs to come from your heart."

"What's in my heart?" she murmured.

Me, I hope. She wasn't as lost as she sounded. She needed a win. He'd help. "Photography."

"I don't know."

"If you let go of the curse and the detractors, what would you gain?"

"I'm not sure," she whispered.

Her words were a breathless hiss. But they didn't sting him, and he prayed the bite wouldn't crush her. "This whole scenario has been pretty remarkable. I wouldn't call it a curse. What are the odds of us meeting up again? And at a moment when you needed help? You get a fresh start; you just have to take it."

Silence stretched.

Had he hurt her? He winced. He didn't want regrets. No matter the outcome, he would be glad for the reunion. "I'm saying this all wrong. I'm pushing. I'm sorry." He stared at the black sky dotted with stars.

The universe was infinite and mysterious. He'd never had much interest in either concept. Truth. Honesty. He respected those character qualities as much as he respected hard work and empathy. "Peanut," he murmured. "I never hoped I'd see you again. My heart couldn't take the pain of hope. But I waited for you anyway.

"I'm here for a quiet life. For peace. I need you to

know how much I love you. I value you. You're unstoppable and incredible. I want you to shine. I want to be part of your life. Maybe this isn't the time for a confession. Or maybe it's the only shot I'll get. I need you to know." He turned towards her. "Molly?"

She was curled into a ball on the cushion, her chest rising and falling in an even tempo. He leaned down, pressing his face against the cushion.

Her eyes were closed. So much for promising not to fall asleep.

He'd let her sleep. Or, at least, he wouldn't call her out for pretending. As her breaths came deeper with each second, she had probably only tricked herself into much-needed rest. What else could she convince herself of? He tucked the blanket around her tighter.

He'd have to carry her downstairs to keep her safe. Or he could stay above and give her the fresh air she needed. Then he'd be up all night.

With Soupy lurking nearby, he wouldn't sleep. He'd stay awake and alert. He'd protect her. For his selfishness, he deserved one indulgence. Lifting his chin to the sky, he sent up a wish. If he could have a real chance, he wouldn't waste it. He'd tell her all over again. For every day of his life, if his luck held.

Chapter Fourteen

Molly pressed her eyes closed, her temples throbbed and her head pounded. Sleep wasn't restorative for her lately. After the fire and then the flood, she'd only had a good night's rest at the inn. Now, she felt hot and nauseous. As she opened her eyes, she remembered where and when she was. And the why.

On the front of the boat, she lay under blankets and the bright morning sun. The vessel rocked back and forth. Ready or not, she had to face him. If she stayed horizontal, she'd be sick. She shoved the blankets off and pushed to sitting, breathing through her nose and calming her aching head. On a boat that operated at the will of the wind and waves, motion sickness was her constant companion.

She'd taken the easy way out of the hard conversation last night. Pretending to sleep until she'd really fallen into a deep slumber had been cowardly. Without the cover of darkness, she'd be on full display for any continued questions. Like how did she feel in return?

He'd told her he loved her. She wanted to tell him the same. With every ounce in her, she'd shut her eyes and held her tongue. Loving him was as easy and necessary and involuntary as breathing. And it solved too many problems for her to ever respect herself.

She needed equality. For that, she had to be her own rescue. Without a firm footing on her own, she'd forever bend towards him, twisting as they grew until, one day, she feared never being sure she was capable of being more than his life partner.

No. She needed success on her own. Fate brought them back together for a purpose, right? Destiny could take a pause while she got herself together.

"Good morning."

She turned and squinted, shielding her eyes with one hand.

Grant cupped his hands around his mouth. "Are you feeling okay?"

On her hands and knees, she scrambled out of the bow and joined him in the cockpit.

He extended a bottle of lukewarm water. "Sorry. Fridges died, too."

"Oh, sure." She nodded and uncapped the drink, taking a long sip. "Thanks. I feel a little better."

"It's not so noticeable back here."

The boat lurched from one side to the other.

He lifted the corner of his mouth. "I stand corrected."

"It's better than lying down."

"You looked quite relaxed out there until a few minutes ago."

Had he watched her? All night? She was touched and flustered at the idea of him standing guard so she could rest. He wasn't a machine. She spotted the bags under his eyes. "Did you get any sleep?"

"No, I'm okay."

Guilt stabbed her. "Are you sure? Don't you want to take a quick nap? I can make sure you don't roll off the side."

"You mean because we're going nowhere and have nothing else to do?" He wiped the corner of his eyes. "I'm okay. I can't sleep under a bright sun. Besides, I doubt I'd have sweet dreams. Like you."

She took another drink, hiding the confusion etched on her face. If he'd slipped into her mind, he'd know the truth. She hadn't dreamed, but that didn't mean she enjoyed the slumber. She fell asleep to the sound of his voice. She'd been too tired to listen. Had she agreed to anything? She really hoped not. No matter how much fun she had, reality still bit into her.

"You smile in your sleep," he said.

"I do?" she squeaked. "Is that all?" She hoped she hadn't talked. Her subconscious might let loose with a whole list of her thoughts and opinions. Because she couldn't shake off one key fact.

She was stranded on the open water with her ex because no one planned ahead.

She couldn't live without a roadmap. She gave it a couple days. At the start, she hadn't fared too poorly. She found him. She almost kissed him.

Her cheeks burned as the silence lengthened. Thank goodness she hadn't made a move. She couldn't compare to whatever model/actress he had dated since moving on from her and finding success. At least she saved herself one embarrassment. "What's the plan? Can we radio for help?"

He shook his head.

Her stomach dropped to her ankles and twisted. She really might be sick. Pressing her hands to her waist, she breathed through the ache. She had to get her life back on track. Somehow. *On my own.*

"Are you hungry?" He reached for a paper grocery store bag, rifling inside.

"More food? I thought we ate everything on board last night."

He threw a plastic bag at her. "Not quite."

She caught the unopened package of marshmallows.

"Breakfast is served," he said with a sly smile.

She rolled her eyes but tore into the package all the same. Sugar wouldn't solve any problems. Neither would a treat make anything worse. She stuffed three jumbo marshmallows into her mouth; chewing momentarily silenced her inner monologue.

"When we get back to land, we can reach out to the company about retrieval."

She finished chewing. "When? Without any method of contacting the outside world, it sounds more like *if.*"

He shook his head and reached for the bag. "Trust me. When."

"No." She cleared her throat and lifted her chin.

"Grant, thank you for everything. But I need to do this on my own."

"You don't have to."

You can't save me. If she couldn't handle negotiations and find success in her own right, what did she have? They'd be an unequal team. She didn't want that. She'd be like a little pet project while he figured out how to spend the next couple of months. Maybe he'd stick around Loon Lake for a year.

But she'd never be his partner and peer. For a while, he might be okay having her as a dependent but not forever. She hated to imagine she'd end up as a quaint, homely anecdote about a brief interlude in his life after work. That he'd tell his gorgeous, future, young wife. She had to stand on her own two feet if only to prepare herself for heartbreak when he moved on. Timing had always been their issue, and she saw nothing different now.

He reached out and rested a hand on hers. "I'll get us to land. I promise."

"How?" Her voice cracked. She pulled back her fingers, tucking her hands in the kangaroo pocket on the oversized sweatshirt. "Do you have rope? Shall we lasso Soupy and let the monster steer us to shore?"

"I'll find a way." He smiled. "I always do."

I don't. If she was really being truly honest, she'd reach the very heart of her pain. She couldn't trust anyone because she had no faith in herself and her abilities. He landed on his feet. He might have forgotten to fill up with gas or have a backup radio or a hundred other things. And he'd be saved.

He was born under a lucky star.

She'd toiled for everything she had. Even in college. She remembered when she learned he was in school for six years without debt, thanks to being born to parents with means. She worked hard to earn her degree as cost effectively as possible. And still, she was behind before she even got started.

But right now, she had a chance. The treasure was real. She had an inheritance. And if all she did was cash in on the building and the timber, she might be able to pay off her loans and at least start over somewhere without debt. Like her mom's spare room?

When Mom returned from her trip, she would be in for a series of shocks. Molly needed a plan before then. Although, she knew Mom would be thrilled about her reunion with Grant. Mom had always liked him.

"Let me help," he said.

She lifted her chin. "I need to do this for me. I have to take charge of my future on my own. I need to act without worrying about anyone else. I'm selfish. I'm sorry."

"Don't apologize. What will you do?"

"Start with the lawyer and work my way from there."

"If you need help, you'll call?"

She held his gaze with an unblinking, unflinching stare. For several beats of her pounding heart, she didn't move. She wanted success, and maybe she was going about everything the wrong way. Maybe she failed her way into freedom. But she couldn't trust her heart not to get snapped in two again if she capitulated now and let him save her. She had to prove herself worthy.

Honk, honk, honk.

She jerked and turned.

As if by magic, a vessel marked Coast Guard appeared. Once again, the universe had provided for him. He trusted his two hands but didn't limit himself to only believing in what he could control. He had faith and was rewarded for his steadfastness time and again.

He chuckled and strode to the stern, waving his arms over his head. "I promised I'd get us back to land. I never break a vow."

She followed him, raising a hand to shield her gaze.

A Coast Guard ship approached. As the vessel neared, the boat rocked and rolled from the wake-created waves.

From the corner of her gaze, she studied him. Inside her chest, her heart burned. She wished she could ignore every single fear and doubt. Nagging worry and insecurity were much louder.

He could have every confidence in the world. But he couldn't make them work just because he wanted it right now. In a few years, what would she have? Would she be entirely indebted to him and still struggling? She needed a future on her own terms. And she'd have to get it by herself.

Grant was glad to sit in the full sun. On the cushioned bench at the stern, he could blame solar exposure for the burn on his skin and not good old-fashioned embarrassment/shame. The wind whipped past his cheeks, whistling in his ears, as the Coast Guard towed the vessel to shore.

His simple mistake—forgetting to fill the tank—had stranded them. At the mercy of the storm, the boat suffered from the electrical currents. He had caused thousands and thousands of dollars of damage. But his error could have proved fatal. They'd been lucky.

He wasn't red-cheeked about his failure with the boat. He was cut to the bone in his romantic ineptitude. Why did he think this second chance encounter held any meaning? It was random. He hadn't deserved her years ago. How much had truly changed? He'd found success. But it was empty. The end of the road led to less and not more.

He'd give anything to circle back to the start. He couldn't imagine anything better than the fresh opportunity to reshape a life like she'd received. Bumping into her again, he imagined a different path for himself. What if he let her control the future like he'd wanted her to do in college? Back then, he'd been immature and lucked into meeting her. Now he understood what he'd lost when they broke up.

Once again, she wanted space. He'd struck out. Should he try a third time? He'd had to block her path and trip her three times in the library before he had captured her attention long enough to ask her if she wanted to go on a date since she was already head over heels for him.

He turned towards her. She was lovely at the seat on the port side, silhouetted against the bright-blue sky. She deserved only good things to come her way. He hated what had happened, especially his role. He'd give her space. He couldn't ignore the board meeting at the end of the week anymore.

Karen had stoked a bit of fear and unease in him about the future of his former business. When he had retired, he had happily handed over the reins. With his former assistant still actively part of the day-to-day operation, however, he stayed more informed than he would have liked. He knew what he'd tell the board, and he didn't need to be in person to do so. But maybe the excuse to get away was one he should take.

"Thank goodness for a quick rescue," she said.

"Well, quick for you. They'll take you back to Loon Lake."

"You're not coming?" she asked.

He shook his head. As much as he longed to see the familiar shoreline, he had a long morning ahead of him. "The boat needs attention at the nearest maintenance yard and that's across the bay. But we're close enough to Loon Lake, you might be able to finagle a ride to shore."

"You really think so?"

"I do."

"I guess I better go grab my bags," she said quickly.

He held up a hand. "Let me. You go and chat with our rescuers."

She opened her mouth. After a long pause, she shut it and nodded.

At least she wasn't going to argue about his basic manners.

She sat down and turned towards the water again, away from him.

He descended the stairs to the cabin and grabbed her purse and duffle. Were these the only belongings she had left? He was sorry for causing her more pain in a horrible week. From the corner of his gaze, he spotted her camera on the mattress. He grabbed it and—although he knew better—he powered it on and flipped through the shots.

The photos of the timber weren't clear. The murky water and overcast skies prevented a perfect shot. He forwarded to the next shot. Him? In her photos, she captured him steering the vessel. He looked calm, collected, and content.

He was all those things and more with her. For her sake, he tapped into an inner resolve. On his own? He wasn't nearly as strong.

She doesn't want me. He turned off the camera and carefully slid the strap over his neck. Whatever she did next, he hoped it involved her heart, wherever that may lead. He had to recalibrate his plans. The more he tried to hold on tight, the more he felt her slipping through his fingers.

A few days back in California would no doubt solidify his choice to stay retired and tucked away in the Midwest. She might be long gone back to Chicago. Or she might stay. Her choice would be hers, and he vowed not to interfere.

He returned above deck, carrying her bags. But she wasn't where he'd left her. Frowning, he turned towards the bow. Again, he saw no one.

"Ahoy," she called. "Over here."

At the stern, a small dinghy had pulled alongside the swim platform.

He'd been so lost in his recriminations that he'd missed the arrival of her transport.

Molly stood on the boat, dressed in a life jacket.

"Leaving already?" He called. He smiled or tried to. The rapid beat of his heart made his breaths come fast and shallow. In a few long strides, he reached her.

"I'm anxious for a shower and dry land." She held out her arms. "Thank you for getting my stuff." Her eyes widened. "And my camera? Oh goodness. Thank you."

He handed her the duffle, then the purse, and, lastly, slipped the camera off his neck. One at a time, he took care with each exchange. If his hands brushed hers excessively in the trade-off, he'd explain he ruined enough for her without destroying her remaining possessions. "Where will you go?"

She blew out a sigh and held the camera tight against her chest. "Right now? I think I'll take another stay at the inn. Then I guess I'll go talk to the lawyer. I've got to find a ride back to my car. Or maybe I'll walk. Probably safer on my own two feet at the moment."

He winced. "Sorry."

"Don't be. Thank you, Grant. I'm sor—"

"Nope." He held up a hand. He couldn't take it if she apologized for the time they spent together. "I'm going away for a few days. You have my number. I'll be back soon. If you need any help, I'll be around." *Not that you'll take it.*

"I appreciate that. And everything."

Stop being so proud. He wasn't sure if he was more frustrated with himself or her. Probably a toss-up. The pair deserved each other and a lifetime of never getting what they wanted because they were too scared of the fallout. He wanted to give her everything. But he couldn't. Maybe he shouldn't. He'd been fine on his own, not living as fully as he wanted, but he was okay.

She had to find her own success. He only hoped she had a clear vision of what that was. Because he didn't have any clue. And he worried his next steps would be more of the same. Taking meetings, checking boxes, and never really living. But she wanted it this way. He couldn't stay and fight for her by battling against her.

The dinghy pulled away.

He stood and waved, watching until she disappeared on the horizon at a pier several miles up.

"Sir? Are we still towing you to the marina?" A sailor shouted.

"Yes, please," Grant called back, cupping his hands around his mouth. "Can I ask something? How did you find me? After the lightning strike, everything on board is fried."

"A call from the inn."

Grant flashed a thumbs-up. Of course. Christopher Lewis would be the one to know Grant was missing. He'd lucked into finding a small town that cared about each other. Not everyone got along at all times, but they looked out for each other. Was it too much to ask for more?

Chapter Fifteen

Molly might have stumbled onto something worse than the walk of shame. The disembarkation of disgrace. The Coast Guard team steered the dinghy close to the public pier—the very visible, crowded dock almost in the center of the Loon Lake boardwalk.

While one man grabbed the dock, the other threw her bags onto the wooden planks, landing with a thud.

If anyone strolling by hadn't been looking before, they definitely were curious now.

Molly tugged the ponytail holder free, combed her fingers through her hair, and created another messy bun. She could only imagine what she looked like in a man's hoodie hanging past her knees. Her smell might be enough to repel anyone daring to venture too close.

"Ready, miss?"

Holding the camera against her chest, she turned towards one of the men and walked to the side. He held her hand as she stepped onto a ladder and climbed. The camera bounced. She was glad for the strap over her neck but kept one hand against the camera on her chest. She didn't want to lose the last thing she cared about like she had lost Grant's good opinion. She shook off the thought and focused on the ladder. At least her rescuer hadn't called her ma'am. She reached the top of the ladder and turned, waving at the rescue team.

What if the crew hadn't appeared?

Gazing out to the horizon, she couldn't spot the Coast Guard ship towing Grant's vessel across the lake. Not seeing him was for the best because it meant his rescue was underway. After an emotionally charged night, she needed to give him some space and time. She had to figure out what to do on her own. It would be easier—and more fun—with him. But she couldn't give in too easily. Nothing had ever come without hard work and sacrifice.

What if I stop being a martyr?

She dropped her hand and turned, grabbing her duffle with one hand and swinging her purse over her arm. Could she stop making things harder on herself and accept when everything went right for no good reason? Maybe part of his no-plan success path was simply staying positive and leaving himself open to being surprised and delighted. She shut down anything catching her off guard. What if she changed? She strolled the length of the pier and reached the end.

A crowd formed on the shore.

She was sure they'd put on quite a show. With her

head down, she focused on her steps. Still, she stumbled over a crack. With a jerk, she stopped herself and glanced up, nearly falling into a person walking in the opposite direction.

"Hey, are you okay?"

Molly stepped back and squinted. "Elise?"

"Oh, it's the heiress." Elise rolled her eyes. "Of course you're out here making a spectacle. What happened now? I heard you tried to flood the street. Did you ram a boat into the breakwater or something?"

Heat burned Molly's cheeks. "Not quite. I... ugh... Grant and I were stranded on the lake last night during a storm."

"Why would you be on the water after dark? I know you didn't grow up out here but that's maritime safety 101. Unless you didn't mean to..." Elise widened her eyes and leaned forward. "You went on the hunt," she whispered.

"You know about that?" Molly tipped her head to the side. Of course she knew Elise did. She'd felt her stare and seen her move in the tree line of nearly every stop.

"Your aunt wanted to leave the sawmill to the town. But she knew how expensive it would be to tackle the extensive repairs and meticulous restoration of the original structure. As the last living Maguire, she knew about the treasure but hadn't ever worked out what to do to retrieve it. After I did research for the town's celebration, I suspected the truth about the logs and scouted the area with Seth on one of his Soupy hunts."

Elise wouldn't have needed to follow Molly to find

the timber. Molly only hindered Elise. "I'm confused. I thought she was converting the mill to condos."

Elise frowned. "No, she'd never do that. Your aunt loved Loon Lake and was devoted to its history. She didn't want the legacy to be destroyed by an outsider and worried that, because of the family tradition, all leads would be exhausted to find an heir. I gave her the idea of a treasure hunt. She hoped whoever came would travel through the region, following our clues, and gain an appreciation of the special community we have. She was worried a new owner would sell the building sight unseen."

Molly's heart skipped a beat. The new information didn't make sense. How could Mr. Baird have been so far off the mark?

"Where did you find the first set of numbers?" Elise asked. "I planted the clues years ago. But Lily held on to the first set. She wasn't sure whether or not she wanted to even let the heir get the opportunity to find the treasure."

"I stumbled onto them by accident on my first night when I was flooded out of the apartment. To be honest, the hunt was... fun. And I did gain an appreciation for the area. This is a special place. Anyone would be lucky to call it home." Molly had enjoyed herself up until the moment she realized she couldn't keep going. "Wait, if you knew, why include the museum in the treasure hunt?"

Elise shrugged. "I wanted repairs done. And now you'll pay for them. I didn't notice anything amiss. You two must make a great team. Seth told me he thought you had good intentions."

Competing thoughts battled for precedence in Molly's mind. *She can't be all bad if sweet Seth loves her* tangled with *who was stalking us?* Elise hadn't prompted the hunt with the water leak and hadn't known that Molly was gone. Perhaps the unease she'd experienced was only a product of Molly's overactive imagination. She focused on the clearest and most fundamental concern. Her future. "Would you hate me if I tried to get the timber out and sold it?"

"I'm sure you'd have your reasons. To be honest, I'd do the same to cover costs for the building. Are you going to move ahead with selling the property to make a clean break?"

Molly shook her head. "I have no place to go. I wish I could stay here, but I don't want any bad blood between us."

"What would you do with the mill?" Elise crossed her arms over her chest. "If you stayed?"

"I like the event space idea. I'm a photographer and having a permanent venue to display my work is appealing. And I need a place to live. I like the idea of using the apartment upstairs as my permanent residence. But it will take a lot of work and money from the sale of those logs. Maybe we could reach a compromise, and I can let you use the mill free of charge for special events?"

"And in exchange?" Elise asked, arching a brow.

"You treat me as a neighbor and friend. I'm not your enemy. I want to be part of this community."

Elise stuck out a hand. "Agreed. I'll work with you if you work with me."

Molly smiled, grabbed the outstretched limb, and

shook vigorously, pumping the interlocked arms up and down several times. "Yes, yes, yes." She let go of Elise and exhaled a sigh that had built up inside her over the years.

"Good. Finish the work by next spring, and we'll be square. Our sesquicentennial celebration must be flawless."

Molly nodded, relieved to have shifted out of the town historian's laser-eyed focus.

"I'm going to head to the inn and check in for another night. Then I'll meet up with Mr. Baird and discuss drawing up new papers. I need a shower."

Elise twitched her nose. "Yes, you do. Do you want me to join you? Mr. Baird can be slippery."

Molly frowned. The man who looked—and acted—like Santa? "How so?"

Elise shook her head. "Don't listen to me. Form your own opinion. I just think..." She shuddered and stuck out her tongue.

"What?"

"Regardless of why he did what he did, exhuming a body to get a DNA sample is strange. There was no foul play in her death. Let her rest in peace." Elise sighed. "Or that could be my envy speaking. I would have used what remained from the treasure to shore up the finances for the historical society. But that's my problem, and I'll come up with another plan. Good luck with your meeting."

Molly couldn't shake the nagging worry that she had missed something about the lawyer. Without his action, she wouldn't be here. She'd be stuck in Chicago looking for a new apartment and a new job and stressed over tomorrow. She wouldn't have reconnected with Grant. Her heart squeezed. With time, she wouldn't ache when she poked near that wound. Walking away now hurt worse than the first time. She'd have to bear the pain. Until she was his equal, she wouldn't be worthy of anyone, including herself. "I'll be in touch."

"If you need anything, you can call me. Can I see your phone? I'll give you my number."

"Thanks, Elise." Molly smiled. "I'm glad to have your support." She slipped the purse off her shoulder, fumbling inside for her cell. She handed it over.

Elise nodded, entered information into the phone, extended it, and stepped back. "I've got to get going. I'm around if you need me."

Should Molly apologize for the damage to the museum? She hated to risk the uneasy truce with a reminder of her bad deed. She gripped the phone tight and waved. "Bye."

She waited until Elise turned before she bent to pick up her duffle. With the strong mid-morning sun high in the sky, Molly felt beat down and too warm. She turned towards the sawmill and trudged along the sidewalk. Ignoring stares was easy when she was so focused on the unshakeable worry that something was missing. Some parts of the puzzle didn't belong.

Because—while she never voiced her concerns to Grant—she was sure they'd been watched. Elise's reaction was genuine. Unless the woman also led the community theater group, she couldn't have been acting. What wasn't Molly seeing? Was it just her own regrets from the inside out? She needed a shower and a nap, and then she'd start to question. She pushed Grant away. She had to do this next part alone.

* * *

Grant's shoulder was sore. He circled his right arm in one direction and then the other. Swinging both arms over his chest, he scanned the horizon as the Chequamegon Bay marina finally came into view. For the better part of the past hour, he'd stood and waved at the gawking boaters and tourists on the ferry's upper deck. He'd put on quite a show. He felt fairly confident he'd become the stuff of local legend for the grand rescue on display today.

He'd have to work doubly hard to overcome this setback. For the sake of his tour boat business and the community counting on him to make it a success, he would. Besides, he had plenty of incentive to stay.

In his pocket, his phone buzzed. Retrieving the cell phone, he frowned at the screen. A few lines flashed. His assistant emailed the details for the board meeting and the room waiting for him at the inn. He'd tell her that he had decided to fly in for the meeting.

He wouldn't shirk his commitments. Wasn't that one of the strikes against him? Along with suddenly being responsible? If he could figure out what she wanted him to be, either an irresponsible loser who needed her or steady and reliable, he had a chance. He'd have plenty of time for contemplation on the long flight to the corporate headquarters.

At the main dock, Jayden stared wide-eyed.

"Morning, Jayden."

The teen scrubbed a hand over his face. "Good morning, Mr. Reem." Jayden turned and whistled over his shoulder.

His brother exited the shop and raced to the dock. "Whoa, what happened?"

"A lot." Grant sighed.

For several minutes, Grant, the kids, and the Coast Guard got to work tying up the yacht to the dock and freeing the tug. With handshakes and waves, the officials departed, leaving Grant with a dead boat and two kids.

"What do you want us to do, Mr. Reem?"

"I need gas. Probably a battery. Can you get the mechanic out?"

Jayden nodded and raced up the dock.

Liam nodded and puffed out his chest. "Our dad is the best around, sir. He'll take care of everything."

Grant nodded. "Let me know what he says." How deep was he in for boat repairs? Maybe he'd earn some sort of points with her for chivalry in the face of a huge bill.

He jogged down the steps and crossed to the cabin, packing up his laptop, tablet, phone, chargers, and a couple days' worth of clothes. The boat held none of his valuables. He wasn't a things person. He invested in people.

That's what he wanted to do for her. Success turned up

empty for him. He did his best when working for others and putting their needs above his own. But she didn't want a rescue, and he couldn't argue with her reasoning.

He'd take a few days and hope he could somehow come up with a plan. Because while he didn't blame her, he didn't agree with her. But telling a woman she was wrong never did him much good.

She wasn't the only one to make a mistake.

After the boys left, Grant realized his problem. He had no ride back to Loon Lake. He stood alone on the dock, staring across the rippling surface.

A fishing boat cut through the water. The metal hull glinted in the sunlight.

Grant frowned. The vessel wasn't much of a match for the depths of the lake. It was a better fit for Loon Lake. Why would someone captain a rather flimsy boat along this stretch of Lake Superior?

As the boat neared, he spotted Seth. Suddenly, all made more sense, if still illogical and unsafe. Grant waved his arms over his head.

Sitting at the motor in the back, Seth steered towards the dock. "Hey, Grant. What are you doing out here?"

"Boat trouble," he said significantly.

"Oh no. Sorry to hear that."

"Are you hunting for Soupy?"

Seth grinned. "Absolutely. After a big storm, I patrol the shore around the channel to see if he was disturbed. He has a few favorite spots."

Grant nodded. He didn't quite have another reply at the ready. "Would you mind giving me a ride back to Loon Lake? Only if you're done. I don't want to interrupt. My boat is docked for the time being. I need to catch a flight. My car is at the boathouse."

"It would be my pleasure. Hop on board."

Grant walked to the edge of the dock and—holding tight to a post—lowered himself into the fishing boat. The boat rocked back and forth, splashing water into the bottom.

"Life jacket, please." Seth pointed to the classic orange life preserver on the floor.

"Of course, thank you." Grant lifted the preserver over his head, fighting the tickle in his nose at the vaguely fishy smell. He secured the strap around his waist. The damp life jacket was a slow sort of seeping into his shirt and skin torture. He'd keep his opinions to himself, lucky to be rescued.

"Anchors aweigh," Seth said and steered towards the channel.

The vessel moved slowly through the water. It was simultaneously peaceful and frustrating. He should relax and enjoy the scenery. He was entirely dependent on Seth to get to his destination. If not for a chance meeting, he'd still be stuck at the marina. Too much had relied on fate lately for his comfort.

Grant turned on the seat, facing his captain. "Thanks again."

"It's no problem. Do you mind if I asked what happened? How did you end up stranded out here?"

Was it Soupy? Grant understood the subtext. He would offer honesty, if not particular encouragement. Because he could neither confirm nor deny the dark shadows and underwater echoes. The only evidence he had was his feelings. Trusting his gut had taken him far in work but not in life.

He would leave his concerns about the area out of the conversation. "Molly and I were stranded on my boat. It got struck by lightning in the storm last night and lost power. We were drifting until the Coast Guard picked us up. I got towed to the marina. She got a ride to Loon Lake."

"The storm was late. Why were you out here after dark? There is nothing around. Unless..." Seth narrowed his gaze. "Treasure hunt?"

Grant nodded. Seth spoke rhetorically. His reaction was at odds with Zach's adamant denial of the topic. "How did you know?"

"Elise told me about it a while ago. She is researching all sorts of myths and legends for her sasquatchcentennial celebration next year. Or the sesiqui..." Seth shook his head. "Whatever it's called, to celebrate the town founding."

"The Maguire treasure is mentioned?"

"Not in so many words." Seth shook his head. "She was curious about the origin of the phrase *A Maguire in possession is prosperity for all*. It's accepted lore. No one has ever challenged the statement." Seth shrugged. "I'm one of those people. When you've always accepted something as fact, you lose your critical evaluation skills. Elise is too smart to accept the status quo. She started to dig into the research." He straightened.

Grant couldn't help but notice how Seth's face softened with each mention of the ice-cold curator. Did Elise deserve Seth? Grant would never pair practical Elise with dreamer Seth. Their differences drew them together like magnets. Grant was envious. He couldn't seem to stop switching polarity and pushing Molly away.

Grant cleared his throat. "What did Elise uncover?"

"The legend started in the mill's early days. Apparently, a hostile takeover pushed out Magnus Maguire. Not too long, a few months tops, a crew lost their entire shipment somewhere in the bay. Their ship nearly sank in the storm, and they lost the whole load of timber. After the men were rescued—by Magnus, who lived in Loon Lake and realized the mill was at a standstill waiting for delivery—they gave him back his company and vowed never to cross him again. Thus sparked the saying. The details of the storm were lost in time, but every generation remembered the saying. It's part of our oral history." Seth narrowed his gaze. "Did you find the treasure? Is the booty actually sunken logs like Elise thinks?"

Grant nodded. If he'd approached Seth and Elise at the start, Grant could have saved himself and Molly a lot of trouble. When Seth had called attention to the Timber Triangle at the ice cream shop, he had been up front. If Grant had asked questions, he would have had answers and a straightforward direction from point A to point Z. In hindsight, the treasure hunt had been completely avoidable. He wouldn't take back a single second of their adventure. He'd cherish the memories forever.

"What are your thoughts about the supernatural?" Seth asked. "Do you believe more exists than we are aware of at the present moment?"

Was Grant being set up? He trusted Seth not to twist his words around to suit his needs. "Yes." Grant scrubbed his hands over his face. "I like believing in something unexplained. Too much of the word is an exact science. I like a little magic."

Seth nodded. "Me too. Did you see or hear anything out of the ordinary while you drifted?"

Grant paused. He hated to disappoint his rescuer. The few peculiar instances of feeling uneasy in the open water had nothing to do with a lake monster. Although, he had that one moment. But then they found the logs, and he must have seen a timber bobbing near the surface, stirred up by the storm. Had Molly seen anything odd? He felt silly to even think about asking her.

Besides her gypsy curse, she'd never believed in the paranormal or otherworldly. If he pressed her about what she may have heard on the water, would he seem ridiculous and unfit to be a partner? She'd already expressed her doubts about a lake monster lurking in the deep. If he was anything less than steady and patient, he'd lose his last chance with her.

Grant shook his head.

"Sorry to give you a hard time," Seth said. "I'm the target of enough questions and disbelieving stares, I should know better."

"I suppose you are."

"I have my own theories about the area where the logs were lost. I'm sorry you were stranded out there." Seth leaned forward. "You ended up in the Timber Triangle, didn't you?"

Grant drew back his chin, unsure of his best response. He had, and the creepy spot had created an unease that morphed into sharp, physical pain in his body. "I should have asked you more questions. I could have saved my boat all the damage." *And protected my heart, too.*

"Mention it to Molly so she is aware," Seth continued. "I don't want her caught by surprise on the open water when she heads back to retrieve the logs."

That's not likely. Nor would Grant get another, real, chance with her. "I think I'd better leave all the explaining to you since it's your theory."

"Any sightings of Soupy?"

The conversation had returned to the lake monster, and with it, the focus shifted off Grant's failures. "Well…" Did he tell Seth exactly what happened? Would he be raising the other man's hopes unnecessarily? Grant couldn't explain his encounters. "No, nothing out there. I'm sorry."

"Too bad. It makes sense if the two could be linked. For all we know, Soupy's size is causing the disruptions in that particular spot. Could be the sight of her nest."

Grant pressed together his lips. Better to swallow his tongue than express disbelief at his rescuer's convictions.

"Did you know Champ, the Lake Champlain monster, is a protected creature? Both New York and Vermont passed laws offering safe harbor. The science doesn't even make sense for his existence. A saltwater plesiosaur living in a freshwater lake? Sure, recent research has indicated that plesiosaurs had the capability to live in freshwater, but how would the creature have reached the lake? Has no one asked how or why? Almost an exact rip off of Nessie." Seth sniggered. "Champ is defended, and Soupy is ignored. Mosasaurs lived in freshwater, and the Great Lakes had been an ocean in the ancient world."

"Soupy won't be overlooked much longer. You'll get the word out. I have faith in you."

"I sure hope so," Seth murmured. "Ashley Hale-Lewis gave me an idea. I'm writing a book."

"A book?"

Seth nodded. "About Soupy."

"Like a children's book? Oh, right, you showed me the toy."

"Yep, that is what I showed you, but no." Seth shook his head. "I haven't been able to connect with a children's book idea. I'm working on non-fiction about my research and my theories. A memoir discussing all the work my dad and I did together. He was the real believer."

Or he really loved his son. Grant appreciated what Soupy meant to the father-son duo, and he liked that everyone in town supported Seth. His lake monster wasn't a known man-eater. Soupy was harmless. Grant hoped the world held a few mysteries. The treasure was real, why not the monster? "I look forward to discussing the specialty tours with you. I think visitors will really love the chance to get out on the water and investigate the lake with a different set of eyes."

"Thank you for the opportunity. We'll make a great team."

They'd reached the channel and slowed even more as they entered Loon Lake.

Grant knew what he had to do. The choice wasn't any easier for understanding how to reach his desired outcome. He had to go forward and hope for a little more magic.

Seth slowed at the outer dock of the boathouse, the pier continued into the building.

Grant patted his pocket. He'd forgotten his door opener for entering from the water. "Just up at the swim ladder is fine."

Seth nodded.

Grant reached for the metal ladder and pulled himself off the boat. "Thanks again."

With a wave, Seth motored away towards the inn.

Grant climbed the algae-covered steps to the dock and strolled down the planks, his steps slapping on each board. He squinted into the distance at the dark figure approaching. Shielding his gaze, he waved an arm over his head. "I owe you my undying gratitude," he shouted at Christopher Lewis.

Shaking his head, Christopher neared and embraced him in a one-arm hug, patting his back. "Undying is the key word in the sentence. I need you to take over this tour business successfully. Hale, hearty, and whole. I can't lose another season, or my guests won't come back."

Grant broke away from the embrace and rolled his eyes.

"Are you okay?" Christopher asked. "For real?" He scanned Grant from head to toe.

"I am. How did you know to call for help? When did you realize I was gone?"

Christopher shrugged. "I stopped by a couple times, and you weren't here. When I talked to housekeeping, I learned you hadn't returned to your room. Once the storm hit, I got worried. I wasn't joking about my commitment to your success."

"I'm glad you have been low-key stalking me. My boat lost power. I might have been drifting for days if not for your interference."

"Do you think you can work that into your next conversation with Zach Jenkins? That my meddling saved your life?" Christopher stroked his chin.

Grant threw back his head and laughed as relief for the rescue and a community that cared enough to search for him washed away every feeling but gratitude. "Better yet, I'll ask if Seth wants the story for the front page of his newspaper. I should have. He gave me a lift back."

Christopher grinned. "Works for me."

"It'll have to wait a few days. I'm heading to California for a meeting."

"Nothing that'll take you away for long, I hope?"

"No, not a long stay. With any luck, I can make headway on the business plans for the tours while I'm there. We're still untangling the legal knots the Prims tied. Whoever had a hand in their business was savvy enough to keep their name off the papers and blame every action on either Carl or Steve or both."

Grant wondered if the podcaster he'd bumped into at the courthouse had any insights. He wasn't sure mentioning a sensationalist journalist—or reaching out personally—would add anything of value. He did not want to make things worse.

Christopher frowned. "I don't know who was

handling their affairs. If I hear anything, I'll let you know. In the meantime, have a good and quick trip."

Grant nodded.

Christopher strode away, his pace more staccato than Grant's.

Grant shared the same wish. He'd do what he always had: put his faith in fate. But he also believed in out of sight, out of mind. He wasn't giving up on her, and he'd prove his loyalty one day at a time for as long as it took.

Chapter Sixteen

Strolling down the street, Molly lifted her face to the sunshine. A shower, clean underwear, and a hot meal did wonders for restoring her spirit. The conversation with Elise helped, too.

Molly wondered about the aunt she'd never known. Would she be frustrated that her heir would be sticking around? Or pleased with the tentative agreement reached between Molly and Elise? What would her aunt say about how she'd managed the treasure hunt?

Molly stumbled. She frowned at the crack in the sidewalk and continued, paying more attention to her destination. And less to Grant. He was gone like she wanted. So what if her instinct was to tell him her changed circumstances or that she could stay? He'd be back in a few days. She had no need to rush. She could wait and maybe impress him.

She slowed and scanned the building on the corner, looking for the address painted on the transom over the front door. She was in the right spot. Reaching for the brass doorknob, she stood still. A shiver wracked her body from her head to the back of her knees.

Turning, she glanced over her shoulder. Had she felt a breeze? Maybe the sundress hadn't been the best choice for the weather. But none of the branches of the trees in the median fluttered. She didn't feel a breeze. And she didn't believe in ghosts.

Maybe she should follow Grant's advice and support those with unshakeable faith in the extraordinary. Maybe she'd be better off. Maybe others would believe her, too. She'd have to be vulnerable first and trust she could handle the response.

She spun the knob and stepped over the threshold. She entered a small vestibule with an open doorway to the right.

A low voice droned.

Shutting the door carefully behind her, she followed the sound, her shoes clicking against hardwood floors. She wanted to make enough noise to be heard but not too much to cause a commotion and disrupt. She stood in the open doorway and frowned.

Instead of greeting a secretary, she spotted Mr. Baird behind the desk with a telephone against his ear.

He didn't immediately acknowledge or greet her.

She raised a fist and softly tapped on the oak trim.

He lifted his gaze and held up a finger. "I've got to let you go. But I'll circle back." He hung up the receiver and stood. "My dear, what timing. I was finishing a call to the insurance company about the flood. I went over myself yesterday and turned the water off. I couldn't get anyone out to start cleaning up, I'm afraid. How have you been faring at the inn?"

I haven't. She couldn't tell him that. She knew enough about small towns to understand how quickly word would spread. "Yes, quite comfortable." She crossed the room and stood in front of the desk. She didn't want to talk about where she'd been or who she'd been with. Because then she'd berate herself all over again for not telling him how she felt. For not sharing that she loved him, too. She had a lot of work to do to ready herself for the time when Grant came back. Hopefully, she wouldn't be too late.

Mr. Baird arched a brow.

She cleared her throat. "It's been nice."

"Please, sit down."

She sank into the chair and dropped her purse on the ground. The hairs raised on the back of her neck. She reached forward and grabbed her cell, holding it in one palm. She was probably being ridiculous. But she had a strange feeling, and she couldn't shake it. She smiled at the lawyer.

He looked as much like Santa today as he had on Monday morning. Nothing changed. The apprehension was her. She had been transformed in a few short days. No one else had had their world entirely rocked and reoriented.

"Well, well, well, to what do I owe the pleasure of this visit?" He pushed a bowl forward.

"I don't know how enjoyable my company is, since I seem to make so much extra work for you." Instinctively, she reached for a wrapped caramel. She crinkled the candy, willing herself to calm down. "Did you have any luck with shutting off the water to the building?"

"By the time I arrived, there was six inches of standing water on the main floor. I opened the garage door and let it flood the pier. I shut off the main water valve to be safe but I'm not sure how long the water flowed. The bill could be significant." He lifted his bushy brows.

Another hit to her bottom line. She had hope for the profitability of retrieving her treasure.

"Speaking of the mill, have you made any decisions about the property?"

She shook her head slowly. "Not yet. I'm still considering all my options. I have a lot to sort through."

"I can make everything a lot clearer for you. Sell to me. I took the liberty of drawing up the papers."

His words should have soothed her after her ramble. Sell and get out of the way. But she was disturbed by his sudden shift. He'd been so insistent that she return, his belief in the legend about local prosperity unflagging. What had happened to cause such a change, when, and, more importantly, why? She frowned. "What would you do with the building?"

"Oh, a little of this and a little of that." He moved his hands from side to side. "Nothing to be concerned about. I'm sure you are anxious to get back to Chicago."

"I don't have much to return to."

"No?" He raised his bushy eyebrows into his hairline. "Well, that's too bad. I'm sure you'll have a lot to tell about your little visit here."

And she had a lot to keep to herself. "Thank you for

drying out the sawmill. I appreciate the help. It'll be nice to sleep under my own roof, safe and dry."

"I did my best. The apartment looked damp when I arrived, but nothing poured from the ceiling. Old sprinkler systems can't be trusted. You could be a lot more comfortable if you took me up on my offer, my dear." He grabbed a stack of papers and slid them in front of her. "Why don't you take a peek at these and sign the last page, and I'll get out of your hair?"

She kept her face calm, as still as she could manage. What was going on? At some point, she must have crossed a portal into an alternate version of Loon Lake. First, Elise was kind and apologetic. Now, Mr. Baird wanted her gone.

He said sprinkler system. The decisive words sliced through her. She wasn't sure the cause of the flooding, and she hadn't mentioned water falling from the apartment's ceiling. But he had known. The hairs on the back of her neck raised. No, she was finding conspiracy where nothing existed.

She reached for the papers with her free hand and scanned the first sheet. Using the stack as cover, she hid her phone and read the document. She wasn't a lawyer. But she had read her share of legal documents over the years and knew to take her time. The wording was absolute, like a quitclaim deed. She flipped through, dragging her finger down the left margin.

And she stopped.

A peculiar word jumped off the page. *Timbers.* Was that a mistake? The specificity rankled her. She hovered her fingertip over the text, rereading. *"Any recovered timbers would be the sole property of the owner of the sawmill, theirs to dispose of as they desired."*

A Maguire in possession is prosperity for all.

The legend never mentioned the logs within the building or the treasure submerged in the lake. At the start of the hunt, at the ice cream shop, Zach had shut down their use of the word. He'd explained how much drama happened earlier in the summer because of rumored treasure. As he elaborated, he had made no mention of her family's involvement.

Why did the document include the specific provision? How could anyone have known about the logs? Unless the lawyer who drafted the document knew everything.

Her throat swelled shut. She kept her breathing even and steady and made a show of darting her gaze side to side and flipping through to the last pages. But she couldn't shake the certainty that her appearance in town had been no coincidence. Up to bumping into Grant, her adventure had been engineered. Or was it destiny? *Is this the end?*

"Come now, my dear. You don't have friends or family here. Let me take the building off your hands. I can make it easy for you. You'll walk away. Back to your real life."

"I just..." she stalled. If she hadn't bumped into Elise, she might have believed him. But now she wasn't alone. She needed to get out of here and get back up. It wasn't Grant. She'd pushed him away.

Maybe they'd never be equals. Maybe at one time or another, one of them would be strong enough to ease the burden of the other. In college, it had been her. But now? It was him. And that was okay. It was fine to be strong and to need strength. She wasn't any less than for feeling down.

He supported her.

And she'd been the fool to push him away.

She'd get out of here first. And then she'd apologize. In person. She had to get to the airport. "You're right. I'm all alone here. I'm expecting a phone call from investigators about my apartment building's fire."

A muscle in his cheek twitched. For a second, he grimaced. He smoothed away his wrinkles with a hand. "I'm sure it's all routine and nothing to work yourself up about. Let's tackle one issue at a time."

She stood pushing back the chair. "I need some air. I'd like to look at the mill one last time. I'll sign the papers at the inn. Come by at five." Reaching for her purse, she stuffed her phone and papers inside and crossed the room at a clip. In seconds, she was through the vestibule and outside on the sidewalk, power walking to the inn.

After the arson, the flood, and the spying, Mr. Baird almost killed her several times. Had she only been collateral damage in a plan involving the inn? Was the key to her problem in the rubble of the lighthouse?

If she had stayed, would he have finally done the deed? She wouldn't go down without a fight. And she needed help.

* * *

"Good morning, Karen," Grant cooed in exaggerated singsong as he drove along the tree-lined highway. She was his second phone call, after informing Ashley and Christopher that he would not be needing the suite for a work call but to please still charge him for the last-minute cancellation and oversight.

He headed to Duluth. If he wanted a more direct flying route to California, he could have driven to Minneapolis and hopped on a nonstop. But he worried he'd turn around and return to Loon Lake at the first chance. Even now, driving the two-lane highway, trees on either side, he continuously scanned the embankments for a side road to pull into.

Karen responded with a deep groan.

Grant chuckled. The only good thing about his impromptu plan was teasing his very capable—but not a morning person—assistant. "Hey, wanted to give you a heads-up. I am flying in today. I emailed you my itinerary. It's a little wonky with a couple layovers. You should have plenty of time to get everything in order for me."

"What changed your mind? Too much fresh air?"

Not enough. He gripped the steering wheel tight, pulling himself straighter. "I figured I could tackle a few other details of my new tour business in person and attend the meeting, too. Hopefully speed up the process for relaunching." And if he gave Molly time and space and she reevaluated her independent plan? All the better.

"How is the new endeavor going? I saw the website. A little basic but serviceable."

Of course Karen wouldn't waste her words. Complimenting him when the comments would be false was beneath her. She was honest but not cruel. "Slow. Expensive. And I don't have much to show for my money so far." He shook his head. A flash of Molly's shock at the outside of the boathouse popped into his mind. She'd still been unaware of his financial position. It had been a moment when she was truly natural around him. He'd had to earn back her unstudied scrutiny. Every opportunity to do so—from jumping into the lake to holing up below in the storm—had been worth all his fortune and then some. She might be the last person to see him for him. She was special.

"Do I detect a change of heart in your hesitation?" Karen asked. "Because we'll take you back. Gladly. Loony Village, or whatever it's called, might not appreciate you. We do."

Loony Village? Really? He rolled his eyes, glad she couldn't witness his reaction. Sure, the townsfolk loved a legend. Myth spread as fast as gossip. A few recent conspiracies had spread rapidly, bringing the community to the attention of legal authorities. But the people weren't out of touch.

They were kind and caring. He'd live in Loon Lake forever, content with the quick recounting of his every move as long as the podcast person didn't track him down. He shivered. "No second guesses." He cleared his throat. "I've made promises to the people of the town. I intend to see those through. And I like the lifestyle here."

"I give you one more winter, and then you're back," she said. "Will you have time to look at real estate this visit? Or should I start doing so on your behalf?"

He rolled his eyes.

"Hold on, I'm opening the email with your flight details." She gasped. "Yikes. Tough travel schedule. Two connections? You really don't need to be here in person. We could easily video conference you in. Don't put yourself through this for us."

"No, I want to be there in person. It'll be a long day. But that's fine." He was hopeful the full day would block out the devastating end to the treasure hunt. Was he wrong for wanting to be a part of Molly's success? Probably. He couldn't shake how much he owed her. Helping her would be the start of repayment. The interest alone would keep him working for her for the rest of his days. He'd be happy to do it.

"If you get stuck at one of your airports, please call. I can get you set up to call in from one of the executive lounges so you won't miss the meeting."

"Great. I'll do that. Hey, have you heard any word from my lawyers about the tour business? I'm trying to sort through the last details."

"Only that the previous owners are in jail."

"Yeah, I know." He shivered, remembering that day at the courthouse. Coincidence was strange sometimes, to put him in the path of his business predecessors like a warning from a higher power. The hair on the back of his neck raised, standing on end like static electricity shot through him. "Why are you bringing that up?"

"Seems like the owners' lawyer might not be the savviest—or most law-abiding—person. I guess part of the complication on this end of the deal was getting out of agreements about forming a utility company."

Grant drew back his chin. "A utility company?"

"Yeah, some sort of high-speed internet business was going to take over land that belongs to someone named Xavier Hale? That would help me out a whole bunch. Make it a lot easier to get in touch with you."

Grant rubbed his eyes and focused on the road. The name sounded vaguely familiar, but he couldn't place it. *Ashley Hale-Lewis.*

The pieces fit. He hadn't reached out to her directly to ask questions. When Christopher shared the real estate slash business opportunity with Grant, he had alluded to his wife's distress about the situation. Grant hadn't pressed her for details.

Had he made a mistake with his reticence? He was missing something else. What was it? In all the talk around Loon Lake, he had never heard about the added deception on behalf of the tour business' former owners. Why? An oversight? Or an omission?

Reclaiming property via eminent domain was a waving red flag. He'd heard about Soupy, the lighthouse fire, and a ghost. He'd set out on a treasure hunt. Why had something very real and very life-altering not been shared?

Did people not know about it?

"Grant? Are you there? Anything else you need from me?" Karen asked.

"I'm good. Thanks."

"Great. I'll get everything set up on my end so you can make a quick trip and get back to your beach bum lifestyle."

Any bumming around was entirely accidental. He

smiled at the turn of phrase. "I'd expect nothing less. Bye." He ended the call.

Should he turn the car around and get answers to questions he didn't realize he hadn't asked? Who could be involved in a scheme to steal? Everyone in town was so nice.

The person was probably long gone. The clench in his gut had to do with his mixed emotions about leaving. He had to get out to California to handle his business and leave her to do hers.

If he returned, he'd go straight to her side. In her own, roundabout, way, she had asked for space. He couldn't force himself on her.

He'd make a note to ask about the latest tangle in a couple days. With any luck, the mess would be resolved without him. If he pushed, he'd be on the outside looking in. He wouldn't risk losing her forever due to his unfounded fears. What could go wrong in forty-eight hours? He gulped. Perhaps the better question was, how much?

Chapter Seventeen

olly reached the boardwalk, doubling over to catch her breath. She'd been glad for the physical exertion, driving back from the lawyer's office to park at the dock. Movement gave her a sense of purpose in the midst of her floundering. The one person she should be able to run to in this scenario was gone, following her direction for space.

Years ago, she pushed him away and had offered him freedom to soar. Repeating the action, she'd condemned herself. Seeing him around town wasn't what she wanted. So why had she convinced them both it was? Too late to beg him to turn around, even if she could track him down. He'd be on a plane by now, or at least too far away to help. After a few more paces, she decided where to go.

Scoops, There It Is looked suspiciously empty. On a sunny day, she expected to find the door in constant motion, welcoming customers. But as she neared, she realized the interior was dark, and no R&B music blared out through the single-pane glass windows.

"No, no, no, no," she murmured as she pressed her glass to the front window and cupped her hands around her eyes for a clearer view. But no matter how much she willed Zach Jenkins to appear in his white overalls, she couldn't make him materialize.

"Do you need help?"

Molly shrieked and spun around.

Seth jumped, eyes wide and staring back at her.

"Oh, Seth. Hi. Hey. Hello." She brushed a loose hair behind her ear.

"Good afternoon." He scanned her face, never settling his gaze in one place for too long.

Was he afraid to make eye contact? How wild-eyed did she look at the moment? She cleared her throat and smoothed her hair. "I was just... When you're craving ice cream, am I right?"

"Like you scream, I scream? We all scream?"

"For ice cream." Her words were too bright, and her smile felt brittle. But what could she do? She didn't want to get Seth involved in her problems. She wasn't exactly sure what help Zach would have been able to offer. Within her sphere of limited town acquaintances, she didn't have a lot of options. "Have you seen Zach? He mentioned keeping an eye on my sawmill for me. I was hoping to follow up with him. Find out how things have been."

"He had to close up early. Some sort of emergency call at the dairy where he gets the cream."

She wasn't sure she'd ever linked those words together before or that anyone would ever do so again. "Huh. Oh."

"For what it's worth, I haven't seen or heard anything."

She nodded, pressing her lips together and studying the passing tourists behind him. No one made a move towards her property. The only person with motive to do so wouldn't need to now. He knew the treasure's location and like a fool she'd led him there.

"About earlier? I was hoping to talk to you," Seth said, interrupting her train of thought. "Not sure if you know, but I picked up Grant and took him to his car. He's headed to the airport, I guess. I was worried I quizzed him too much about what he may or may not have seen out on the water. I don't want to put you on the spot. But I'm always around to talk. And I'd love to find out what happened from your perspective."

On the water? Flashing back, she wracked her brain for any idea of what he was talking about. Was he after the treasure, too? She couldn't imagine the kindhearted man angling for her inheritance, but her first impression of Mr. Baird as Santa was way off the mark.

She hated to think Seth had an ulterior motive, too, concerning the events out past the mouth of the channel in his Timber Triangle. *Soupy?* She had had that strange moment when she swore something hit the boat from underneath. She couldn't trust what she may or may not have experienced. Her heightened emotions controlled her at that point, and she was once again operating in survival mode. Only this time, the stakes were even more dire. Dying at the hands of nature felt like fate. Succumbing to a terrible end thanks to a respected member of the community was a joke.

Seth held out a hand and hovered it over her shoulder. "Are you okay? I don't mean to interrogate you. I just figured maybe you had an encounter with Soupy."

She drew in a sharp breath and lifted her chin. If she could be honest with anyone in town and be heard, she'd bumped into the right person. "No, I didn't see Soupy. Sorry, Seth. Wish I had better news for you. And I'm not okay. Mr. Baird is behind everything."

"What do you mean? What's everything?"

"The apartment fire, losing my job, probably the flood at the sawmill, all of it. He tricked me into coming here, used me for his own purposes, and now I'm in danger, and I don't know what to do."

Seth nodded, solemn and thoughtful. He reached up to stroke his chin.

"I shouldn't unload on you. I'm sorry. Forget it. Please." She waved her hands. "I'll be fine. I'm good."

"Forgive me, but what you just told me doesn't sound *fine*." He air-quoted the word.

She reached up to cover her mouth and physically restrain herself from more conversation, or worse, tears. A sob built in her throat, burning her airways.

"You need to assemble a team. Let's go to the inn."

"Team?"

"Sure. A couple of months ago, there was a kidnapping and attempted murder."

Molly's jaw dropped. "Here?" She pointed to the boardwalk. "In this quaint town?"

Seth shrugged. "Crime can happen anywhere. It involved an explosion at the lighthouse folly by the inn. If anyone can help you, I know who can."

She wasn't sure what Seth had in mind. For once, she didn't care. He stepped up to help her, and she wouldn't ask for specifics to vet the assistance. "After you, please."

She followed him down the boardwalk, not asking questions when he pulled out his phone or meeting the curious gazes of people greeting Seth as they strolled past. If she lived through the next few hours, she'd spend a lifetime getting to know her neighbors and making amends for any poor first impressions. By the time they reached the inn, she was utterly drained of the last of her adrenaline rush from fear.

Seth strolled through the open accessibility door and steered her towards the staircase, leading the way to the top and a door at the end of the hallway. He knocked three times and entered.

Behind an enormous partner's desk, Ashley Hale-Lewis rose, Elise at her side.

Molly gaped. She was sure her fledgling friend would balk at providing assistance so quickly after their peace treaty. To her credit, Elise was here.

"Molly?" Ashley tipped her head to the side. "I don't understand. What's the emergency, Seth?'

"I'm in danger. And I need help." Molly's voice cracked.

"Of course, sit, please." Ashley waved her to the chairs in front of the desk.

Elise poured her a glass of water.

"I'm sorry, but I have to go. I was on the way to a

meeting when I bumped into her at the ice cream shop," Seth apologized.

"We can take it from here," Elise replied. "Thank you for alerting us."

Seth flushed. "You're the smartest people I know. Bye, Molly, if you need anything, let me know. Okay?"

Molly nodded and accepted the water on the desk, drinking long and soothing her dry throat. "First, I have a question that might be important." Or not. If Leonard Baird had covered her hotel room, had he also bugged her room? How had he known she'd end up at the inn? She didn't remember anyone else in the restaurant at closing. She hadn't paid much attention to her surroundings. Being in Grant's company pushed everything else to the periphery of her mind. "The night I stayed here, who paid for my room?"

"Grant Reem," Ashley said without turning on her computer or searching through her records. "He caught me before my shift ended and the overnight manager took over."

Molly sagged. Before the treasure hunt, the revelation would have upset her. First, for worrying how he'd pay for it and then for being a burden to him. With the benefit of those conversations on board, however, she only felt gratitude.

"Why? What does that have to do with anything?" Ashley asked.

"Not much," Molly answered. Her heart disagreed. A warmth and lightness filled her with hope. She would make it through this situation and find her way back to him. No more pride pushing love aside.

* * *

Grant shook the bag of honey-roasted peanuts into his hand. Since the grocery store near his office stopped stocking them, he hadn't found his favorite snack in years. But of course, the last place he'd think to look, the store at the Duluth airport, supplied him. If only he could find aa simple a solution for the unease plaguing him, he'd be happy.

He stretched his legs out in front of him and studied the board. In thirty minutes, the crew would begin priority boarding. He'd head to Chicago and, after a layover, on to California. He'd land late, grab a cab to his hotel, and crash. In the morning, he'd rise early for the meeting and hopefully catch a flight back before he got roped into staying.

Not that he had any reason to return.

Molly had returned to his life at the moment he least expected her. Instead of reaching for their second chance and holding on forever, he'd messed up. She'd been pretty clear about where they stood. She wanted space again.

In this one instance, she was wrong. And he hated that they were both collateral damage. Goodbye to their shared happiness for the sake of her pride. After living through a breakup once before, however, he knew what to do this time. He refused to give up. He'd head back and stick around and make her understand he wasn't moving on.

But something else bugged him that he couldn't make sense of. A gnawing unease that he couldn't shake.

The unsettling feeling was more than frustration from being on opposite sides of an argument.

While he believed in fate and found opportunities in every moment, he couldn't fully accept that her situation had been about bringing them back into each other's lives. There were too many heavy-handed moments in the work of an all-powerful and benevolent being.

In his pocket, he pulled out his cell phone and hit redial.

"Don't tell me you're changing your travel plans already," Karen greeted.

"And hello to you too, Karen. I'm wondering if you can do a little digging for me."

"Oooh! I haven't had the chance to play private investigator for a while. Who's the mark?"

Grant rolled his eyes and scanned his surroundings. He didn't want to besmirch someone in public, even if he was having a private conversation. Too many curious ears had a tendency to start an unfortunate game of telephone for his liking. "Give me a second. I need to move to get some…"

"Privacy?" she stage whispered.

He grabbed his bag and rolled back towards the bathrooms before every head at the gate turned to stare. "I'm wondering what you can find out about a lawyer named Leonard Baird."

"What's wrong with Franklin? Are you firing him? Should I? He's updating my will."

"No, no, no. This isn't someone I'll be working with. A friend hired him. Or he tracked her down." Grant pinched the bridge of his nose. The twisted knot had frayed edges and had to be untangled.

"Oh, okay. In that small town, then?" The tapping of fingers flying across a keyboard echoed over the line. "Well, this isn't good."

"What isn't?" A pit formed in his stomach.

"He's been disbarred."

"You found that out already? What databases do you have access to?"

"Just the same basic internet browser you have on the device you're calling me with."

Grant heard the admonishment in her tone. But he didn't let it prick him. He had enough on his mind to let a little insubordination slide. Although, she wasn't his employee anymore, and this was, strictly speaking, a favor. "Does it say why?"

"Hmmm...."

His mind filled in the worst with that stall. A conviction?

"Looks like a series of standard complaints. Neglecting clients and violating ethics. It's pretty vague, but I guess it must have been well-documented or reported many times to warrant his removal. It happened pretty recently. Within the past month."

Grant's chest tightened. "If there's a sign, the situation has happened more than once."

"Ahh. You remembered my mom's advice? And yes. Where there is smoke, there's a fire. If this man is presenting himself as a reputable attorney, you need to tell whoever is involved with him to run away. Or else."

Grant paced, his pulse pounding and his body

thrumming. He'd bumped into the attorney the day he spotted Molly at the brewery. Nothing about the man stuck out then. Grant had been too focused on Molly to worry about his surroundings. "You're right."

She sighed. "You're not getting on that flight."

"No. I have to go back. I think my friend is in danger."

"Grant. Be careful. Please."

"I will, but let me tell you what I plan to formally announce to the board. I'm not coming back. And I want you to officially be in charge of our former division. No one knows the operation as well as you. It's a horrible oversight that you haven't be promoted yet. And I won't stand it any longer."

"Really? Do you mean that?" She sounded winded.

"I do, and I'm sorry it's taken so long for me to realize."

"Thank you. You don't know what that means to me," Karen murmured. "I just looked over the results and found something else. This Leonard Baird was the lawyer working for the bankrupt company you bought."

"What?" Grant gasped and turned. He spotted several disapproving frowns from his fellow passengers near the store.

Grabbing his suitcase handle, he rolled past and stopped near the water fountain. How had he missed that piece of information? Wracking his memory, he couldn't recall seeing the name on any of the documents he'd been sent to review. Although he hadn't received too many yet.

After bumping into Molly, Grant left for the courthouse. It was a reasonable assumption at the time that while the pair were being arraigned, they'd have representation. But of course, they'd need someone legally allowed to do so. Unbeknownst to Grant, their disbarred attorney was meeting with Molly. What was he playing at? Why seek her out?

"Just what I said. Please be smart. Don't do anything rash."

At his side, Grant clenched and unclenched his free hand until the tight squeeze ached through his knuckles. He shouldn't have needed the reminder, but he did. Because now he feared the worst. A man with nothing to lose was the most dangerous of all. "Thank you. I appreciate the heads up."

"Of course. Be careful. I'll update the bosses."

"Bye, Karen. Thank you." Grant ended the call and slid the phone into his pocket.

Grant and Molly had been followed on their treasure hunt. The person he spotted with the binoculars had a name and criminal intent. His blood turned to ice, and if he didn't keep moving and keep his blood pumping, he might faint.

Worst-case scenarios flashed in his mind. While he'd been praising fate, he hadn't noticed the work of a villain. Most people didn't suffer multiple calamities over the course of their lifetimes. And yet she had been susceptible to several back-to-back-to-back. She had been in danger the whole time. He'd been oblivious, and then he left. He did as she asked and walked away. But he knew better.

He went against his conscience to give her the space

she said she needed. Now, his gut instinct screamed so loud he couldn't muffle the sound any longer. He strolled out of the terminal and through the airport. The wheels on his carry-on rolled smoothly as he wove through and around other travelers. He knew where he belonged, and as long as she was safe, she could yell at him as much as she wanted.

Chapter Eighteen

Molly scanned the lobby, smoothing her hair behind her ears. Her heart pounded. Could everyone hear the thud? Were her eyes wild?

Grant would know in an instant. She scrunched her burning nose. Up until the electrical storm out on the water, she thought she could rewrite her path. He'd been there. Against all odds, he stepped up for her exactly when and how she needed. He would have now, if she'd let him.

She gave herself a little shake. He was Mr. No Plan. He wouldn't have been ready for her quick reset. She could do this because she had to.

And she wasn't alone.

At the armchair next to the fireplace, Elise lowered a newspaper and met her gaze. She tilted her head to the two men sitting with books in the area opposite near the doors to the back patio.

Molly rubbed the side of her nose and continued like

normal to her position in the sting setup near Elise. Or at least she hoped she didn't draw any attention. Her body pulsated with energy. She willed a calm she didn't feel as she sank into the other chair. "Hey, thank you again for helping to set this up."

"Of course." Elise folded the newspaper she hid behind and tucked it into the side of her chair. "I can't believe how much I missed. His wife left six months ago and moved in with her sister in Superior. Rumor is she wants a divorce. He wouldn't be the first to get scared and desperate with the threat of exposure of business dealings. And I heard he can't practice law anymore."

"Was he involved with the tour boat businesspeople?" Molly's stomach twisted and soured. She hated to think about what Grant might be involved with—albeit accidentally.

"I wouldn't be surprised," Elise murmured. "The Prims aren't the brightest. They are thugs. I should have realized they weren't working alone. Doesn't line up with their personalities. They had to have had help to formulate their attempted coup of the island from the inn. We just didn't see it. Once they landed behind bars, we all wanted to get back to normal. No one wanted more problems, so no one dug any deeper. I'm sorry."

Molly was just glad she wasn't dismissed. Because she was afraid of how truly dangerous a person with nothing to lose could be. She couldn't shake the fear that he caused everything, starting with the fire.

And if he had, he didn't care who lived or died as long as he was in the clear. His ghoulish behavior proved his extreme narcissism. "He must have decided to dig up

Lily when he learned the treasure was real," Molly said. "He only came to find me to lead him to a payday. How did he know? Small town gossip?"

"It's my fault." Elise blanched and covered her mouth with both hands. "She was exhumed because of me."

"Are you alright?" Molly hovered her hand over Elise's shoulder. "Do you need water?"

"No, I'm not. I can't believe I caused that."

"You are not responsible in the least for what happened to Lily postmortem."

"Oh, believe me. I am. Because...," Elise said through her fingers, her voice muffled. She dropped her hands to her sides. "I was talking to Seth about the treasure at the coffee shop a few years ago." She shook her head. "I've been researching for our big celebration for a long time. I remember when I learned about a lost shipment of timbers. Seth and I were at the coffee shop, and I said the Maguire treasure is real." Her cheeks flushed. "That was my exact phrase. I remember a few heads turning to stare. I lowered my voice as I explained my theory. This whole thing is my fault. I didn't think we were being too loud, but we weren't in private. I guess once Mr. Baird grew desperate, and with his life falling apart, he took extreme measures to track you down. Oh poor Lily. Did he confront her? Or snoop through her home?"

Molly had no answer that would offer reassurance. Mr. Baird had a lot of misdeeds in the recent past. She couldn't imagine his villainous behavior came out of nowhere. There must have been signs of his treachery.

"Can I ask what you meant when you told Grant I

was too late?" Molly crossed her arms over her chest. "Was it about the property deadline? Or the treasure?"

"What deadline?"

"If I don't accept the sawmill by Sunday, the town gets it."

Elise gaped. "I wish! That would have made things easy for me."

Molly appreciated the honest response, but her stomach twisted at the realization of another lie.

"There is no deadline." Elise shook her head. "It's your inheritance but maybe Leonard Baird wanted to speed up proceedings to try to claim the building from you. I wanted to scare you off. I thought you and Grant were in cahoots with the lawyer. I'm sorry. I'm the cause of all of your troubles." Elise dropped her chin to her chest. "Lily was a friend of mine. I'm sure you've heard by now that I don't have many. But I promised her I'd take care of the sawmill, and I was ultimately responsible for disturbing her eternal slumber."

"You are not to blame. Let's get Mr. Baird off the streets. Okay?" Molly glanced at the clock near the restaurant. "He'll be here soon."

Elise unfolded the newspaper again.

Molly stood and retreated to her position. Seated in one of the rocking chairs, with her back towards the lake, she had a clear view of the busy lobby. She lifted the legs and started the chair. The forward and back motion felt as unsettling as the waves hitting the boat during the storm. Like then, she couldn't stop. She dragged in a shaky breath, nausea and dizziness fighting for top complaint.

I can do this. She was glad for the presence of mind to move to a public ground. And grateful the small town meant her unexpected ally knew the owners of the inn. They immediately called the sheriff's office.

The front doors opened.

Mr. Baird crossed the threshold. His white hair and beard caught the light, and he was almost blinding in his seersucker suit.

He hadn't spotted her. Free to study him, she didn't see the kindly old Santa Claus. This time, she saw a big man with a determined scowl. He could be a powerful enemy.

She got to her feet and waved, forcing a smile when he met her gaze. She faced straight ahead but studied the men in her peripheral vision. Wearing hats and glasses, they weren't disguised as much as hidden. With the phone in her pocket recording the conversation, she had every hope she could get to the truth. Safely.

"My dear. Forgive my bold lack of civility, but I am concerned for your health. Did you nap? You need rest."

She sat back in the rocking chair and motioned to the other at her side. "I got some lunch." *In the inn's office upstairs...* "I don't think I can sleep. It's been a rather long week. I think everything caught up to me at once. Maybe I'll be able to rest tonight."

"I understand. And I'm certain you are ready to sign your troubles away." He chuckled and slipped a hand inside his jacket.

Don't pull out a gun. She winced. Acting as bait required more skill than she possessed. And she steeled herself for impact.

He brandished a folded stack of papers and a pen. Extending the sheets, he frowned. "My dear, are you well? Should we call a doctor? Perhaps too much sun from boating has worn you out."

"Oh no, I'm fine." She grabbed the papers, crinkling in her tight grip. "I'm a little on edge. The insurance company isn't covering my full premium for my apartment. The fire is suspected arson."

He held steady, not flinching. He was ice-cold. She fought off a shiver.

"That is a shame," he drawled. "But you'll do well enough with your inheritance. I've already fielded a few offers. Maybe you'll be able to buy your own boat. Seemed like you had fun with Mr. Reem." Leonard waggled his bushy eyebrows.

"But... What?" She gasped. "How did you know I was on a boat?"

His lips twitched. "You told me, my dear." He didn't break from her stare. "And your lovely tan betrays you. If you flip to the last page and sign, you can return to your normal life."

She crossed her arms. "No, I never told you what I was doing or where I was. And why does this quitclaim mention timber? The mill hasn't been operational in years."

"It does?" He frowned. "I confess, I thought I grabbed boilerplate off the internet. How very strange. Of course, it was from another sawmill business, makes sense to include it. But that'll teach me to cut corners." He stroked his chin. "Just go ahead and sign, and I'll fix it at the office. No sweat."

"No." She held his gaze with a steady stare. She wasn't backing down. She had to prove to herself she could look trouble in the face and win. And then she'd trust she was strong enough when she needed so she could be weak at other times.

In the past, her relationship with Grant swung from one extreme to the next. It didn't have to be that way. He wanted to be there for her and not override her. If she could do this, she could move forward and forgive herself enough to let him love her.

"Listen, you don't know what you're getting yourself into with this property. I'll fix everything."

"For me? Or for you?" She gripped her upper arms.

"What a question. Why for you, of course! You have no home. No job. No friends."

If you hurt him... she wouldn't rise to the bait. Grant was safe. He was fine. She lifted her chin. She couldn't take his mirthless laugh any longer. "Yes, you've seen to all that, haven't you?"

"No one needs to get hurt, my dear." His smile tightened into a grimace.

"No thanks to you. You could have killed someone."

"Dial back the melodrama and consider your situation. You can't get that timber out without help. I have all the contacts. You have none. You think anyone will believe your word against mine? You're from out of town. You're some upstart who is going to steal a prime piece of lakefront property out from under everyone. You think anyone will believe you?"

"Did you set fire to the apartment building? Did you sabotage the mill?"

He shrugged. "It's neither here nor there. The past can't be rewritten. Get out. While you can."

"Mr. Baird, are you threatening my life?"

He leveled her with a hot-eyed stare. She got to her feet and took three steps.

He scrambled forward and reached for her, clammy, pudgy fingers grasping her elbow. "Don't go anywhere."

She turned, her pulse pounding.

The plainclothes deputy got to his feet and pulled back Leonard Baird, breaking his hold on Molly.

"What is the meaning of this?" He sputtered and swiveled his neck from the deputy to Sheriff Hanks, approaching him in full uniform. "Sheriff, there is a mistake."

Sheriff Hanks shook his head slowly and read the Miranda rights as the deputy slapped on cuffs.

Ashley Hale-Lewis approached from the office behind the front desk.

If looks could kill... Molly stiffened and forced her shoulders down. She wasn't in trouble.

Ashley stopped next to Sheriff Hanks. "Let me know what you need from the inn to press additional charges. We will give our full cooperation."

Leonard Baird stared at the ground.

Sheriff Hanks nodded and walked Leonard out of the inn.

Ashley strode towards Molly, her limbs shaking. "Oh, I am so angry at myself for my part in this. We should have realized the Prims had help with their schemes. They would never have attempted a takeover on their own. If we had uncovered the plot, we would have put

Leonard Baird in jail alongside them months ago. I'm sorry you were put in harm's way."

Molly shrugged. "It's okay."

Elise crossed the lobby, tucking the newspaper under her arm as she clapped. "Well done. Your aunt had her concerns, but I never thought they were valid."

"I'm glad she did." Molly shuddered. Her deceased, distant aunt had been exhumed by that foul man for his own greed. Molly's life was forever changed by a selfish decision. Guilt didn't begin to describe her conflicted feelings. Her future success was at the expense of others and had disturbed someone's eternal slumber. She couldn't help but feel unworthy of the gift of a second chance. "I was completely fooled."

Ashley crossed her arms low over her belly. "We all were."

"Thanks for your help," Molly said. "Both of you."

"Anytime," Elise said. "Although, maybe let's do with a little less big city showmanship and a little more community care in the future."

Ashley rolled her eyes.

"I understand," Molly replied. She agreed whole-heartedly "I want to be part of this town, not fight against it."

Elise nodded.

"My dad invented a story about cursed treasure on the lighthouse island as a marketing ploy in the nineties," Ashley said. "Guess I know now he didn't come up with the idea out of thin air. No wonder the story caught on since it already had roots in the past. That answers one question I always had."

This time, Elise shot her gaze heavenward.

The two women had history. Molly would learn all about the connections as she settled in town. She was looking forward to it.

"Let me know if you need anything else from me or the inn," Ashley added.

Molly smiled and shook her head. With any luck, she would never be a part of a sting ever again. "I appreciate that. Can I keep my room for a little longer?"

"Absolutely. Let me update the reservation," Ashley said and strolled back to the front desk.

The front door opened.

A man in a suit rushed in, passing the officers on their way out. "Was that Leonard Baird?" he asked, striding to the front desk. "What is going on here? I left for a couple of meetings, and I come back to an arrest in the lobby?"

"The last missing piece of the Prim's puzzle," Ashley said, spinning and meeting him halfway. "Sorry, honey. Everything happened very fast. Mr. Baird was responsible for the Prim's imminent domain scheme. When his payday fell apart, he turned his attention to Lily Maguire's estate." Ashley tilted her head towards Molly.

Molly stepped forward, extending her hand. "Hello, I'm Molly Maguire."

"It's a pleasure to meet you. I'm Christopher Lewis," he said, darting his gaze between Elise and Ashley as he shook Molly's hand.

"Leonard Baird was out of options," Molly said. "He tried to gain control of my family's tr..." She couldn't say treasure. Zach had impressed on her how delicate the word was to the inn. She cleared her throat. "My family's legacy."

"I'm sorry if this in any way involved the inn," he continued. "If we had known earlier, we could have apprehended him before your life became so complicated."

And I wouldn't have found where I was meant to be. She didn't thank Mr. Baird for his underhanded dealings. Without him, however, she'd be at a dead-end job in Chicago with no chance of improving her prospects. "Thank you for your generosity. You are not responsible. I appreciate your kindness all the same," Molly said. "I'm sorry to have brought such notoriety to your door."

Ashley waved a hand in a nonchalant gesture. "Oh, trust me. I've done plenty of that on my own."

Molly lifted her mouth in a half-hearted smile, glad for commiseration but suddenly very tired.

With the lawyer arrested, Molly was drained of the rush of adrenaline. She glanced at her watch. The last flight of the day left from Duluth in an hour and a half. Could she stop him in time to apologize? Did she even have the energy to try? She glanced at Elise. "Thanks for everything. I've got somewhere to be." The words rolled off her tongue unbidden and reawakened her flagging spirit.

"Go get him." Elise winked.

With murmured goodbyes to the innkeepers, she raced out of the building. She had to trust she'd reach him in time. She finally believed the universe had reunited them. She didn't want to waste even a day without him. The gypsy curse had been a blessing in disguise the whole time.

Molly raced to her car, turned the key in the ignition, and peeled out of the parking lot. She had to make it to the airport. With no time to spare, she had to tell Grant what had become clear to her when she quieted her doubts and listened to her inner voice.

She didn't need him. She didn't have to rely on him. When she wanted to, however, she could count on him, and that meant everything. He'd be her backup and her equal. She could stand on her own. Life was better with love and a partner.

If she didn't catch him? She shook her head, refusing to worry about that. Instead, she followed her heart like he would and hoped for the best. She'd stop planning every single second. She'd start living.

What else could go wrong after the worst had already happened? She'd lost everything. But in the end, she still had what mattered. And she could rebuild better than ever. She drove through town, past the boardwalk and her dock. She'd build a good life here. It would be hard. The sawmill needed extensive repairs. But she never gave up on a challenge before and wouldn't start now.

On the other side of town, she drove down the two-lane highway. There was nothing but bright-blue sky, puffy white clouds, and the deep green of the forest and grass. A picturesque day perfect for racing across the state to stop a flight. Until all of a sudden, she heard a pop, and her car jerked and jolted.

"No, no, no, no, no, no, no, no, no." She steered the car onto the shoulder. She was well past town. And with no car coming on either side of the road, she might be there for a while. She reached into her purse and pulled out her cell phone. Dead. She looked for the phone charger, remembering she'd left it at the inn in the room with her belongings before the confrontation.

Spontaneity was clearly an art form. She'd have to be a bit of a hybrid planner and by the seat of her pants person. At least she knew she couldn't blame this on the lawyer.

She let out a merciless chuckle and got out of the car. She walked around to the back of the vehicle. Sure enough, the rear right tire was gone, and the rubber was completely blown apart. It was amazing she hadn't sparked a fire by driving on a rim.

What were the chances the rental car insurance would cover this? She hadn't had much luck with claims lately. She sighed and shook her head she'd have to just wait until some helpful person took pity on the woman stranded on the road. So much for stopping a plane. Could she even come up with a Plan B? Or would that fall apart the second she thought it?

Thunder cracked. She jumped. Falling backward in a tangle of limbs. The low rumble that followed shook the earth. She turned her face up to the sky. The white puffy clouds darkened to an unforgiving chrome in a matter of seconds. Of course it had.

A streak of lightning flashed in the distance. Fat drops of rain smacked against her face. She laughed. The chortle started deep in her belly, ripping out from her throat. She leaned back on her hands behind her and opened her mouth, catching the rain. Because what else was she going to do? She might as well enjoy herself.

In seconds, as the rain poured over her, she was soaked to the bone. And the chill of a sudden, twenty drop in temperature, promised her she'd get sick if she stayed where she was. But still, she didn't get in the car. Not yet. For a moment, she wanted to sit outside in the rain and let it wash away all the worries and troubles, every ounce of pain she'd bottled inside her for the last decade plus.

Another rumble and roar echoed. But this time, it sounded mechanical. Opening her eyes, she got to her feet and rounded the bumper of the car. And her heart caught in her throat.

On the other side of the highway, Grant waved both arms over his head in sharp frantic motions. *Are you okay?* He might have yelled, but she couldn't hear him. She read his lips.

Holding her arms out at shoulder height, she spun, dancing in the rain. She heard his footfall crashing into puddles as he raced across the road.

She stopped spinning. He reached for her, resting his hands on her shoulders, forcing her to stay still. Then, with one hand, he lifted her chin and knit together his brow, narrowing his gaze. Looking for any signs of injury? She shook out of his hold. "I'm fine. Why are you here? What about the big meeting?"

"I couldn't get on the plane. I couldn't shake a bad feeling. And then I called Karen and learned about your crooked lawyer. Are you really all right? Did you crash? Hit your head?"

"No. Nothing like that, I..." She didn't want to tell him about the dangers she had been in. But now she felt silly for keeping anything to herself. Because that wasn't fair to either of them. "I'm okay. I was on my way to you. I needed to stop you."

"Consider me stopped."

"It was... Mr. Baird. Everything, the fire at my apartment, the flood, being followed on the hunt."

Grant's chocolate brown eyes hardened. "What? Where is he now? Did he threaten you?"

"I'm fine. He gave me a scare. With Elise's help, I set up a trap. He's been arrested. He was working with the tour boat people?"

Grant shuddered. "I should have dug into it more. I'm so sorry. If I had..." He shook his head. "I put you in danger."

She reached for his hands, interlacing their fingers and bringing the clasp to her lips. "You have nothing to apologize for because I wouldn't be here. And I'm not looking back. I can't."

He squeezed her hands before brushing back a strand of hair from her forehead. "When Karen told me he'd been disbarred, I came to find you."

"I can't believe he managed to keep that a secret from Loon Lake. But he did. I don't want to waste another second on him. He's in the past. What's important is you and me. Moving forward. Thank you for giving me the space to see things through. But I realized something, too."

"And what's that?"

"That just because I can do something on my own

doesn't mean I should. And just because I have an image of what success should be, doesn't mean I'm not blind to what it actually is."

"A lot of revelations for one morning. I had some, too. Just because you ask me to give you space doesn't mean I have to take it literally and fly to the other side of the country." Grant lifted the corner of his mouth. "I let you push me away once. If I let it happen twice, shame on me."

"So... we're both wrong?"

He reached for her waist and held her tight. "No, I think we're both right." He lowered his head to hers and pressed his lips to hers in a soft, sweet kiss promising a thousand more. She was glad they eventually found their way back to one another. And she'd stop overanalyzing and micromanaging every second of whatever came next.

* * *

Grant parked at the sawmill, angling between two pickups and a large panel van. When he got out of the vehicle, he wasn't greeted with the silence that had been Loon Lake's hallmark for years. Noise ricocheted off every building in town.

With the inn's lighthouse reconstruction and the renovations of the boathouse and sawmill, the towns-people lived in one giant work zone. Not that he'd heard any complaints. Finding enough skilled labor was only the first challenge.

Grant had hired every construction crew he could find in a fifty-mile radius to help with the boat house and her project. The boathouse work was straightforward. The building had nothing of historical significance to warrant special consideration.

Rip out and replace became his crew's motto. The sawmill was more complicated. As such, the work demanded almost double the manpower, and the decibel level of power tools and manual labor was the highest around. Most days, he couldn't hear himself think at her property.

But he was happy every time he stopped by, and he wasted no time. In the month since their kiss in the rain, the weather had started to cool, and the days shortened. Everyone was renewed with a sense of urgency to complete their updates by the spring. The celebration year loomed. Loon Lake had to be ready.

Or they'd face the wrath of Elise McKenna.

He'd already stared her down once in recent weeks and—ultimately—lost. Pretending he had no idea what had happened at the museum fooled no one. She'd told him off in a few choice words. He wasn't looking for more of her ire. After adding improvements to the museum to his list, he was on her good side following her discovery of the damage to the trim. Elise's favor was fickle and conditional.

The mismatched, rusted siding had been ripped off the building. The crew was in the process of removing everything rotten and broken and using new materials to replace things, mimicking the original design. With some sections missing, the building should look monstrous. The old wooden exterior—even with its wear and knot holes—was a huge improvement on the nineteen seventies attempt at preservation. He navigated around the vehicles and entered through the open front door. He stepped over a toolbox as he reached the center of the room.

Light poured into the space, illuminating the work and a rare positive of losing the roof and the apartment.

She planned to rebuild the living quarters but in a style more in keeping with the original timber structure, blending into the lakeshore better than before.

He spotted her standing next to one of the original supports, discussing plans with the foreman.

Dressed in a hard hat and overalls, she fit in perfectly. She could lose the headgear and help scoop ice cream with Zach. In almost no time, she had become part of the fabric of the town. He was so happy for both of them.

"Hey, how's it going?" Grant called over the buzz of saws.

She spun.

The second she met his gaze, she grinned. His heart skipped a beat. Every day, he fell a little more in love with her. At her side, he marveled at how she managed the project with ease. She had a clear vision of what she wanted and a knack for anticipating problems. He was in awe and asked for her guidance on the boathouse project.

He neared, reaching for her hand.

She interlaced her fingers with his and leaned close. "Come outside, you'll never guess what I have to tell you."

He stiffened. Her tone ramped up his nerves. After every unbelievable situation they had lived through, he didn't know he could handle another. What could she possibly say that necessitated her stoic delivery? That she was leaving? That it was too much work? As he let her lead him to the dock via a side door, he spotted a cardboard box with frames.

"What's this?" he asked, dropping her hand and stooping to rummage through the contents.

"Just some... I had an idea. I don't know if it's any good."

Her words were halting and short and very un-Molly. He reached inside and pulled out a frame, holding a black-and-white image of the inn. The photo captured everything that made visitors return to the resort. While a game of bocce was played in the background, a family assembled sandcastles on the beach, and smiling staff served diners at the restaurant's patio. The image held the nostalgia and warmth that made the business so special.

The photos would be perfect for the town's celebrations next year. He could already visualize the ad campaigns. "Wow. Where did Elise find these?" he asked.

"She didn't." Molly grabbed the frame's edge, her cheeks pink. "I took it."

"You're getting back into photography? For real?"

She deposited the frame back into the box and shrugged. "I am."

"Is that what you want to talk about?"

She glanced up and frowned. "Well, no... it's not—"

The loud whir of tools cut her off.

She reached for his hand again and tugged him outside. Once through the door, she pulled off her hard hat and finger combed her hair, continuing to the side.

He envied her pier. He followed her to the railing

overlooking the mouth of the channel. Despite the chaos, her side of the lake was peaceful. "Is it a Soupy sighting? Because Seth should be informed first."

She chuckled. "No, not Soupy. And not about my photography. Although, I've adapted Elise's event space idea to serve as a gallery for my art, too. I think it's a pretty good one."

He dropped his jaw.

"You don't think I can? I'm not good enough? My work is too cheap?" Molly scrunched her nose.

"The opposite." He beamed, flashing her a knowing grin. "I'm jealous I didn't think of it myself. And impressed Elise did."

"Fixing the damage at the museum and getting started here has been enough to earn a smidge of kindness," Molly said, tucking a strand of hair behind her ear.

"Very well-deserved. You'll struggle to keep enough inventory stocked for shows to last more than one evening."

She blushed.

He rubbed his hands together. "And it seems like work is on track here. So? Don't leave me in suspense. What is your news?"

"More of Mr. Baird's deceptions are being revealed as Sheriff Hanks continues the investigation and has reached out to other law enforcement agencies. Mr. Baird was behind everything. I don't have to worry about a curse or conspiracy."

Grant widened his gaze. He'd had his suspicions, but confirmation still shocked him. If the dastardly lawyer hadn't been pulling the strings, would Grant and

Molly have reunited at all? In his heart, he knew the answer.

Yes. Of course. They were fated to be together. Eventually, they would have found one another again—perhaps with less life-fearing moments. He wouldn't look back and wonder what if. He only looked forward.

"Yes, I am cleared. The insurance money hit my account, and I heard from my former employer's lawyer that I'll be getting an additional payout from them to avoid litigation for wrongful termination."

"Really?"

She nodded. "I have a feeling if investigated, we'd find Mr. Baird tampered with the sprinkler system at the sawmill, too. I gain nothing by adding to Sheriff Hanks's workload with my suspicions. I'm focused on moving forward. And now, with the payout, I'm paying off my student debt." She extended her arms. "I'm really starting over fresh here. I'm so happy. I didn't realize how relieved I'd feel without the burden of those bills."

Money couldn't buy happiness. Financial security afforded a freedom that definitely mimicked contentment. With independence, she could do something a little reckless. He leaned close. "Does that mean we're going after the treasure?" he murmured.

"Yes. And I was looking over some plans to incorporate the lumber into the building. I don't want to sell it. I want to preserve. *A Maguire in possession is prosperity for all.*"

He wanted to pump his fist in the air. She'd fully embraced Loon Lake's love of lore. He wouldn't crow his victory. At least, not excessively. "Now you believe in the legend?"

"Oooorrr...." She held him steady with her piercing gaze. "I'm grateful for both my good fortune and my family legacy. Elise will have a whole display on the Maguire Mill and the...Timber Triangle." She air quoted. "I really don't believe there is an active Bermuda triangle-like phenomenon happening in the lake."

Grant held up his hands, facing his palms out. "I'm merely Seth's messenger. I'd hate to get stuck out there again."

"It wasn't all bad. We talked and laughed. We lifted a curse thanks to true love."

He rolled his eyes and reached for her, pulling her in close. "No curses. I'll concede something unusual is occurring out on the open water. But on this I won't budge. Curses aren't real. Monsters? Maybe."

"Says you," she murmured.

He pressed his lips to hers and marked her with his own vow. She was right on one count. They were true love. And he'd never let her go again. How much could go wrong in the Timber Triangle? Another boat sinking wasn't likely. Legends lingered under the surface of Loon Lake. As far as he was concerned, that's where the myths could stay.

If a monster lived in Loon Lake, Grant wasn't about to disturb its peace.

About the Author

Rachelle Paige Campbell writes contemporary romance novels filled with heart and hope. She believes love and laughter can change lives, and every story needs a happily ever after. Learn more at her website https://rachellepaigecampbell.com/

About the Publisher

Harbor Lane Books, LLC is a US-based independent digital publisher of commercial fiction, non-fiction, and poetry.

Connect with Harbor Lane Books on their website (www.harborlanebooks.com) and social media @harborlanebooks.

facebook.com/harborlanebooks

x.com/harborlanebooks

instagram.com/harborlanebooks

bsky.app/profile/harborlanebooks.bsky.social

tiktok.com/@harborlanebooks

threads.net/harborlanebooks

youtube.com/harborlanebooks

pinterest.com/harborlanebooks

www.ingramcontent.com/pod-product-compliance
Lightning Source LLC
Chambersburg PA
CBHW061118310726
48974CB00002B/589